MW00917616

When It Counts

book two in the *2016* series

Lauren Hopkins

cover art by Sarah Hopkins

As always, love and thanks to Mom, Dad, Ricky, and Sarah.

Thursday, June 23, 2016
43 days left

"The Han documents at least show glimpses of compassion toward the lower classes, but in their own documents, the Romans show only indifference at best. Was the empire truly a 'glorious' one?"

Suck it, Ancient Rome! I aggressively slam my pencil onto the desk, practically dance my way up to Mrs. Farnsworth's desk under the jealous glares of my still-suffering classmates, drop my blue book on my teacher's desk, whisper a hasty goodbye, and bid good riddance to AP World History and to my sophomore year.

Two weeks ago, my life changed. But really? It didn't, at all. Everything is still exactly the same, like I didn't just win a gold medal at nationals and I'm not on my way to a potential spot on the United States women's gymnastics team at the Olympic Games.

In Boston, we were superstars. People recognized us at the airport, and not just my vastly more famous teammates. *Me*. They knew who I was and asked me to take pictures and sign autographs while I was getting coffee. When our flight landed in Seattle, dozens of people were swarming outside the terminal with balloons and streamers, and cameras from the local news filmed it all, calling it a "hero's welcome."

Now I'm normal old Amalia Blanchard again, nerdy high school kid who does homework and washes the dishes and casually trains for Rio in her spare time.

"Get in, loser. We're going shopping."

Okay, not *everything* in my life is normal. It's definitely not normal to have Emerson Bedford waiting for you outside of your high school, top down on her BMW, blond hair glinting in the sun, quoting *Mean Girls*. Emerson Bedford, once my gym obsession, then my mortal enemy, and now one of my best friends. Life is weird.

"How were exams?"

I dump my backpack into the back of the car and hop into the passenger seat, slipping my sunglasses down over my eyes. "Great. I think. If not, who cares? I'll just sign with Nike and become a Kardashian."

"Good plan. Speaking of, did you give more thought to the whole agent thing?"

"I have a meeting with that lady who stalked me at nationals next week, actually, but my parents want me to wait until after the Olympics so I have time to give it more serious thought. Oh, and they also wanted me to talk to you and Ruby to get some perspective, hint hint."

"Well, I went pro when I was still a junior, so I'm probably not the best person to ask."

"Do you regret it?"

"Nah." She doesn't think about her response for even a nanosecond.

"Okay, so…you'd say go for it?"

"I *personally* don't regret it because I was lucky. Everything worked out perfectly for me. I won world titles, I had the look advertisers were into, and I made a lot of money. One busted ankle, or a fall in the all-around final? I wouldn't have anything I have today, and I would have regretted it for sure. I wouldn't recommend going pro to anyone who didn't have my exact career path, to be honest. And you can't predict that, so you just have to hope for the same luck."

I nod, trying to take it in, but it's so overwhelming. She sounds braggy, but for real, so many girls go pro after even the smallest bit of success when they first start out, but then they get injured or realize they peaked too soon and will never make a major team. They got an agent, signed the contracts, made meager amounts of money, but no more will come in *and* they've forfeited their NCAA eligibility. They trained for years and years, and got nothing in the end. No big endorsements, no college scholarships, nothing.

For literally every sport but gymnastics, this isn't even an issue. Football players, baseball players, soccer players...they're normal kids in high school, get recruited into NCAA programs on full scholarships, play for four years in college, and then the big leagues pick them up and give them millions.

Gymnasts, though, we usually peak *before* we get to college. We have to choose between the scholarship and making money, sometimes as young as fourteen, like Emerson. It worked out for her, but if your career implodes like a dying star, you're screwed. You've made your choice and you can never take it back.

So that's where I am right now. If I don't make the Olympic team, or if I make it but fail miserably, no one's gonna want to give me any money. But even if I make it, win a medal, have my face splashed all over TV and magazines, I could probably have a solid income for a couple of years before the hype dies down and I fade into oblivion.

To me, going pro sucks no matter how your career pans out, especially because I really want to go to college. Stanford has been my dream since I was in kindergarten, and if I don't get in there, the University of Washington's gymnastics program has been drooling over me since I was ten.

But how cool would it be to kill it in Rio and star in a Nike ad, win *Dancing with the Stars*, and do a guest role on *Grey's Anatomy* or something, and then use *that* money to pay for college? The best of both worlds.

"I don't know *what* I want," I exhale, my anxiety bubbling out of every cell in my body, which Emerson senses.

"Chill, Mal. This is the absolute last thing you need to worry about right now. Just make it to Rio. That's the goal. Cancel with the agent if you need to. Put all of that energy into training and making the team. *Then* make the decision."

That's easy for her to say. She has an Olympic team spot and the huge endorsement deals locked down. Maybe nationals didn't exactly go her way, and she's been beating herself up about her beam fall for the past two weeks, but not one person doubts that she's going to Rio.

Everyone doubts me.

***

After practice, I absent-mindedly push my balsamic honey chicken around my plate, leftovers from Monday heated up all week long because my paralegal mom is working late on a case and my dad's stuck in the middle of nowhere for his new job changing the world at an underprivileged school. He's only in Seattle on weekends now, and we probably won't even get him back this week because he has too many meetings.

Now that finals are over, I can't even distract myself with studying. As long as I'm awake, the Olympics are the only thing on my mind, which is pure, heinous, beautiful torture.

Tomorrow's the two-week point before trials, and in seventeen days we'll know who's going to Rio. It's mind-blowing. My future will be decided just like that, and I'm not supposed to think about it.

That's what Natasha says, anyway. My coach, Natasha Malkina, was a superstar champion Olympic gymnast before she retired and opened her gym — the Malkina Gold Medal Academy — and her advice is to take the process one day at a time. "Don't think about the future!" she yells at me three thousand times a day. "Stay in the moment! Be present! Focus on the task at hand!"

Great advice, when the task at hand is hurtling myself over the vault table or trying to stick my floor passes. But when I'm sitting at my kitchen table with nothing else to do, I'm going to freak out.

Since nationals, practice has been all about perfecting everything in our routines, building on what we've already accomplished, looking at the mistakes we've made, and figuring out how to never make them again.

For most of my life, the mindset I use to get me through competitions has been like, okay, if I make a mistake, it's not the end of the world. There's always next time. Even at the open and nationals this year, I still had a next time. But with trials? That's literally it. No next time. If I don't hit here, if I don't prove I am one of the best in the country, I'm done.

Overdramatic much? For real, life will go on, but my Olympic dreams will be over forever. 2020 is out there, but I'll be nineteen. It's not old by any means for normal humans, but for gymnasts, four years is an eternity. There's no way in hell I'll be able to make it through doing this all over again.

When my teammate and best friend Ruby Spencer got injured right before the Olympics in 2012, she was my age. She was the best in the country and didn't get to go to the Olympic Games because she ruptured her Achilles. Everyone assumed she was done forever, but because she's Ruby, she doesn't give up on anything without an epic fight. That's how she won the national title two weeks ago, and that's why she's a lock for the Olympic team this year.

Ruby proved that coming back at nineteen and kicking butt is totally possible, but I'm not Ruby. No one is, honestly. She's not human. I know my body and my limits. I definitely don't have another four years at the elite level of this sport in me. If 2016 doesn't happen, 2020 certainly won't.

I groan, loudly, taking advantage of the one benefit that comes from an empty house — being fully ridiculous in a judgment-free zone. I scroll through my iPod until I land on Taylor Swift, blast "Shake It Off," and start scream-singing my way through the house while I wash my dishes and get my bath ready.

Tonight, instead of studying the history terms I had taped up to the bathtub wall, I will binge *America's Next Top Model*. My dad bought me a million bath bombs over the weekend — apparently they make up for his absence and are going to parent me in his place — and I'm going full Zen, forgetting everything on my mind and saving myself from my full-blown midlife crisis at fifteen.

"TYRA, SAVE MEEEEEEEEEEEEE!" I bellow from my oatmeal and honey bubble cave, my laptop perched on the counter across from me.

"Who's Tyra?" my mom yells back, after apparently sneaking into the house like a ninja. "Amalia, are you okay?"

I burst out laughing and sink into the water. Yes, I am totally losing it.

Friday, June 24, 2016
42 days left

"Your first day of total freedom!" Ruby grins in the locker room before morning practice. She holds her hairbrush up to my face like a reporter with a microphone. "Amalia Blanchard, with school done for the summer, *what* are you going to do between workouts?!"

"I have literally no idea," I shrug, waving her brush away, always grumpy on early mornings. "Seriously, the only appealing option right now is building a fort out of mats and sleeping the entire time."

"We're getting lunch," Emerson butts in. "My treat. You can even pick the place."

"How generous!" Ruby patronizes. "Does she get to pick the music on the car ride over, or is that taking it too far?"

"Don't make me uninvite you."

Ruby laughs. She and Emerson have never gotten along, and their career-long animosity became an all-out war when Emerson came to our gym a few months ago. They've actually become pretty good friends since nationals, where Emerson's mom caused the most insane drama. The stress destroyed her mentally, costing Emerson what could've been her third all-around title in a row. Ever since, Ruby has been much more understanding, and the two have actually bonded over their different but similarly rough experiences in the sport.

Emerson's mom has been trying to get money out of her ever since she went pro, and while Ruby's own family has been nothing but super supportive of her career, her injury four years ago nearly ruined her life. Before the mama drama, Emerson came off like this untouchable diva who stepped on everyone to get what she wanted, but after learning her story and struggles, Ruby said she totally gets it.

"She's trying to protect herself," Ruby had said, psychoanalyzing Emerson after we returned from Boston. "It's fight or flight. She feels threatened by everything and so she chooses to go on the offensive rather than waiting for the attack."

"You're the same way," I had responded, and Ruby, always hyper self-aware, fully agreed.

"Exactly. That's why we hated each other for so long. We're both just trying to protect ourselves by lashing out at whatever we see as a potential threat."

They understand each other, they are loyal to one another, and they're incredibly supportive teammates, but they still fight like first graders about everything under the sun. Even when there's absolutely nothing to fight about, you can always count on them to figure something out.

"Two weeks!" Natasha yells from the floor. "Why am I out here before you?! You'd think with two weeks until trials, you'd be getting early starts, not showing up late! Ten minutes of extra conditioning for every minute I have to wait!"

Yeah, we are muddling through the morning. At least I have a week of finals as an excuse for my sluggishness. Ruby and Em are so lucky they're done with high school and can focus solely on gym.

I finish pinning my hair up and we run into the gym right into our laps before the national team warmup. Once we're sweaty and out of breath, we form a line in front of Natasha for a few announcements.

"As I yelled earlier, we're down to two weeks until our first day of competition in Atlanta," she smiles. "That's twenty practices left here in Seattle. Twenty workouts to turn you from national-level competitors to Olympic athletes. Is that sinking in yet?"

No, I'm only slowly turning into an anxiety-ridden clump of muscle and skin as my brain deteriorates into mush.

"Your next twenty workouts are fully planned," Sergei Vanyushkin, a former US Olympian and Emerson's personal coach who moved here with her from Chicago, continues. "For conditioning, we'll alternate between strength, cardio, shaping, and plyometrics. We'll take it somewhat easy with full routines and hard landings for now so we don't burn you out, so if it's a hard-landing vault day, we'll use the tumble track for floor, and if it's a hard-landing floor day, we'll vault into the pit. This morning we have vault drills, bars skills, beam routines on the floor, and one full floor routine before a half hour of strength and cardio. Ready to work?"

"Yes," we respond in unison.

"...*Sir*," Ruby giggles. Sergei winks at her.

I roll my eyes. I'm pretty sure Ruby has been lying to me about her relationship with Sergei since he arrived at our gym two months ago, pretending like there's nothing going on, but constantly sneaking off to hang out with him, flirting with him at practice, and generally acting like an idiot. Emerson and Natasha are so wrapped up in other things — ahem, themselves, ahem! — so they've never picked up on the little things I've seen, but while it's super creepy and against the rules to date a coach, it's not my business to clue them in.

Morning workout is actually pretty easy, all things considered. Compared to doing full routines, getting through skills on their own is easy, and doing beam routines on the floor? It's not even work! If I could do beam on the floor in competition, I'd get a perfect execution score every single time.

As a drill, floor beam helps us get through full routines without worrying about falling, something that keeps us up at night enough as it is. Sometimes it's good to just make things a bit easier so we can focus on perfecting our movements, making our connections fluid, and letting our muscles memorize the feeling of being steady on each big skill.

"Perfect, Amalia," Polina, our assistant coach, says after my full set. "I have faith that you can do it just as well on the beam."

"I totally can," I grin, dusting my chalky hands on my thighs. "One more time?"

"No, just throw your dismount into the pit. Three times, please."

I climb onto the beam and work a few jumps and then a back handspring to get my bearings. My dismount is one of the most difficult in the world, but for me it's just a matter of focus. As long as I hit the sweet spot and get my big punch off the end, I have more than enough power to rotate both flips fully around, and more than enough finesse to stick the blind landing. And I don't even have to stick today. Blammo. The good life.

"One!" Polina yells as I soar into the pit. Seriously, the hardest part about this morning's workout has been freeing myself from our pit's foam blocks.

Back up on the beam, I repeat the dismount. "Two!" Lather, rinse, repeat. "Three!" Polina claps and I only have floor left.

"One more routine until we're free!" Ruby sings. "I'm gonna nap so hard."

"I'm with you, actually," Emerson yawns. "It's almost like this practice was *too* easy. Boring, in a way. It's putting me to sleep."

"Yes, boring is *exactly* the word I'm looking for when describing the first workout of my life that hasn't made me sweat out through my internal organs or need to encase myself in an ice tomb for a year," Ruby laughs.

"It's not about being easy!" Sergei yells, clearing his throat. "It's about making sure we don't burn out. Appreciate it now because the last few days leading up to our departure are all about pressure sets and nothing else."

Polina fiddles with Ruby's floor music and then we work our routines at full performance level, which is actually really hard to do without a crowd here. Ruby always manages to bust out something good, though, and I'll never stop being jealous. With the energetic "King of Swing" by Big Bad Voodoo Daddy blasting through the sound system, her huge personality is explosive even in front of the five of us watching here in the gym; when she steps out in front of thousands in an arena, it's practically a Beyoncé concert. People lose their minds.

Emerson's routine, set to a song called "Arwen's Virgil" by the Piano Guys, is slower and more dramatic like mine, but she forms this insane emotional connection with the crowd and can seriously make people cry with her expression and movement.

It's actually blasphemous to have me going last. They're both seriously so good, it makes me look like literal garbage in comparison. I'm not terrible in front of a crowd — hearing people cheer really gives me that little extra *oomph* I need to get in the zone — but performing in the gym is super awkward and I can barely get through it.

When choreographing my routine, Natasha and Polina jokingly decided that I best portray "creepy." Ahem. At first it was a joke, but Natasha ran with it, had our music guy put together a ninety-second mix of the final theme from the horror movie *Saw*, and that was that. My creeptastic but effing awesome routine was born.

I try my best to be *on* today so Polina doesn't once again laugh about my inability to relate to human emotions enough to portray them in front of other humans, but my focus is always more on my tumbling. I have endurance issues, so passes that should be easy for me end up looking terrible at the end of a routine when my energy is completely zapped.

Thankfully, the beginning of my set today goes well, but with only one pass left, I'm feeling a little sluggish, like I need to stop for an energy gel pack or something. But that would mean starting over and doing this whole routine again. I'm not stupid.

I half-ass the rest of my choreo and gear up for my final pass, a roundoff back handspring into a double tuck, the easiest of my four tumbling runs, but tacked at the end of a long routine, it's the one I'm most likely to screw up.

The run feels off from the beginning. My back handspring doesn't get low enough, my set doesn't reach the height I need, and I know in the middle of my first flip that I'm not going to make it around a second time and still land on my feet.

In gymnastics, the first thing we learn is how to fall. I know I have a way out of this, a way to save my ankles and knees from the disaster of a crunched landing, but my reaction time lags and I'm rotating through the second flip before I start readying myself for a crashed but safe landing.

I prep, planning to drop onto my hands and knees. Bent elbows, forearms first, stomach and ribs pulled in, almost like a plank. But the ground approaches faster than I'd like, and I miss a crucial piece of the puzzle — turning my head to the side.

My face smashes into the floor and my head snaps back from the impact. I stay still for a minute, breathe in, breathe out, listen to the noises of the gym around me, register my coaches and teammates rushing toward me, see flashes of light through my closed eyelids.

"I'm fine," I whisper.

Then everything goes black.

***

"We'll keep her a few more hours for observation, but it's only a mild concussion and a hairline nasal fracture. She can go home tonight."

"When can I go back to the gym?"

"No kid I know is that eager about getting back to working out," Dr. Fairchild guffaws. "A couple of weeks. Take it easy. Think of it as an extended vacation."

I can't hold back the tears. Natasha holds my hand, my surrogate mom for the day because my actual parents are stuck at work. I'm usually pretty hardcore and almost never betray my emotions, especially in front of Natasha. But now, everything's blubbering out of me like a feelings tornado.

"We'll see the national team doctor," Natasha whispers, trying to reassure me. "If it's as mild as they say, you'll be back conditioning right away."

"What doctor?" Dr. Fairchild inquires.

"She's a national-level gymnast," Natasha explains. "She has Olympic team trials in two weeks. Exactly two weeks from right now. The national team staff is going to want their doctor to look at her and clear her to compete."

Dr. Fairchild looks impressed, but also concerned. "The Olympics, huh?"

"She has a shot," Natasha says proudly. "A big one."

"Well, that's incredible. I've never treated an almost-Olympian before." The doctor jots something down on his notepad. "Listen, your prognosis looks good, and I don't think two weeks is a reach. But if you push it and try to get back to the gym too soon, you'll only make it worse."

"No one is pushing anything," Natasha hisses, clearly offended. "Obviously her health is our biggest concern."

"My biggest concern as well." Dr. Fairchild clears his throat and unnecessarily shuffles his papers. "The nurse will be in to check on you in a few minutes."

"My one wish in this universe is for people to stop basing their opinions about gymnastics on books and documentaries that came out twenty years ago," Natasha grumbles after he leaves. "Trust me, I was still competing in the glory days of abuse. Shit still goes down, but it's like a whole new world now. You kids don't know how lucky you have it. In my day, we walked barefoot through the snow to every competition, and my mom used to give me concussions right before every meet as an extra challenge."

She's trying in her own irreverent way to make me laugh, but I can't stop the tears, no matter how hard I fight to pull them back. All I can think about is not being in shape for trials and missing out on competing and not getting to go to the Olympics and seeing my dreams crushed into dust all because my energy was a little too low today. Seriously?

"You'll be fine, kid." Natasha senses my fears. "At least school's out and you won't have to worry about missing that, too. Sunday's a day off, so you're really only missing this afternoon and tomorrow. That's nothing. Monday, we'll reevaluate and get you back to non-impact conditioning, and then we'll take it from there. I've seen girls with far worse concussions than yours come back within a week."

"I just can't have this be it," I finally utter. "What if I lose my skills?"

"Mal, you're not going to lose your skills! You've taken a week off for vacation before, right? Think about it like that."

"As if you'd let me casually take a vacation two weeks before trials, or *any* competition? Come on."

"No, I would never. But still. We have to approach it from that mindset. It's only a week, not the end of the world. It's not like you broke your leg or ended up in a neck brace, or...ruptured your Achilles."

That stings. Poor Ruby. She's probably more upset than I am, having gone through a pre-Olympic injury drama of her own about a million times worse than this, given that her injury ended her season entirely. She's probably hella worried that my prognosis will be just as harrowing.

I sigh. I'm on an IV cocktail of pain meds so I can't even feel my busted up nose, which bled all over the floor at the gym. Trying to keep me from going insane after I came back from my one-second knockout, Ruby pretended to be a vampire and volunteered to clean the floor with her tongue. I better text her and let her know it's not so bad.

"Call your mom," Natasha says, pushing herself up off my bed to grab my phone. "She still doesn't know."

"Nah, I'll wait until she comes home. It'll be easier if she sees me so she knows it's not so bad. She's crazy busy at work and I don't want her to think she has to leave early or something. It's fine."

"Fine. I'm going to get something to eat. Don't play with your phone. It's bad for concussions. I'll grab some fruit and yogurt for you, okay?" I nod. "I'll check in with Sergei and Polina as well, give them an update and make sure your teammates are working twice as hard in your honor."

I smile meekly.

"Cheer up, Mal. Focus on right now. Don't think about the future. Everything will work out."

When she leaves, I sink back into the pillows and sigh again, long and low, tears beginning to fall once again. I don't close my eyes because based on my medical knowledge from every TV show ever, if you shut your eyes for even a second with a concussion, you'll most likely fall asleep and immediately die. I listen to Natasha and don't mess with my phone, either, since the bright screen will also make things worse.

My only option is staring into space, breathing in and out, counting to ten repeatedly to stay centered and focused.

But counting and focused breathing never works for me. Instead, my mind produces a never-ending streams of f-bombs. Centered and focused my ass.

Saturday, June 25, 2016
41 days left

"*Why* didn't you call me, Amalia?!"

"You were at work! You always freak out when anything happens. I'm fine, I was fine. If I called you, you would've assumed I had a gaping flesh wound or severe paralysis or something. When I broke my finger, you reacted like the doctors said they'd have to amputate all of my limbs. The last thing I need right now is you overreacting."

"This sounds like a private family only conversation," my best non-gym friend Jack says nonchalantly, picking up his backpack and laptop. "I'll come by later, Mal."

"Bye, Jack."

He waves and happily slips away from our drama through the front door.

"If anyone should be overreacting, it's *me*, just FYI," I huff, running my calf muscles over my black foam roller. Gotta do something, right? "You're the one who didn't come home all night and didn't answer her phone all morning and showed up at noon like that's normal. Naturally I assumed you had been brutally murdered."

"I told you, Amalia, I worked until three in the morning. The firm said they'd pay for a car home or a hotel by the office. I opted for the latter so I could finish a few things in the office this morning. I drove up assuming you'd already be long gone, at the gym. I had no reason to suspect otherwise."

"But you couldn't call me or text me back? I called you a million times this morning."

"My cell phone was on do not disturb, as it always is when I'm busy with a project. You know that. Again, I had no reason to think you'd even know I was gone."

"Whatever."

I'm still pissed about my injuries and am just redirecting that rage toward my mom. Natasha ended up spending the night with me, and then she had Jack and his mom come over this morning when she had to leave for the gym.

"No work all weekend," she promises, ruffling my hair like I'm six. "God, Amalia, your nose. You look like Rocky. 'Eye of the Tiger' is going to be even more meaningful to you now."

"Yep, that's me. The underdog fighter."

She goes into the kitchen to make lunch while I do leg lifts, listening to but not watching a marathon of *Law and Order: SVU*. My head already feels a billion times better, and I never got dizzy or nauseous, so I assume I'm pretty much fine, but I can't shake the feeling that I won't be back at a hundred percent in time to get in a good enough number of routines before we leave for trials.

With everything going on with my various head traumas and my missing-presumed-murdered mother, the upside is that it made my reunion with Jack way less intense. The last time we saw each other was after nationals in Boston, where we shared a ridiculously embarrassing moment in the hotel and then a long and painfully awkward flight home before retreating into our respective finals bubbles. Going to different schools in addition to me spending every non-school second either at the gym, studying, or asleep meant this morning was the long-awaited first meeting back in Seattle.

Having his mom tag along also didn't hurt. By the time she trusted him enough to watch me on his own so she could go back next door and work in her garden, we were communicating with each other like two champions of the spoken word. We completely talked our way around our confessions of love, and let the mundane chatter about school, gym (my obsession), computers (his obsession), and concussions fill the air instead. What happens in Boston stays in Boston.

"Natasha said she got you all set for a follow-up at the hospital tomorrow," my mom shouts over the running sink. "Very quick turnaround, no?"

"The doctor said it was mild. I seriously don't even feel...concussed. Neurologically, I'm totally intact. They're just playing it safe."

"How are you supposed to tumble with a broken face?"

"It's *barely* broken. Hairline fracture. I've done worse damage dropping my phone on my face." No joke. I gave myself a black eye from this act of self-violence two years ago. "Do not use while lying in bed" should be a warning label on every iPhone box.

"Amalia, I know the Olympics are your dream and this is the chance of a lifetime, but you need to know that no matter how you feel right now, your health is the most important. I can't let you risk your health."

"So what, that's it? I'm done? All this work for nothing?"

"No. Maybe you *are* fine. But we're going to need several opinions here. Natasha already emailed me about the national team doctor. I've read about team doctors giving air casts to girls with broken legs while telling them it's fine to keep training. The national team cares about team results, not your long-term health. You can see the team doctor for clearance, but you're also going to see that neurologist from the hospital as well as your pediatrician before I let you back into the gym."

I grit my teeth but it's not like I have any say in the matter. Which is probably a good thing. If it was up to me, I'd be back in the gym doing double backs this very second, ignoring the pain and potential long-term damage because I don't have my priorities straight at all.

"The chicken is done!" my mom announces like a fifties housewife a few minutes later as I'm working on my nine-billionth scissor kick. I figure my lower extremities are far enough away from my head that I'm safe getting a few leg workouts in. One last set, and then I gingerly push myself off the couch and head to the kitchen, scowling the entire time.

"Oh, don't take it out on me," she scolds with a bit of an eye roll. "I know I'm just your mean old mother, but I'm only trying to protect you. That's what mothers do."

Protect me? More like ruin my life. How's *that* for overreacting?

Sunday, June 26, 2016
40 days left

"This has a very *SVU* opening feel to it. Like when the maid walks in and finds the body and screams her face off."

"Except I don't think they ever find bodies in this position on *SVU*."

I'm flat out on my bed in a full middle split, my butt facing the bedroom door, so yeah, it's a weird look.

I push myself back up and swing my legs around to face Ruby and Emerson, who have a tub of sliced strawberries and a little vase with three daisies, my favorite fruit and my favorite flower. These guys are keepers.

"Didn't the doctor tell you to take some time off?" Ruby asks. "I guess a day is more than enough."

"Are you okay?" Emerson follows up. "Natasha told us about the concussion, and I can see the whole nose...*situation* is pretty rough as well."

"I'm fine," I grunt, hopping off of my bed to go over and give them hugs. This is the first time I'm seeing them since *the incident*, though I did text both of them voraciously last night. "Actually, I went back to the ER doctor this morning and then had an emergency appointment with my regular doctor, and they both cleared me, concussion-wise. I have zero symptoms left and am totally fine. The nose, though..."

"When can you come back to practice?"

"Tomorrow," I grin. "Nothing crazy at first, no tumbling or anything, but I can do cardio and conditioning. Maybe bars and beam."

"Dedication," Ruby crosses her arms. "I'm impressed."

"Yeah, well, if we didn't have twelve days until trials I'd fully take advantage of this mess, but like, seriously universe? As if I wasn't freaking out enough about making the team. Now I'm in a full-blown panic. The only good thing to come out of all of this was my mom canceling my meeting with the agent. She said I have to put all of my focus into gymnastics first, and told her we'd give her a ring if I end up making the team. One less thing to worry about, but now every ounce of nervous energy is hyper-focused on recovery."

"You'll be fine," Emerson counsels, sprawling out on my bed. "At least it's not your ankle or knee. You can deal with a nose. You'll be back to full routines by Wednesday."

"My doctor consulted with the national team doctor and they said next Monday," I shrug. "Gives me exactly two full days in the gym before we leave for Atlanta. Doesn't exactly inspire confidence."

The prognosis this morning at the hospital didn't seem so bad, but now that I'm saying the words out loud, my mind starts racing. Two days of full training before the most important meet of my life? It's impossible. It's never going to happen. I'm doomed.

"They're just saving their asses by giving you a week. See how you feel tomorrow and then tell the doctor you're fine. A broken nose is seriously nothing. Just stock up on meds and ignore every sign of pain until you get that team spot," Ruby laughs. "Seriously, Mal, when you hear your name called for the team, trust me. You won't even know your nose exists."

Guilt forcefully smacks me in the face when I realize what a dick I'm being about this. Ruby's ruptured Achilles four years ago took her almost a year to recover from physically, and I still don't think she's over it mentally, even though she hides it well.

Here I am feeling sorry for myself because I'm going to miss a week of practice, max. I can get through a few days off if I keep my goal in sight. Rio. Rio. Rio. I didn't make it this far to let a tiny setback end my career before it even begins.

"You're right, Ruby. As always."

"I know. Wanna get out of here? I'm guessing you're ridiculously bored."

"Shouldn't she rest?" Emerson asks.

"No. More. Resting." I exhale loudly, and then grab a pair of jeans to throw over my booty shorts. "I'm up for anything, seriously. I just need to get out of this house. My mother is being a nightmare. I am being smothered by her love."

I cringe as soon as these words leave my mouth, knowing Emerson would probably kill to be smothered by a mother's love, given that her own mother is a sociopath actively trying to run Emerson's life. I'm two-for-two with my insensitivity today. Tact, Amalia. Seriously, I have so much good in my life and I'm the whiniest person in the world. God forbid I ever actually have a real problem.

"Where to? Lunch? The movies? Mani-pedis?" Emerson, our chauffeur, digs for her keys as we head downstairs.

"Boring, boring, and boring," I shoot her down not-so-gently. "I want to do something spontaneous and fun and unexpected. This could be our last day of freedom in months."

Ruby's face lights up. "I know exactly the place. You guys are gonna die. I've wanted to do this ever since I moved here. Squeeee, Emerson, let me drive! I want it to be a total surprise."

Emerson tosses her the keys. "Fine with me. You gonna blindfold us, too?"

"Mom, I'm going out!" I yell, slamming the front door behind me before she can protest. It feels good to rebel. I'm almost a real live teenager.

I jump into the front seat with a renewed energy, happy to be out of the slump that's been slowly drowning me for the past two days. Ruby cranks the radio volume, gives me a smile, and we back out of the driveway into a brilliant sunshiney day.

***

"This. Smells. SO. BAD."

Ruby and I crack up. Emerson can deal with pretty much anything in the gym, but outside of the sport, she's a total girly girl and a bit of a wimp. On a boat in the middle of the San Juan Islands surrounded by whales isn't exactly her scene.

Yeah, so it turns out Ruby's plan was better than anything anyone has ever come up with in the history of the world.

WHALE WATCHING.

Seriously, it's magical. Like, this is something we're actually doing in real life even though it's straight out of an early 2000s Disney Channel movie about BFFs running around being carefree and whimsical. It's also great for me because I feel like I'm doing something exciting and adventurous but at the same time I can sit still on a bench without worrying about my smashed up skull.

There's a brief lull in the whale action and Emerson clears her throat.

"You're doing awfully well for someone who came scarily close to blowing her Olympic shot," she finally says. "You said you were freaking out, but really, you seem super chill."

I'm stunned for a moment but then shrug it off. "But I didn't blow it."

"No, but if I was in your shoes I'd be losing my mind right now. Every second of training counts and here you are, missing full days of workouts and you're not even concerned."

"Lay off, Em," Ruby cautions without even turning her head away from the water.

"Don't you think I know that?" I retort. "I was freaking out. Obviously. But things look good right now. It ended up not being as big as I thought. I'll be fine and back to training almost immediately. I've stressed about it enough and now I've made my peace. Why keep worrying? It'll only make things worse."

When I say these words out in the open in front of people, I realize it's more about quieting my own fears than about trying to prove something to her.

"I competed at nationals in 2011 with three broken toes and I won the junior title," Ruby chimes in. "I missed two full weeks of training right before the meet and I was fine. The physical pain, you get through that. Especially with the Olympics on the line. If I broke my foot right now, I'd totally still vault on it and do my floor routine. I wouldn't care if I never walked again. It's the Olympics. It's worth everything."

"Seriously? Never walking again? A lifetime of pain for a few weeks of glory?"

"Hell yeah, and you'd make the same choice, otherwise you wouldn't be here," Ruby laughs. "We're already in for a lifetime of pain whether we go to the Olympics or not. I know girls who didn't make it past level eight who got diagnosed with arthritis in their twenties. If it wasn't physically impossible to compete with an effed up Achilles, I would've gone for it in 2012."

After a moment of silence, Ruby turns to me.

"You need to be in a good mindset, Mal. Whether you're busted to bits or in perfect health, your mental game is what matters."

"All I'm saying is that concussions are risky and that fall could have jeopardized your shot at Rio." Emerson crosses her tan legs, adjusts her yellow sundress, and pushes her sunglasses down to cover her eyes. "If it was me, I wouldn't be this calm."

"Good thing you're not me."

I now have a headache, and it's zero percent related to my injury, hashtag Emerson problems.

Mini-drama aside, we enjoy the rest of the boat ride and I pass out immediately on the car right home, like I did after a long day at the amusement park when I was six.

I quietly latch the door behind me when I get home, but my mother's waiting in the foyer, and ambushes me with eight million questions about my current state of health and well-being.

When she sets me free, I curl up in bed and switch my phone back on. Because I'm super popular, in addition to the four hundred voicemails from my mom, I have exactly one text. Natasha.

"Got the report from the doc. See you at practice tomorrow."

Wednesday, June 29, 2016
37 days left

"One week!" Sergei high fives me as I walk into the gym bright and early Wednesday morning.

"One week!" I cringe back.

My first two days at practice following my injury were boring but essential in getting me back on track. If I never have to see another treadmill or stationary bike again, I'll die the happiest woman on earth, but my choreo is now so perfect I can do it backwards in my dreams, and I'm pretty sure my flexibility has never been so good. I could totally retire from artistic gymnastics and be a rhythmic star. Stretching nonstop all weekend will do that to you.

My pediatrician who cleared me for Monday's practice put me on "strictly limited" training this week. I probably could've started working on routines already, but Natasha didn't want to push anything.

"It's a blessing in disguise," she'd reasoned. "You'll conserve energy for trials."

Conserving energy is great, but we're blissfully ignoring a huge setback as we're supposed to be working toward my peak, I can't help thinking. I'm sure Natasha was thinking the same thing, but no reason to actually say it out loud and make it real, right?

We've been working all season with the goal of peaking in August, so we'd be at our best when it counts, not a second sooner or a day too late. I've missed the better part of a week at this point, which is a huge wrench thrown into our plans, and I can't help getting a little nervous thinking about how I'll look easing my way back in today. Especially if the nerves turn into mental lapses and I have another stupid fall.

I'm the first one at MGMA today, and can enjoy a little me time before

Emerson and Ruby burst in like small bombs. I turn on the shower in the last stall and shut the door, positioning myself on the bench with my knees folded up into my chest so I stay dry.

I know, kill me, what a waste of water. Sorry California. But it's the only thing that soothes my anxiety, as if the steady pounding of water against the tile can iron out the kinks in my brain the same way actually taking a shower relieves my muscles.

Sitting there, eyes closed, counting back until my heart rate steadies, I begin to visualize my routines, performing them in my head the way I want to hit them for real today, zero bumps or struggles.

It's funny, because the same little nuisances that exist in my actual routines also find their way into my brain, like I know deep down I'll never be able to tap into a giant without piking my hips ever so slightly, but everything I *can* control — wobbles, steps on landings, falls — is taken care of.

I don't snap out of my trance until I hear Ruby and Emerson yammering back and forth at each other as they enter the locker room, my cue to turn the nozzle off and join them.

"Early shower?" Ruby asks.

"Mmmm," I respond, still kind of dazed from my mental exercises.

"Your hair's not wet," Emerson mentions, wrinkling her nose.

"Maybe she forgot," Ruby laughs. "Symptom of her concussion."

I roll my eyes. "I was just shaving my legs, Nancy Drew." I feel Emerson's eyes wander to my bare calves and I'm thankful I actually shaved them last night, lest she keep asking questions. We're together a billion hours a day and everyone thinks I'm crazy enough as it is. I deserve to keep some of my weirdo rituals to myself.

"I'll meet you out there!" I call cheerfully, rushing to the door. Now that I'm in my happy place, I'm not in the mood to listen to them bitch while they get dressed.

Out on the floor, I catch Natasha's eye and the nerves come back. She jogs over, grabs my shoulders, and whispers "breathe." I nod, close my eyes, inhale, count, exhale, and repeat. Nothing has changed. It's impossible to lose an entire lifetime of workouts and skill progressions in less than a week. I got this. I. Got. This.

***

"Good, Mal!" Natasha yells. "Up, up, up!"

I listen to her, using the push and pull of the high bar combined with my own power and strength to release up into my Gienger, completing the flip and catching easily, not too close, not too far. It's seamless.

This was the one and only skill I'd missed in my first set of the day, and that was a fluke. My hand slipped when I let go of the bar, giving me less propulsion than I normally need. I still completed the skill, but I caught way too close, ruining my flow and throwing me into a dead hang. After the error, we work the skill a few times on its own, and it's back to perfection.

"You got it!" Natasha screams. "Keep going!"

I swing through my transitions, another release, and up, up, up again into my double front dismount, landing it solid on the mat. Pause, hold it, salute to no one, and then hold my hands up for a double high five.

"What concussion?!" Sergei yells from across the gym, and I grin sheepishly.

"You look great, kid. Your whole dilemma didn't even affect you." Natasha gives me a big hug and then starts into her notes. "We'll work casts and shapes for the rest of the hour and then I have some shoulder conditioning for you, but seriously, if I knew your recovery was going to be this effortless, I would've given you the week off. Kidding, obviously, but really. Great job."

Today's training plan is a few steps up from the "strictly limited" plan I'm supposed to follow, but I'm still not pushing anything. I skipped vault and tumbling completely, using that hour for my floor choreography instead.

The hope is to ease me into tumbling with my beam acro, which I'll do on floor or the low beam instead of up on the four-foot-high competition beam just in case my sense of balance is totally off. If all goes well, we'll try some vault and tumbling basics on the trampoline tomorrow.

"If worst comes to worst, we'll pull you from the all-around at trials," Natasha had decided reluctantly this morning. "That's a big *if*, but we do have to at least consider it a possibility. You can do bars and beam, and Vera knows your Amanar's good enough, so you can still make the team. She does love all-arounders, so coming in as a specialist could hurt us, but she knows what you can do when you're healthy and she knows you're coming in with an injury that will be gone and forgotten by the Olympics. It shouldn't hurt your chances at all."

I don't think Natasha actually believed that last part, but honestly, we all know I'm not going anywhere near floor at the Olympic Games. Why would it matter if I competed it at trials? Maybe she's right.

"Go work on acro with Polina" Natasha gestures to the floor. "And if you're feeling particularly impressive, feel free to bust out a double back or something."

"Excellent work on your details this week, Amalia," Polina compliments me on my walk over. And I know it's a real compliment, not a "sorry you're injured" compliment, because Polina is a tough old Russian broad who tells it like it is. No sugarcoating ever comes out of her mouth.

"Not good enough that the judges will be able to tell the difference, I'm afraid," she continues, criticizing my jerky arm movements on beam and my still relatively stiff performance ability on floor. See? She's like a Sour Patch Kids commercial. "But I see the difference. That and a Metrocard will get you on the subway, but I appreciate it."

How one woman can go back and forth between praising me and throwing shade at me a million times in a single sentence is beyond me.

We work my beam skills, and I'm so thankful for the forgiving bounce of the floor, which makes it feel like I'm performing my routine on a cloud. Because that goes well, Polina dares me to try out my double back, the same skill that busted me up last week.

I'm a little worried, not gonna lie, but I also don't want to fear it more than I already have, so I compromise. I position myself on the floor in a way that will allow me to land the skill into the pit, and I think about everything that went wrong in last week's attempt.

"Focus," I breathe. "Low back handspring, high set. You got this."

Before I can think about it too much, I start running. I hurdle into the roundoff, stay tight and low to the ground as I flip backwards into the handspring, and then, just like on bars, I think "up, up, up!" as I set into the flips, rotating through the two tucks exactly the way I need to do it in the routine.

Though the pit softens the blow of the landing and I don't have a way to gauge how good my position would be on the actual floor, everything *feels* right.

"Nice work." Polina gives me a hand to help me out of the pit, and I can see Natasha giving me a thumbs up from across the gym. "But your knees were loose and your chest was a bit low. It could be better."

That's my Polina.

Saturday, July 2, 2016
34 days left

"Can you believe it? In eight days you'll know if you're going to the Olympics!"

I know my dad means well but I can't help rolling my eyes. I've only heard this from every single person in the universe this week, from my coaches and teammates to random people at restaurants and the mall who saw my story in the paper. *I get it.*

"It's so surreal, kiddo," he goes on. "A lifetime of work all for this one moment that will determine the rest of your life."

"Yeah, dad. It's huge."

I gaze out the window for the rest of the ride home. Dad drove back from his job as superintendent for a struggling little school district four hours away in the middle of nowhere and surprised me by picking me up at the gym. Not that I don't love him and want to see him, but it was *slightly* annoying, because I had mani-pedi plans with Emerson and Ruby. But he's my dad, and he's actually around for once, and I'm grateful. Blah, blah, blah.

"Your mom and I have a little surprise tonight," he grins, peeking back through the rearview mirror. I sat in the back so I can sit against the door with my legs straight out in front of me, feet on a pillow with ice packs around my sore ankles, which totally breaks every seatbelt law in the universe, but shh. I won't tell if you don't.

"What is it? You bought me the remote from *Click* so I can fast-forward through this week before I bite my nails down so far I start chewing on my finger bones?"

He doesn't answer, keeping the goofy grin on his face while singing along to Prince's "1999" which is almost meta in 2016. RIP.

I exhale. Practice is completely one hundred percent back to normal, like my minor head injuries never even happened. Even my nose doesn't look quite as horrifying, which is awesome because I'm sick of people staring at me like they're either sorry for me or afraid I'll fight them.

Natasha got me back to tumbling by Thursday morning, we doubled our efforts that afternoon and Friday, and then this morning it was like a normal Saturday, like nothing ever happened, as if the past week was some hellscape nightmare thrown at me just for fun because everything in my life was working out a little too well.

"Dad, for real, you know I'm recovering from a head injury and have the biggest meet of my life in a week? I don't think I can physically, mentally, or emotionally handle any surprises. *Please* tell me. Please, please, please, please, please..."

He shushes me and then laughs. You can handle it. Trust me. Relax."

I shrink back in my seat and drum my fingers against my thigh to the beat of the music. My phone is on flight mode almost all the time now. When the press isn't calling and I'm not trying to dodge calls from the agent trying to recruit me as a client, I'm getting random texts from classmates I've never spoken to and Facebook messages from my aunt's hairstylist's daughter's dog's veterinarian's nephew. I totally get why Britney lost it in 2007.

Because I'm the worst, I ask again. "You're killing me, dad," I whine. "Does mom know the surprise?"

"She might be in on it," he winks. "That's all I'm saying, so save your energy."

"Okay, but like, last time you sprung something on me, you said you were moving away. Do you really blame me for getting antsy?"

"Nice try, but you were better at the guilt trip thing when you were three. And besides, you know as well as I do that if I hadn't taken that job, I'd be begging in the streets for the money to buy your grips and ankle tape."

Where's the lie, though?

"Just trust me, Mally Pally. Don't get your hopes up, we're not sending you to space camp or buying you a pony or anything, but you will fully enjoy yourself."

We ride in silence the rest of the way home, and to be honest, by the time we pull into the driveway, I've almost completely forgotten about *the surprise*. I drag my gym bag into the house and see a flutter of movement through the screen door on the back porch, but don't think anything of it. It's obviously my mom.

"I'm home!" I yell. "Moooo-ooom, I'm home, and I brought a strange man with me!"

"I'm out back, Amalia!" she yells back. It's a nice night, and I'm crossing my fingers hoping that *the surprise* is chicken on the grill, mixing things up from the usual chicken baked in the oven or sautéed on the stove. I slide open the screen door and peer my head around the newly power-washed deck.

"SURPRISE!"

My extended family, some people from the neighborhood (yes, including *Jack*), and a whole hoard of my MGMA teammates — including my elite crew — jump out from behind the hedges that separate us from our neighbors. That's when I notice the red, white, and blue streamers and balloons adorning the back porch, the coolers full of beverages, the meat on the grill, the clearing set up for horseshoes and badminton, and a fire going in the pit.

"What is this?!" I realize my dad has joined the masses, sneaking around the side of the house rather than going through. "This is awesome!"

"Don't thank me," my dad responds, a twinkle in his eye. "It was all Jack's idea. Your mom and I did do all the work, though, so yeah, you're welcome."

Jack blushes when I look over at him, his face nearly matching the red balloon he's holding.

"I know you have to miss the usual neighborhood 4th of July bash on Monday because of practice, and you've been so stressed...I thought this might be a nice way to relax before your competition."

I leap into his arms for a hug, shocking both him and myself.

"It's perfect." If I were a manic pixie dream girl from a John Green novel I'd probably kiss him and our legions of shippers would cheer, but this is already too much for reserved little old me. I unwrap from his arms and step back. "Seriously, you think of everything. You're awesome."

"Yeah, well, I figured you were sick of sitting in front of the TV. Or not, but it's my civic duty to drag you away from the garbage you watch...and usually force me to watch."

Ruby has already roundoff double-backed into the pool, some of our younger teammates following her lead as Polina watched nervously from the porch. I realize I'm still in my sweaty practice gear, and excuse myself to go change.

This is the eight-billionth time Jack has done something brilliant and epic and adorable and perfect while I've done nothing but bitch and moan and force him to listen to my daily dramas. I literally don't deserve him. Once this whole Olympics thing is over, I'm gonna have to figure out a way to pay him back.

***

"What would you do if you didn't make the team?"

"Emerson, *no gym talk*," Ruby moans. The party has died down and the three of us are sitting by the fire in my parents' old striped lawn chairs, battling mosquitos and enjoying melty red, white, and blue popsicles. "Can't we just enjoy being actual human people for once?"

"I'm serious, and don't tell me it's something you haven't thought about," Emerson huffs. "It's always a possibility, no matter how good you are or where you stand right now. Anything can happen."

"In case you've forgotten, I've lived it," Ruby snaps.

"We get it," Emerson rolls her eyes. "I just keep thinking about all of these 'what ifs' and want to know that I'm not the only crazy person putting my anxiety ahead of years of experience."

"You're not," I smile, in an attempt to bond. "Though my spot is quite a bit more precarious than yours, so I guess I have reason."

No one disagrees.

"I don't know what I'd do if I missed out a second time," Ruby finally admits. "Once was bad enough. If I had no shot and kept missing, that's one thing. I'd understand why I wasn't going. But to be leading the game both years and then miss out on *two* Olympics in a row? The first time it happened almost killed me. I can't even think about it happening again because I don't think I could survive. The day after trials, you'd find my body floating in Elliott Bay."

She's joking, but this is still way too dark and deep for my liking, and we sit in silence for a minute. I bend my popsicle stick back and forth until it finally snaps, breaking the tension along with it.

"I'm not *really* gonna throw myself off the ferry," Ruby laughs. "I'm just saying...I mean, I've trained in this sport my entire life. I've already had one huge unexpected against-the-odds comeback. My body and my pride won't last another four years. What comes next? I don't know how to cook on a stove or hang curtains, let alone possess marketable skills that would qualify me for literally any job. I'd have to move back in with my parents and go to community college or trade school or something."

"I can totally see you repairing air conditioners for a living," I joke.

"Try clown college," Emerson offers. "You'd fit right in."

"You're gonna make it, Rubes." I toss my splintery popsicle stick onto the fire. "That was a freak thing in 2012. It's not going to happen again."

"At least if it ends for you guys, you have families and people who will help you out," Emerson whispers, hugging her knees. "I'd have no money without my sponsors, nowhere to live without my host family, nothing to do in life without this sport. I've never done anything else. You both have options. I am no one without gymnastics."

It's quiet again. I look up at the house and see a silhouette of my parents through the screen door in the kitchen. My mom's arms are wrapped around my dad's neck and I smile as he bends down to kiss her on the forehead.

With my dad gone all the time and my mom basically living at the office and me *actually* living in the gym, it's weird and amazing and comforting to have everyone home like a normal family for once. I can't imagine being Emerson and not having people in my life who make sacrifices and support me every second and make sure I'm well-rounded and a regular kid despite everything that's going on.

"You'll figure it out, Emerson." Ruby picks at a rip on her palm. "We all will. Gymnastics will end one day and it'll suck, but we'll move on."

"Speaking of, I think I should probably move on," Emerson segues. She pushes herself out of the lawn chair and wipes her hands on her shorts. "Ruby, ride?"

"Actually, I kinda want to spend the night if it's okay with Mal?"

"Fine with me." I stand up and start cleaning up our mess. I want to put out the fire, too, but realize I have no idea how. Water, obviously, but like…do I just dump it on? Ruby's spot on about this whole "zero life skills" thing. "Emerson, do you wanna sleep over too?"

She thinks for a second. "Might as well. Maybe if I stay here long enough your perfect parents will adopt me and I won't have to worry about my future anymore."

Ruby jumps into the pool for a few cool-down laps to tire her body before bed, and Emerson and I head into the house. I need my dad for this whole fire situation, but my parents have disappeared.

"Dad?"

"He went to the store," Emerson says. "He said he had to go pick up milk for breakfast tomorrow."

"I just saw him in the kitchen, like, five seconds ago."

I hear a toilet flush and this guy I only vaguely recognize steps out of our little half-bathroom next to the laundry room.

"Hi, Amalia," he smiles. "I was just saying goodnight to your mom before I hit the road. Good luck next week at your national championships."

He's a lawyer at her firm, I slowly realize. A partner. Jasper or Casper or something.

"It's actually the United States Olympic Trials," Emerson steps in.

"Right, the trials. I'll be watching you guys on TV. See ya, kiddo." Jasper-or-Casper waves before walking through the front door, and I shudder. Kiddo is what my dad always calls me.

I watch this guy leave just as my dad's car pulls in. The two exchange pleasantries in the driveway and my dad runs up to the house, a bulging brown bag in his arms.

"I know, I was only supposed to get milk, but I couldn't help also grabbing Eggos, strawberries, bananas, and whipped cream," he says excitedly. "And eggs, and avocado. Get ready for the best breakfast of your life, kiddo."

As he carries the bag into the kitchen, I stand open-mouthed, staring out the front door. Time doesn't feel real and my heart starts to flutter deep in my chest.

"What's wrong?" Emerson whispers.

I have no idea how to respond.

Tuesday, July 5, 2016
31 days left

"Today's first order of business is Amalia's head. How goes it, Lady Blanchard?" Sergei asks at the start of our final practice before we leave for trials. *Gulp.*

"I am one hundred percent a-okay," I smile. "Fully cleared by every doctor on the planet and ready to kick ass."

"That's what I like to hear. Okay," he clears his throat. "Tomorrow we leave for Atlanta, bright and early. Five o'clock flight. Blame Natasha for booking these seats. As you know, we're skipping afternoon practice today, but that doesn't mean you should run off and go wild. Lunch, massages, maybe go for a swim, and in bed by seven. That should help us get used to east coast time."

We nod. We know it all by heart, our detailed itineraries landing in our inboxes last week. I've studied mine over and over again, and have everything fully memorized, down to our flight number, our rotation groups, and even the route between the hotel and the arena. What can I say? I'm super into organization.

"We practice like we compete today," Natasha joins in. "National team warmup, a brief touch on each event, then competition sets, one at a time, just like we'll do on Friday and Sunday. When we're done, I'm letting each of you pick what you think your five biggest problem areas will be with the judges. We'll break into three groups and work on all of them. It'll be interesting to see how insightful you are with your own work. Make me proud."

The national team warmup is twenty minutes of huffing and puffing, the conditioning and strengthening required by our sport sometimes more difficult to get through than our actual routines. I found early on that I'm able to push through the pain by basically pretending I don't exist. I go on autopilot and tell myself stories in my head. It's great. One time, during an especially lengthy session, I even recited most of the movie *Grease*.

Today, though, the only thing on my mind as I run and jump and stretch and flip is my mom's arms around Jasper-or-Casper while my dad innocently drove around picking up breakfast for his family.

I go extra hard, scream-singing along to the classic rock pumping through the speakers in an effort to drive these disgusting images away.

"You're a live wire today, Mal!" Natasha yells.

"Just feeling that Rolling Stones spirit!" I yell back, feigning extreme happiness to hide my rage. "Man, was I born in the wrong decade or what?!"

Putting on a happy face has always been easy for me, and so Sunday wasn't too awkward, until my friends went home and my dad drove back to his new life, after which I've managed to successfully avoid my mother ever since.

I am consciously trying not to think about what happened, because this is the last thing I need right now. If my mother wants to have a midlife crisis and cheat on her husband, that's her deal. My deal is making this freaking team, and I'm not going to let her drama ruin this. Every so often, though, the image of her with Jasper-or-Casper flashes into my brain and I wish I could get a lobotomy or have electric shock therapy or something so I can destroy it forever.

Once we move into actual routine work, my body and brain come off of autopilot and I can push it all out of my head. I channel my rage and annoyances into hardcore focus, and I kill it, getting major thumbs up of approval from everyone in the gym.

"Okay, problem areas!" Natasha yells once we've gone through our sets, zero falls for any of us. "Ruby with Polina, Emerson with Sergei, and Amalia with me."

"Endurance," I exhale, appropriately out-of-breath. "That's my number one, in case you were unaware."

"Judges can't deduct for you looking like an asthmatic pug in the middle of your floor routine, though," Natasha jokes. "I mean, if you look super pained and start dragging, there's probably a good artistry deduction or two in there, but we already know you're getting docked in that area."

"Rude."

"Okay, for real. Five problem areas. Go."

"Hips and general body alignment in my post-flight on vault. Handstands on bars, they're always a teensy bit short. Lack of control when landing tumbling on floor. Ummm..."

"Come on, that's only three. You're good, but you're not *that* good. I, personally, can think of at least ten."

"You're so mean," I laugh. "Okay, my back leg on every leap on beam and floor, and...sticking with floor, I guess, my knees or legs coming apart on some passes."

"Good insight. What do you think is *most* fixable?"

"They're all so built into my foundation, I'm afraid none of these will ever improve and so therefore I have nothing to work on today." I grin, hoping to get away with it, but Natasha just rolls her eyes. "Okay, I'm gonna go with the legs apart on my tumbling, because this adds up a lot, generally I only need a few minor corrections to make it better, and I need to work on tumbling more than anything else, so why not start there?"

"Fantastic. Tumble track, now."

I look at the clock and see there's only an hour left until practice ends, so I practically skip to the trampoline, excited to be only a few drills away from finishing the final workout before we leave.

This is what matters, this feeling right now and everything that will come later this week. I need to remember this, and vow not to let anything outside of my gymnastics get to me. That stuff is important, I guess, but it can wait until after the Olympics. It doesn't mean anything to me right now. It's nothing, vapor, air.

Ignorance is bliss.

Wednesday, July 6, 2016
30 days left

Our plane touches down in Atlanta shortly after four in the afternoon. We've been awake since three in the morning on the west coast, and the time change is screwing with my brain.

A burst of billion-degree steam engulfs us as we step off the plane and onto the jetway and no matter how dry my lips are, I'm desperate to climb back into the freezing comfort of the cabin.

"Hotlanta!" Ruby remarks, hosting her bag over her shoulder.

"Hilarious," Emerson rolls her eyes. We're all just a tiny bit grumpy.

Our shuttle speeds down the highway and I'm happy to be missing all of the traffic coming out of the city from the opposite direction. All I want to do is get to the hotel and sleep forever.

Finally, we veer off the highway and down Marietta Street to the Omni, which I know from my repeated googlings is right across the street from the Centennial Olympic Park, where I can't wait to stop and pay tribute or burn sage or whatever people do when they visit sacred sites.

We get our room assignments, Emerson on her own while I share with Ruby, as usual. I throw myself onto the bed once we're upstairs, and Ruby marvels at the city views from our eleventh-floor room.

"I wish we flew into these cities a day early so we could actually get to see things," she groans. "There's an awesome music scene in Atlanta."

"We have Saturday free," I remind her, but she quickly shoots me down — it's recovery day between the two days of competition. There's absolutely no way Natasha will let us roam around.

"It would probably suck, anyway." Ruby falls back onto her bed and begins a series of crunches without even thinking, as if her brain subconsciously knows it's been a full day without training and automatically launches her into workout mode.

"One year when we were in St. Louis for nationals, I went to the Arch with my family on the day off between meets and one little girl noticed me and asked for a handstand picture," she continues. "Why not? She was adorable. I mean, can you imagine being ten and seeing your favorite gymnast out in public in the perfect handstand picture setting? I'd one hundred percent want that picture, and I was thrilled to make this girl happy. But then a million other little girls and their families noticed me, and before long, a fun day out with my parents and brothers turned into a two-hour autograph and photo session in the heinous Missouri heat. Never again."

I roll over to face her. "Nervous yet?"

"Nope. This is just another competition. You?"

"Nah," I lie. "It's like any other day."

"You wanna swim tonight? My legs feel like they atrophied overnight."

"Yeah, funny how a day off feels like a year. I'd be up for the pool."

Ruby texts Natasha, who seems to be impressed with our enthusiasm and commitment. "Bring Emerson," she replies. "Then room service by seven and bed by ten."

We change into swimsuits and I text Emerson, telling her to meet us on the roof. Our pool workouts are actually pretty epic, and I hope no lifeguards or other guests are around so we can flip into the water and splash like maniacs. It's how we train when we're messing around in my backyard, though hotels generally don't tend to love us.

Thankfully, the coast is clear, so I run and front flip in, my knees tucked up to my chest and my pointed toes breaking the water. I love the feeling of being weightless in the pool. There's nothing like doing a ring leap and holding the shape forever while I float, analyzing how my body feels in that position, something I later try to emulate on beam and floor but never quite get it. Eat me, gravity.

Emerson, Ruby, and I swim laps, plank on noodles, do press handstands on the pool's edge, and push through thousands of resistance exercises that work our abs and shoulders harder than anything we do when conditioning in the gym. It feels amazing after the long flight, much better than a nap would've felt, if you can believe it. The water also calms me, melting my tense muscles and clearing my nervous brain.

I gulp down Gatorade when we finish, never realizing how thirsty I get in the water until I'm done. We hop into the steamy hot tub to cool down, which is kind of an oxymoron, but it does its job.

"No gym talk, and I mean it this time," Ruby pants, still out of breath.

"I promise," Emerson responds, sliding into the water.

"Have you heard anything about your mom?" Ruby asks. "Is she coming this weekend?"

"If gymnastics is off-limits, so is my mother," Emerson bites. "And no. I have no idea."

"Isn't there a way you can get security to, like…keep her from getting inside the arena?" I ask, probably naively, but it's a genuine question slash suggestion. If I had a crazy mom trying to psyche me out and blackmail me for cash, I'd have security all over her in a heartbeat.

"If she buys a ticket, I don't think there's any way I can get her locked out," she shrugs. "I guess if I had a restraining order or something, but I don't think there is a way for me to legally keep her out of my life right now."

"That sucks," I commiserate, biting my nails. Yeah, I'm the queen of responses.

"Are your parents gonna make it?" Emerson asks me.

"Yeah, actually." I sigh. Neither of them knows anything that's been going on with my mom and I'm trying to keep it that way.

"You seem thrilled," Ruby laughs. "My whole family is coming and I can't freaking wait to see them, but I think I'm gonna have to put it off until after the team is named. They make me so nervous and crazy with their questions. Even when they say things like 'you're gonna make it!' I'm like, shut your mouths, you're jinxing me! I hate saying it, but they just get me too worked up."

"Same," I respond. "They always call me their little Olympian and think they're psyching me up by telling me how great I am and how well I'm going to do, but it actually does exactly the opposite and psyches me *out*. I go crazy when they say stuff like that. Like, way to add to the pressure."

"So, your dad can make it, then?" Ruby asks, closing her eyes as a cloud moves, opening the sky to the painfully bright sun. "At your party, he said he wasn't sure if he could work it out."

"Yeah, he surprised me yesterday. He can't get the week off but he'll fly out Friday morning with my mom, I think."

"That's awesome."

"Mmmm." I lean back against the side of the tub and stretch my legs out in front of me, stretching every muscle from my quads to my toes. The hot water feels unbelievable and my body loosens up even more once we add in the jets. Paradise on a rooftop in Atlanta.

"You don't seem that excited," Ruby can't help prying.

"She just said they add a tremendous amount of pressure," Emerson answers for me, eyeing me the whole time. "Ten more minutes and we should get ready for dinner."

"Okay, mom," Ruby sighs, stretching out her own thick, muscular legs and pointing her feet as hard as she can, circling her ankles in each direction.

I whisper a "thank you" to Emerson, who raises an eyebrow at me. I shake my head as if to say "don't even ask," and she nods. She gets me, and leaves it alone.

Thursday, July 7, 2016
29 days left

"You have interviews right after podium training," the media rep from the United States Gymnastics Association reminds the fourteen of us here at trials. "Things are a bit fancier here than they were at nationals...you each have your own chair in the press room, personalized with your last name above. Stay at your chair until the entire session is over. No wandering off. There are dozens of journalists here this time, so you might have to wait a bit before they all get to you."

We nod in unison, lined up in height order, our national team warmups on over red, white, and blue national team workout leotards instead of our usual club gym gear. At this level, everything is all about Team USA, not our personal gyms, and no detail is left untouched.

"General stretch and warmups will last a half hour, and then you'll go into your rotation groups for the timed training, twenty minutes per event. I have Malkina Gold Medal, Vanyushkin, Waimea, Texas Tornadoes, and Reynolds starting on floor, and then Windy City, Great Plains, Sawyer Burke, and Nashville starting on vault."

Our group includes the three of us as well as Zara Morgan, her club teammate Beatrice Turner, Amaya Logan, and Brooklyn Farrow. The latter three definitely won't make the team, but are here because they made the cut at nationals, which opened up trials spots to the top fourteen all-arounders and specialists regardless of anyone's team chances. I could maybe see Amaya getting an alternate spot, but even that would be a long shot. She's good, but not a threat.

Zara, though...she's someone I'm excited to see. She's been consistently killing it on vault and floor, and her bars are pretty sweet as well when she hits. She hasn't beaten me yet this season in the all-around because her beam is kind of a nightmare, but she's absolutely strong enough on vault and floor to go to the Games just for those events.

The other group has all four Windy City girls who made it, nearly all of whom have a shot at Rio. They probably would've had five here had Bailey Dawson not gotten injured at nationals, effectively ending her dreams in a panic-inducing flash of insanity when she threw a brand-new and monstrously difficult triple Yurchenko vault, but the four they have here are scary enough.

Maddy Zhang and Charlotte Kessler were third and fourth at nationals, both beating me. Olivia Nguyen is solid on all four events, and Irina Borovskaya is a pro, winning bars gold at world championships last year. This year, she had a world-class meltdown on this event at nationals, so I don't know if she'll be serious competition, but she might just be saving her best for when it counts.

The Windy City rotation group also has Madison Kerr, Kaitlin Abrams, and Sophia Harper, and while the first two are more examples of girls who did a good job at nationals but won't factor in here at all, Sophia is a top-notch bars and beam specialist, and the returning Olympic all-around champion who could definitely challenge for the spot I want.

Basically, I'm in the middle here. I'm not a lock to make it in the way Ruby and Emerson are, but I'm not a total blow-off name either. Five make the team, and my odds right now are about fifty-fifty. It could be worse, but there's still reason enough to keep me on my toes.

I'm feeling good about warmups as we march over to the floor, our strategy this morning to be quick and solid, doing a few of our best skills to start, and then hitting one routine apiece. If we fall, we get back up and finish the routine just like we'd do in competition, and then we repeat the problem skill on our next turn up. We're not allowed to lose our minds over any mistakes. It's all about staying in the moment and moving on to what's next.

"Lineup for floor is Zara, Emerson, Amaya, Brooklyn, Ruby, Beatrice, and Amalia," Natasha calls out, taking charge of the event even though there are four other coaches and their assistants in this rotation.

Podium training on floor is usually little more than organized chaos, with everyone throwing passes one at a time while the rest do leaps and spins on the sidelines. We start out with simple layout passes to get started, though Zara casually busts out a double tuck right away, easy for her. The rest of the passes in her routine are bananas. She can definitely win a medal on this event in Rio, I realize, and I mentally insert her onto the team I have running in my mind.

She's the first one up when we run through full routines, and her music is this awesome Broadway musical version of the Elvis Presley song "Jailhouse Rock." Girl can tumble, and she's selling the crap out of this, even without a crowd here to beef up her performance.

I watch her passes, really paying attention for the first time. She has a layout double double, a one-and-a-half through to triple full to punch front tuck, a tucked double double, and a double front half-out to finish it off. No big deal. I would literally die after the first half of that routine.

"I'll do your beam if you do my floor!" I shout to her, giving her a high five after her coaches free her from their critique.

"Thanks," she smiles shyly, out of breath but still somehow functioning like a human. Seriously, give me all of your powers.

My own teammates are great, no mistakes, and I also somehow manage to make it through with no major problems. My landings are actually some of my strongest, and I can't help thinking that while annoying and awful, my whole concussion ordeal actually came with benefits. I got a break and time off to rest my body, and then had to deal with the pressure of prepping for this meet with less time than I was supposed to have, kicking my butt into high gear right when I needed it.

"You guys are done early," Sergei calls out once I finish. "Still five minutes left until vault. Stay warm. Run and jump."

I run down the length of the vault track along the side of the arena since we're not officially allowed onto the podium until the bell rings, even though all of the vaulters are done. I jog back, catching my breath, and then prep to make the run a second time when bam, there's Maddy.

"Nice face. Run into a brick wall?" Good God, she has gotten even more atrocious in the few weeks since nationals, which I didn't think was possible.

"Your dad punched her because she was so beautiful, your mom couldn't look away." Ruby comes to my aid, using an attack that is actually more biting to *me* at the moment, given my whole mom situation.

"You're disgusting," Maddy says before storming off.

"That didn't even make sense," I laugh.

"My dad almost punched my friend Jill once," Ruby says. "I was having a sleepover in my basement and my brothers and their friends kept trying to break in via the garage, so when we heard footsteps outside for the nine-billionth time, Jill hid next to the door to scare them. The door opened, Jill screamed in the face of the intruder, which turned out to be my dad, and he naturally assumed she was a murderer. He whipped his arm back to prep for a punch, but *thankfully* stopped himself when he saw her face. Can you imagine? He totally would've gone to jail for beating up a teenage girl. We really lucked out there."

I crack up laughing. Ruby needs to win every medal in Rio just so she can tell her insanely hilarious stories on every late night talk show once she gets back.

"I'm keeping you from your sprints," she apologizes. "Get on with it before Natasha loses her shiz."

This time as I prep, I do my entire pre-vault ritual so I can run through my Amanar, like I do before every single time I throw it in competition. The run-through helps a ton on an apparatus that demands perfection. I can count my steps, figure out the mechanic of my run, and then even though I'm not really vaulting over the table, once I slow down, I can practice my mid-air and landing positioning.

Ruby cheers me on for this, even though I'm not really doing anything except running. I have to say, I don't think I'd make it through this week at all if it wasn't for her. Whether she's cheering or giving me advice or even sharing her stupid stories and trying to make me laugh, she always says exactly what I need to hear so I can be at my best. She's amazing, and my heart flips and twists with the love I have for her.

***

"Well, *helloooooooooo*, Amalia!"

I take a deep breath and close my eyes, cringing at the voice I know and hate.

Anna Young, she devil reporter whose one goal in life is to get me riled up about nothing before and after every competition. Picture Rita Skeeter from *Harry Potter* and don't change a thing in your brain. That's her. I will not be a bitch, I will not be a bitch, I will not be a bitch.

I paste on my biggest smile and return her greeting.

"How was practice?"

"It was great." It's only my nine hundredth time answering this question in the past ten minutes. "I hit all of my routines with no falls, and while there's definitely room to perfect a few of my skills, if I compete the way I trained today, I should have a fantastic weekend."

"When you say there's still room to perfect skills, do you think this is something that should've been taken care of before getting here? Or are you waiting to peak until the absolute last minute?"

She somehow makes everything she says seem like a jab.

"We're not expected to be at a hundred percent here," I explain. "Even though we're working to make the team, Vera and our coaches wanted us to be at seventy percent at the open, eighty at nationals, ninety this weekend, and a hundred percent at the Olympics. I'd say personally I'm almost at my full potential, but as always, there are a few tiny things that I'll do my best to nail this weekend, though if I don't, they're not things that will keep me from making the team."

"Your nose has seen better days," she smiles brightly, jotting something down in her notebook even though she's recording our interview on her phone. "Gymnastics injury?"

"Yes, actually." No reason to lie, but I decide not to mention the concussion so people don't freak out about how cruel gymnastics coaches are, forcing "little girls" to risk their lives all for the chance at the Olympics. Give me a break. "I was working on tumbling at the gym and my air awareness was way off. Thankfully I controlled the fall and managed to save my ankles and knees, so it could've been a lot worse, though I did end up with a messed up face for a bit."

"Did you miss any training?"

"Less than a week. Thankfully it happened just before the start of my weekend, so the bulk of my recovery got out of the way with almost no break in my training schedule, and I was able to get back to limited practices with only one day off."

"Is there a mental side effect that comes with something like this? You know, a lasting memory of the injury that replays in your head when you attempt the skill now?"

"Not at all," I smile, forcing harder than ever. "Thankfully it was a fluke. Never happened before, won't ever happen again. Training the skill has been no problem, and my mind is so busy with cues during the routine, I don't have time to think about what could go wrong, not even subconsciously. My coach has been working with me on what she calls mental gymnastics since I came to her, way before elite was in the cards for me, and I've been able to apply her teachings at every step of my career, including now."

"What's your biggest goal this weekend?" A welcome change of subject. I really thought she was gonna drill me on the nose thing forever.

"The Olympic team, obviously. That's everyone's goal here, whether it's realistic or not."

"Do you think it's realistic for you?"

"I'm not the best here and may not be a top contender, but I *am* on the cusp. It'll all depend on what Vera thinks makes the most sense for the team. It could be me for what I have to offer on vault and beam, but what if she's trying to pad the floor lineup? I definitely wouldn't go in that case. So yes, it's realistic. It's not a given, but it's not out of my reach. Not at all."

"What do you think you need to prove to Vera? Why should you be the gymnast who fits into her puzzle?"

"Number one is my beam. I need to prove that I can hit two flawless sets this weekend, with zero wobbles or form breaks. If I can get a score around a 15.5 or higher, it would set me apart from pretty much everyone else on the planet, so I'd be helping the team out and could probably also get an individual medal. I'll also need to stick my Amanar with no form problems, since they might want me in the team final there, and I'd need to hit a clean bars set as well. On floor, my routine isn't even worthy of qualifications unless there's some kind of emergency, but obviously I still want to hit there. To show that I can."

"Say you do fall on floor one day. Is the Olympic dream over for you?"

"No. Again, because it's not one of my strong suits, it won't be a huge deal. It's nice to have me as a reliable fifth option on that event in case someone gets injured or something, so I do think it's important for me to look solid and consistent, but if I do make a mistake, I won't be too hard on myself."

"Will your parents be here to watch you?"

"Yes, they both arrive from Seattle tomorrow."

"Any plans for celebrations when it's over?"

"I don't want to count my chickens before they hatch, so I'm just taking it one day at a time. I know the naming of the team is out there in the very near future and it's definitely something I think about deep down, but the focus right now is just on hitting. If we get to celebrate on Sunday night, great, but it's *so* not a priority at the moment."

"Thanks, Amalia. Best of luck this weekend. As a journalist, I'm supposed to be impartial, but I have to admit, I'm really rooting for you."

I'm taken aback at this and the surprisingly chill vibe from the whole interview compared to the usual torture I endure at her hands. She did have a field day with my nose for a minute, but I didn't feel any desire to stab her in the eyes, which is a welcome change.

"Thanks!" I finally utter, and she moves on to her next victim.

The media zone here is much busier than anything I've ever experienced before, with journalists from what seems like every newspaper and magazine in the country, most of whom don't even know gymnastics exists outside of this month-long period every four years. It's a lot, but most of the questions are so basic, I don't have to get too involved with my responses.

It helps that most don't know who I am, of course. Ruby and Emerson are both surrounded by a million journalists apiece, and they're basically hosting mini press conferences, complete with reporters raising their hands for questions so they don't all speak at once.

As soon as the half hour is up, the USGA media rep shuts everything down, leading all fourteen of us back through the winding backstage path to the locker room.

We're actually competing in a football stadium, the Georgia Dome, where the US women's gymnastics team won its first Olympic team gold medal back in 1996. It's way bigger than any arena I've ever competed in, so big in fact that more than half of the seats are actually blocked off with ginormous black curtains since there's no way this meet would bring in 70,000 people. The backstage area is massive and confusing, and many of the people working here are zooming around on golf carts to get from place to place.

"Ice baths at the hotel," Natasha says as we file in. "Not here."

Natasha hates the whole community aspect in the locker room, and I don't blame her, considering Maddy is on a mission to mentally destroy every girl here. She really is the new Emerson, or at least the public version of the Emerson I saw from afar before I actually knew her. Except Maddy has no tragic backstory and this isn't a front. She's just a stone-cold diva bitch, which wouldn't annoy me if she was more talented and actually had a reason to act like that. Good thing she's the first one to jump into the ice bath because that was a *burn*.

"Yo, turn off the sun!" Ruby yells once we find our way outside after a century of searching for the exit. Our hotel is only a little over a five-minute walk from the arena, but this heat makes it feel like five miles.

"We should seriously just stay at the Dome," Emerson whines.

"You have five hours before evening training," Sergei reminds us. "Get room service for lunch, take a bath, watch TV. All at the same time if you're feeling particularly fancy."

"Red leos tonight, guys," Natasha remembers to inform us before we get onto the elevator at the Omni. "The one with the swirly thing on the front. Meet out front 45 minutes before we have to be there. No full routines tonight. Plan on working problem areas and then we'll do routines in two parts with a break at the halfway point. I think that's everything! You're free. Free to lock yourselves in your rooms."

Ruby presses the door close button repeatedly and Emerson asks if she can join us in our room for the lunch portion of the afternoon. After that, I plan on throwing a bath bomb in the tub along with my ice and shivering through an episode of *How to Get Away with Murder* before taking the best nap ever.

What life-changing competition tomorrow? I'm totally chill.

Friday, July 8, 2016
28 days left

It's today, it's today, it's today, *it's today.*

Oh, nothing. It's only one of the two most important days of my life, and yet it dares to present itself just as any other day does on the calendar, with zero significance or meaning, because to 99.9999% of people in the world right now, it means nothing.

But to me, it's everything. July 8 is one of today days that will decide my entire future, whether I go to Rio in a month and win medals and become famous and get endorsements and spend my adulthood telling people I peaked at fifteen, or whether I fail and watch the Olympics on TV like a normal person and go back to high school and do gymnastics in college and get a job in PR or something.

Yeah, I definitely haven't given this any thought.

"I can't believe how ready you are," Ruby says as we lounge in our room this morning. "You're just chugging on through like this is a YMCA rec meet. Seriously proud of you, bro."

"I was more nervous for nationals, to be honest," I reply. "I had that pressure coming away from the open to beat Maddy, and it didn't happen, but no one thought any less of me. I was the one responsible for all that pressure, and now that I'm doing exactly what Natasha taught us, staying in the moment and going one step at a time, that pressure doesn't exist anymore. I can just...*be.*"

"Deep. Hey, I'm gonna run out for a bit, you want anything?"

"Is there something in Sergei's room that we don't already have here?" I tease.

Ruby rolls her eyes in response. "I know you have this whole relationship concocted in your annoying brain, but how many times do I have to tell you it's nothing?"

"Then why are you so secretive if it's *nothing*?"

"Sergei's my friend. One of my best friends. He gets me. It's hard to explain. But I promise you, I'm not stupid enough to blow my reputation by hooking up with a coach."

"Whatever." If booty calls with hot Russian boys help her be a better competitor, who am I to judge?

Today's a low-key one before the meet. It's all about breakfast in bed, bad Lifetime movies, bath bombs, Sudoku, and a quick team lunch just outside the hotel before we suit up for tonight. It's laid-back enough to keep us focused on the task at hand, but with enough busy little distractions thrown in so we don't lose our minds thinking about tonight.

In other words, it's exactly what I need.

***

I go blind when we march out into the arena during the introductions. The spotlights have something to do with it, but I'm not gonna lie. There are also some tears.

Usually at meets, we walk out with our rotation groups, wave to the crowd, no big deal. But tonight the arena is totally blacked out. Dramatic music like the kind you hear before commercial breaks during the Super Bowl fills my ears, and we make our entrance one at a time, each of us paired with a random volunteer guy leading us like we're making our grand entrance at the ball in *Cinderella*.

When the announcer bellows my name, actually pronouncing *Ah-mahhhhhl-ya* correctly, the applause crashes over me like a wave. I climb onto the floor podium, see my headshot flash onto the jumbotron, and then the hot white spotlight finds me in the darkness, making the crowd cheer even louder. I can't breathe, it's so beautiful and terrifying.

I think of my parents up in the stands, trying to hide their sobs, because they're both overemotional disasters who try to pretend otherwise, and I laugh at the mental image of them trying to keep it together.

But while I thought I'd personally be numb to it all, I'm *also* crying because it's all so overwhelming. I must be up in the stands watching, not down here *being*...right?

One by one, the floor fills with gymnasts. Ruby and Emerson get the biggest applause, but that doesn't matter. It's all about Team USA right now, our leos all throwbacks to various Olympic leos over the years, the national anthem singer reaching Whitney Houston levels of diva, and the jumbotron highlighting some of the best moments in US women's gymnastics history. It's borderline Soviet propaganda, actually, but even so, every moment is perfect and I can't help melting with pride for my country and this team.

It all happens so fast, I try to take mental videos of it all, but before I can imprint every piece of this into my brain, I'm standing on the vault podium waiting for the green light to allow us to start the touch warmup.

Today, I'm third after Ruby and Beatrice. It's a good place to start because it lacks both the pressure that comes with going up first as well as the antagonizing wait you have when you're last. Of course, I'll end up being last on floor, which is the longest wait *ever*, but I don't care. I can only control my performance, not the rotation order, not the judging, and not the outcome.

We go one at a time here, alternating between vault and bars, so in a way it's kind of like being back at the national team training center, which is how we verify routines in front of Vera at our monthly camps.

Watching the start of the rotation, I get major déjà vu going back to
when I was last there in April, where I kicked ass. It comforts me.
I keep telling myself "it's just a regular competition" because at the end
of the day, everything is the same. But no matter how often I say it, the
part of me deep down that knows the significance of being at trials
laughs in my face. Finding another competition to compare it to, like
that April camp verification, helps me channel my nervous energy into
adrenaline. When it's my turn to vault, I've never been more ready.

***

"On vault, from Malkina Gold Medal Academy, Amalia Blanchard."

The crowd roars and I get into the zone, waiting for my signal to go. I
salute, take a deep breath, and the ritual begins. My stride feels long
and powerful, like I'm a gazelle, not wholly human. My feet hit the
sweet spot on the springboard, launching me backwards into the hard
suede-covered table, where my hands make brief but powerful contact
before I go air-bound.

Everything happens so quickly from this point on. It's impossible to
know for sure how I look in the air, but I can tell from my block off the
table that my height is exactly where it needs to be. I pull my arms
inward and remember to lock my ankles together as I twist, twist, twist,
two and a half times before hitting the mat.

The landing shocks everyone, I think, but mostly me. There's no fight,
no struggle, no second-guessing. I simply drop down from the sky, no
need to pike down or even bend my knees to absorb the impact because
I'm that perfect. I finish with my chest fully up and feet firmly planted,
a position I hold onto for a brief moment before saluting and bolting to
the stairs.

"Amaliaaaaaaaaaaa!" Natasha is screaming. Actually, the whole crowd
is losing it, but I don't hear them. The only voice among the 20,000
that matters is Natasha's.

Natasha yanks me off the podium and into a bear hug, spinning me around as three television cameras follow me back to my seat, one on a crane from high above and the other two held by aggressive guys being chased by even more guys carrying boom mics and cables. It's actually fascinating, how all of this works, and I have so many questions as I struggle to walk around them. Which camera is the one showing up on TV? How do they decide? Normal questions after you've just done the best vault of your career.

"I can't *believe it*," Ruby squeals when we meet up. "You were literally perfect."

Ruby's own Amanar was also impressive, probably even with a little more distance than mine because she's a powerful monster who always explodes off the table. But my landing was better and that's what everyone remembers.

Congratulations come from all around me and someone's on bars but I have no idea who. I sip water and try to regain my composure, breathing in and out to get centered and grounded because as thrilling as this was, it's only one down and three to go.

Just as the wave of calm finally comes, the crowd starts screaming again and whoever's on bars isn't even done yet. I know instinctively that my score has just flashed on the jumbotron, but I'm a crazy person and refuse to look because I fully believe that it will jinx the rest of my competition.

Ruby, Natasha, Emerson, Sergei, and Polina have all seen it, though. They're whooping and hollering along with the crowd, so I shoot them my "don't say a word" look before burying my face in my bag to pretend to search for my grips. I know my score is huge. I know it's the best score I've ever gotten on any event in my life. But I'm staying present, focusing on the *now*, and I'm not letting myself celebrate yet.

On the outside, anyway. Inside, I'm screaming.

***

When I land my double front dismount off bars, the crowd's reaction tells me that like vault, this was probably my best bars set of all time, but all I can think about is that I made it through with no mistakes and now have the entire remainder of the rotation to relax and get my head straight before going up first on beam.

I can't watch anyone else because I know if I see a fall or a mistake, I'll start thinking about myself making those same mistakes, and I'm not about to let that happen. I stay in my bubble, judging routines by the crowd's reactions, so I at least know that my own teammates have hit and I can give them the appropriate hugs and squeals when they finish, even though they know I haven't seen a thing.

Before the rotation officially ends, I slip on my noise-cancelling headphones so I can't hear the announcer yelling the scores and rankings as we walk over to beam. Life would be ideal if I could do the touch warmup with these babies strapped to my head, but alas. At least when I'm on the podium training the skills, the only sound I register is my own brain yelling my mental cues, making it easy to drown out anything that might otherwise distract me.

Going up first on any other event would send me into a blind panic, but I can handle beam. I don't trust anything in the world as much as I trust myself on beam, where I attack the precise movements and skills like I'm playing a real-life game of Operation and the patient would die if I was even a hair away from grazing the sides of his open flesh wounds with my tweezers.

In the touch, I go through the motions, throwing a few skills to get a feel for the beam before hopping off and chalking my legs and feet until I'm satisfied with their gritty texture. The bell dings, the other girls clear the podium, and it's just me and the balance beam, alone together in this world.

Inch by inch, skill by skill, I put on a clinic up there, feeling like Taylor

Swift in front of a sold-out crowd at CenturyLink Field every single time I land a skill. The added confidence from my first two events carries over to beam, helping me hit everything a little bit better than I might usually do it. My face is brighter, my toes are pointier, my connections are more fluid than they've ever been, and my landings? They're perfect.

I want the same landing on my double arabian dismount that I had with my Amanar earlier, so when my brain screams "up, up, up!" as I punch off the beam, I listen.

The first flip is at such a great height that I'm still above the beam as I continue rotating into the second. My knees give a little on the landing, but my chest is up and the stick is good, making this my third killer routine of the day.

"You can go home now," Natasha is beaming as I yet again leap off of the podium into her arms. "You've done your job. If Vera doesn't see that, if you don't make this team, I'm losing all faith in humanity."

More hugs from teammates and the other girls in my rotation group. More cheers from the crowd. More of me ignoring everything except thinking about tackling my final routine, which I want to be my best floor ever. Eff my fall two weeks ago. Screw the concussion and the broken nose. I'm better than ever and nothing's gonna stop me now.

***

"That was Amalia Blanchard on floor exercise."

It's over. My best competition in history. Lock it up and throw away the key. There's nothing else to say.

I don't expect too much from my score there, because I know even with a hit routine I'm severely lacking, but the point is that I looked good and polished and confident. I can compete this event at the Olympic Games if I need to, and while it wouldn't be the greatest routine out there, I can do it. That's what matters.

Going from first in the beam rotation to last on floor was an interminable torture, but I survived. Now we're done, and I can get my scores and breathe a sigh of relief because I've done everything in my power to be amazing today.

"In third place is Amalia Blanchard of Malkina Gold Medal Academy with a 60.7."

I almost pass out from happiness. It's not only my personal best, but it's only two tenths behind Ruby, who has a 60.9, and less than a point behind Emerson, who leads with a 61.6.

"You win the battle," Ruby grins, hugging Emerson as we begin collecting our belongings. "But I'm going to win the war."

Maddy Zhang is right on my tail with a 60.4, Zara Morgan is only a tenth behind that, and Irina Borovskaya has a flat 60, so as great as I was today, I'm going to have to do it all over again on Sunday, lest one of these other ladies steal my thunder. If I can seal a third place all-around finish, there's no way they can leave me off of this team, but anything beyond that puts my spot in question.

From Natasha, I hear that Sophia Harper looked out-of-this-galaxy on bars and beam, and Charlotte Kessler fell on vault, which limited her overall ranking, though she looked great on her other three events. So yeah. It's tight. I'm not done yet.

Our entourage passes through a sea of people yelling "congratulations" on our way to the mixed zone, and I want to skip press, but I'm a good girl and sit in my chair answering questions while thinking about pizza.

"You were great tonight," Anna Young remarks, waiting for the hype around me to die down before she approaches. "Want to walk me through it?"

"Well, I don't follow my scores throughout the competition, so the end result was definitely a surprise, but I felt confident the whole way through. I tried to stay in my bubble and focus on everything I was doing instead of what was going on around me. That mindset really helped, and I was able to pull off what was easily my best performance ever."

"Anything you're working on fixing before Sunday?" Only Anna Young would force me to get über critical after I literally killed it tonight.

"It's always about the little things," I smile back. "I can always look a little more crisp or get a little more height or focus harder on my form. But the only thing I'm focusing on between now and Sunday is how I feel in this moment right now, and how if I do it all again, I'm going to the Olympic Games."

Saturday, July 9, 2016
27 days left

My phone is a nonstop parade of texts and social media notifications and missed calls. I eventually turn it to airplane mode because otherwise I'd be doing nothing but responding to people, which is getting stressful.

"What do you want for breakfast?" Ruby asks, bright and early, poring over the room service menu, which is bomb, by the way. We're getting so spoiled here.

I'm super groggy from a lack of quality sleep after tossing and turning due to the excitement, but today's a chill day, so I can nap all I want. We'll probably go to the hotel gym or the pool, and we have massages scheduled for the afternoon, but otherwise it's a day of bliss.

Emerson stops by after I text her to let her know what we're up to, because I know if I don't, she'll yell at us for not including her, even though she's the one who demands the private rooms. She collapses onto my bed, exhausted, and asks if we're as tired as she is.

"I barely slept," I admit. "Too excited."

"It's a good thing the Olympics are happening *now* because I'm getting too old for this," Emerson whines. "Less than two hours at the meet, four minutes of actual routines, and I feel like I've been run over by a steamroller and then pushed into a ravine and then stepped on by a dinosaur. I need to be in a retirement home by 22."

"Same," Ruby yawns.

Physically I'm good, just the usual nagging pain that comes with the territory, but nothing more. Hooray for being fifteen. But the mental aspect is what wiped me out. It's hard keeping yourself in a self-imposed brain lockdown for an entire meet.

Our breakfast arrives and we eat in silence, the others scrolling through their phones and occasionally yelling out new follower counts on Twitter and Instagram while I just play Candy Crush, still too overwhelmed to read my texts and social media.

Suddenly Ruby gasps.

"What?!" Emerson and I practically jump out of our skin at Ruby's outburst.

"Don't, um...ugh, I shouldn't have said anything. Emerson, don't google yourself."

"What? Why?! You can't just tell me not to google myself and then expect me to be like okay, great, thanks for the tip!"

"Well, if you *do* google yourself, which we all know you were going to do anyway, now at least you won't be blindsided. It's good having a warning, right? Think of me as your tornado siren."

"Blindsided by *what*?! What could possibly be so bad? I'm leading trials. It's not like anyone can possibly skew that into how terrible I am."

"Your mom can," Ruby coughs.

Emerson turns as white as the hotel-issue robe she's wearing. Clearly, changing her phone number did nothing to thwart her mother's attacks. Instead of going straight to Emerson, now she has the press at her disposal, which is even worse.

She opens the browser on her phone and taps into her bookmarks, where she has a Google news search with her name already saved.

"Here we go. 'Top Olympic contender Emerson Bedford's demons threaten team,'" she reads aloud, her hand going to her mouth. "What the hell. 'Star's mom opens up about Emerson's shady past and mental illnesses.' Mental illnesses, *plural*? What does 'shady past' even mean? The only thing shady about my past is her, like, I don't know, when she all but forced me away from her when I was a kid because of her inability to be a parent."

"Ignore it, Em. I'm serious," Ruby warns. "Don't turn this into another nationals. Your mom doesn't matter. And no one even reads this. It's a gossip mag."

"She *does* matter, Ruby!" Emerson cries. "She knows that I care about my reputation. She knows how to get to me. My mother had a very clear motive in going to the press with this. Gossip mag or not, people are going to read it and believe it."

"So what? Even if they do, no one's gonna say anything to you about it. At least not until after tomorrow's competition. None of the ten-year-old girls in the crowd tomorrow will know or care what some trashy website has to say. They're there to watch some of the best gymnasts in the world make their country's Olympic team. Everything else is background noise. Say it."

"Everything else is background noise," Emerson whispers.

"After the weekend is over, you can take your response to basically any journalist in the country," I add, wanting to be helpful but not really knowing what to say in a situation like this. "Who do you think they'll believe, America's sweetheart or some woman no one cares about who basically abandoned her child?"

"Harsh," Emerson blows her nose. "But accurate."

"I'm not really into this tradition of you losing your shit in the middle of the biggest meets of our careers," Ruby says, returning to her scrambled eggs, signaling that this conversation will soon be over and that she'll have the last word. "Seriously, this *can't* ruin you again. You have to kill it tomorrow. There's still more than 24 hours until we compete, so watch stupid TV, enjoy your massage, or do something else that will keep you from focusing on this crap that isn't worth your time. There's so much more you deserve in this world, but you need to be on your game to get it."

"I know."

"Good. Now for real, go take a bath so your muscles are all warm and gooey before your massage. We'll see you at lunch? And then we can swim later today?"

Emerson finishes a few pieces of fruit before dropping her fork on her plate, saying "see ya," and booking it out of our room. Ruby sighs.

"Would you believe me if I said I missed the Emerson we knew before we actually got to know her? Like, superbitch Emerson who was a dick to everyone and had a perfect life?" Ruby laughs. "Real life sad and conflicted Emerson bums me out. It's like finding out Santa Claus isn't real. Let's be happy and grateful that we're drama-free."

"Yeah," I sigh, obviously thinking about my own mama drama in this moment and how badly it totally effed with me earlier in the week. But like Ruby said to Emerson, everything else in our lives right now is background noise. Keep shoving it into the back of your mind, Mal. Last night was epic and tomorrow has to be as well. Focus. There's no room for real life right now. There's no room for drama.

I push around the food left on my plate while Ruby scarfs hers down, whining about how it's getting cold and gross. I'm not hungry, or not in the mood to eat, and I just want to nap until lunch. That's probably not the healthiest decision, but I'm hella tired and getting grumpier by the second. The day's only going to get worse if I don't combat this immediately.

The old Emerson would probably suggest hot yoga and some sort of super juice or something, I muse. But she's not here right now to force me into making good choices. Sleep it is.

Sunday, July 10, 2016
26 days left

"You've got to get up every morning with a smile on your face and show the world all the love in your heaaaaaart."

Someone is singing directly into my ear and I'm not loving it.

"Mmmmmmgggggghhhhhhuuuuuuffffffff," I moan into my pillow before rubbing my eyes. In a shocking twist, it's Emerson standing above me. "You're chipper for six in the morning."

"Uh, yeah. It's kind of going to be the best day of my life? I don't know about you, but *I'm* making the Olympic team today."

Yep, there it is. Holy crap. I bolt up onto my feet, pulling Emerson onto the bed, and we jump up and down, shrieking loudly enough to make anyone with rooms on this floor hate us.

Ruby steps out of the bathroom, towel wrapped around her impossibly toned body.

"I've been up since five," she smiles. "I don't know, I *might* be excited or something."

"No one ask me how I feel while staring at me with puppy dog eyes," Emerson cautions. "Today is Dreams Come True Day. Literally nothing else in the world matters as much as this. If there's anything else happening on this planet that affects my life, anything at all, I don't want to know about it."

"Amen!" I cheer, jumping to the floor and running into the bathroom.

We tried to keep things as normal as possible for Emerson yesterday, but almost everyone we ran into knew what had happened with her mom spreading nonsense to the press. Including our coaches, who gingerly and expertly tap danced around the subject, but obviously wanted to make sure their star was doing okay. It was a weird day, but we ate and swam and watched TV and chatted about fictional people's drama in an effort to pretend our own doesn't exist.

It's impossible to know what's going on in Emerson's head, but on the outside, she really does seem okay with everything. Her face is radiating light and happiness, and we need to keep it that way.

According to Natasha's itinerary, we have breakfast at seven, chill time, a quick physical therapy session in her room at eleven, lunch at noon, a little over an hour to mess around with hair and makeup, and then we'll meet in the lobby before walking to the arena. Warmups start at three, and finally, the competition begins at five. By around seven tonight, aka a little over twelve hours from now, we'll know who's going to Rio.

I could just die.

***

"I'm not going to tell you how important this meet is," Natasha begins at our team meeting following warmups. "You get it. But what you need to think about right now is that this isn't the end of the road. This is an important step in the process, yes. One of the most important steps. But anyone who makes the Olympic team still has weeks of training left before actually competing at the Games and becoming an Olympian. Making the team isn't the goal. Competing in Rio is the goal."

She gulps from her water. It's sweltering backstage.

"Emerson and Ruby have been through selection for other international teams before," she continues. "It's a big relief once the selection camp ends, but they know what it's like to have to go from that high of making the team straight into the weeks of training at the farm, traveling abroad, podium training at an unfamiliar venue in a country they've never been to before, and then, finally, competing in the qualifying rounds. It's a long journey before you get to any of the finals.

Anything can happen in that time. Getting selected today is something you check off the list before moving on to the next step, so think about that today."

I start biting my nails out of habit, wanting to take in everything she's saying, but honestly, it's only making me more nervous. I just need to get out on the floor. Then I'll be okay.

"This competition is like any other. You do your job, you stay in the moment, you control what you can, and if you make the team, you celebrate, but then you keep moving forward. You still have a lot to prove after today. I've personally seen girls tossed off of teams in the weeks leading up to the Olympics because they either settle or can't handle the pressure and their routines start to deteriorate. I tell you this not to scare you, but because you need to be reminded of your future beyond today. You can't think of today as the be-all end-all of your careers, because you *will* get in your head, and that's not good. Be present, be in the moment, and take it one step at a time. Do what you know how to do, what you've been training for your whole lives. Beyond that, it's out of everyone's control but Vera's."

I loop my thumbs through the little holes in my red, white, and blue warmup jacket and grip the sleeves tight, the only thing I can do to keep my fingernails from my mouth. I know this is supposed to be like any other meet, but anyone who says they're totally chill in this moment is a big fat liar. No matter how much "mental gymnastics" we do, no matter how much we try to fool ourselves into being calm, it's totally impossible to forget the implication.

Emerson and Ruby are literally locks. They could fall on every single event today and still make it. That's how good they are, that's how far ahead they are compared to everyone else. Sure, I can get close on a good day, but so can Maddy, so can Charlotte, so can pretty much anyone else who's been in the top five at any meet this season. We're all interchangeable. Emerson and Ruby aren't. They're a step above the rest of us. They're in. They know it. Natasha and Sergei and Polina and Vera know it. Everyone knows it.

Me? I could have the best performance of my life today and still not make it. I'm good, but it's not about me. It's about the team. If I'm not the best choice for the team, it doesn't matter what I do.

Natasha's right, though. I have zero control over the outcome, so I might as well just go out there and forget about everything except doing what I know how to do.

In the end, it's out of my hands, but there's still this part of me that wants to go for broke and use this last shot to show Vera that I *need* to go to Rio.

I'm nodding along to the rest of Natasha's pep talk, only half-listening, when I notice the lights in the arena go out. The dramatic entrance music starts a split second later.

"That's our cue," Natasha whispers. "You got this. Bring it home."

***

Rub, rub, rub. Clap, clap, blow. Repeat.

I'm almost glad bars is first today. My grip chalking ritual is one of few things in the world that can calm me, so while I don't always have the best track record on this event, it's like a blessing in disguise. Or at least that's what I tell myself to cover up the overwhelming sense of panic that runs through my veins.

"Mental cues, Mal!" Natasha yells from off the podium. She climbs the stairs and walks over to the low bar, triple-checking the chalk situation there, a nervous habit of hers I try to ignore.

I'm second-to-last on this event today. Beatrice Turner went up before me and fell twice. The wait for her score is never-ending, the judges taking their sweet time adding up all of her deductions and bickering about whether or not they should credit one of her connections, as if this score even *matters*. Damn you, Beatrice.

If you're an adrenaline junkie and love thrilling activities like skydiving, bungee jumping, or climbing Everest, may I suggest standing on a podium in a leo in front of 20,000 totally silent gym fans as you wait to compete for a spot on the Olympic team? There are only so many times I can chalk my hands before it becomes overkill.

Rub, rub, rub. Clap, clap, blow. Repeat.

Finally, seven thousand hours later, Beatrice gets her score, an 11.7. I can't help hearing the announcer share her score. Rough.

I get into position for my mount, just me and the low bar, face to face. The green light finally allows me to begin, and I glide kip my way into the first routine of the final competition before the Olympics. No big deal.

It's not until I stick my double front that I realize I've made it through with my stupid brain completely letting my body take control for once. Everything came together exactly as I needed it to, and I did my job, my mind fading into the background while my muscle memory took me from skill to skill.

While I'm admittedly awful on floor, mentally, it's not a problem routine for me. I am simply terrible at keeping my endurance up during the entirety of a routine, and I'm also the worst performer alive. I get it. I deal. But bars, physically, I should be great. I *am* great. And yet for some reason, my brain plays tricks on me, makes me think I'm awful there, and I let it.

I don't know why, but today's different. I don't overthink a single skill, and it's a big success.

"Amalia Blanchard on the uneven bars," the announcer proclaims as I salute, clap my hands together to celebrate, and then run into Natasha's arms.

"One down," she squeals, wrapping one arm over my shoulders and squeezing. "You looked good. Your form was superb. Excellent height off the high bar into the dismount. You let go of the bar at the perfect moment. I couldn't have asked for much more...the little things, like your hip angle on your giants and in your swing, they could've been a *little* more exact. But it was a good big picture routine. I want the same thing on beam. Until we rotate, go over your dance elements, and then you can work on your acro while the first couple of competitors go up."

I nod, sip from my water bottle, and sit still for a second to catch my breath, a camera directly in my face. I get congratulatory hugs from Ruby and Emerson, both of whom have already gone up, and then I try to meditate for a minute until I have to focus on beam, headphones on so I don't hear my score if the announcer decides to say it over the speakers. Sometimes he does, sometimes he doesn't. It's hella annoying if you're trying to shield yourself from your scores, but I'm good at blocking out all sounds.

When Zara goes up for her routine, I push up from my chair and jog off to the side of the podium to warm up my dance elements for beam. Emerson, foam rolling her hip nearby, gives me a thumbs up. After a few switch leaps and pirouettes, I walk over to her.

"How did yours go?" I ask. Watching my teammates freaks me out, but once they're done and I can't be mentally rattled, I don't care if they share.

"Perfect," she grins. She's cocky in her answer, but she deserves to be cocky. I'm sure she was literally perfect.

I don't want to be the one to bring her mom up, especially in the arena, but I'm dying to know if she's here, planning to cause a crazy scene the way she did at nationals. Right as Emerson mounted beam, her mom screamed "that's my baby!" from a few rows away. Needless to say, it shook her up, and she fell.

As if reading my mind, Emerson glances up into the crowd skittishly and then sighs deeply, an attempt to soothe her nerves.

"She here?" I ask, trying to keep it as cool as possible.

"I don't think so," she responds. "I don't think she's even in Atlanta, honestly. She'd find a way to get to me if she was. Hotel room phone or waiting outside the arena or something. She hasn't tried anything yet. I'm pretty sure the interview was her way of tormenting me since she couldn't physically be here to do it."

Emerson sticks her hot pink foam roller under her left armpit and leans back onto her right hand, pushing through a back walkover to go from sitting to standing up. Casual. I've always wanted to try out that skill — a Valdez — on beam, actually.

The rotation bell rings and we head over to pack up our stuff.

"Clear mind," I remind her as we grab our bags. "Don't think about anything but this moment. And especially don't think about your mom."

Emerson smirks. "What mom?"

***

Just like bars, I don't remember a second of my beam. How annoying is that? It's like when Katniss conveniently gets knocked out and doesn't see any of the big final battle in *Mockingjay*.

I once heard that when you're under extreme stress, your body has ways of protecting you from mentally losing it, and that must be what's going on. I don't like Autopilot Amalia, but if it helps me hit my routines today, I'm not complaining.

"Perfect." Ruby gives me a double high five after I half-listen to Natasha's notes, still in a fog. "You could do beam in your sleep."

I don't tell her I basically *was* asleep.

Emerson's up last this time around, and I definitely don't have the mental strength to watch her, so I run over to the side of the arena and jump up and down in place facing the opposite direction, headphones on and eyes closed. In an instant, I make everything in the world fade away.

It's not until Natasha gently touches her fingers against my shoulders, causing me to jolt a bit, that I know it's time to get ready for floor.

I yank off my headphones to the sound of the crowd going berserk, so I know Emerson must've hit. Good for her. I mean, we all know she's going to Rio, but no one wants her Olympic moment tainted by a fall that wouldn't even have mattered.

The march to the floor podium is like boarding an airplane, too frustratingly slow for my painfully impatient Type A brain. I just want to get floor *over with*. Come on. Two events left. I'm halfway there.

My heart leaps into my throat while my stomach is simultaneously flipping over itself, and I feel nauseous. I try to breathe. Get it together, Mal. Now is not the time to lose it.

The seven of us climb onto the podium and line up in front of the judges, presenting ourselves and saluting, the weirdest tradition in gymnastics. We stand there, tense but antsy, waiting an eternity for the touch warmup.

I smile awkwardly at the judges beneath us, most of whom used to be gymnasts but don't seem to remember exactly how intimidating this process is. The head judge does talk to us a little, giving us some words of encouragement, but I can't help feeling super uncomfortable.

When the judges tell us we can start, I throw my double arabian and triple full right away, trying to get a sense for my adrenaline level, which is about the same now as it will be when I compete in a few minutes.

I'm fourth here today, smack in the middle of the rotation, which I reason will be good for me. Before I go up, I'll have time to mentally slow down and think about all of my cues, and on the other side, when I'm done, I'll have time to chill and catch my breath before vault. Win-win.

I feel good, especially on the triple, which I sometimes land either a hair short or with my left foot stepping out and over my right to control myself from adding an extra half twist. I hate that I either give too much or too little instead of being right on the money. It's truly the biggest pain in my ass. But right now, I'm close to being on target, coming in with a little too much power in the touch, which I should be able to reel in when I actually perform.

"Compete like that!" Natasha gives me a pat on the back. "And grab an energy chew. You need a little boost."

"Give her Pixy Stix," Ruby chimes in. "It works on *Toddlers and Tiaras.*"

"Kill it," I tell her. She's second up.

"I will," Ruby grins, and I know she will.

In the meantime, I go back to my can't-hear, can't-see, "no senses allowed" zone in the corner until it's my turn, letting the fruit punch energy chew release a party in my mouth while I do a few sets of jumping jacks to stay warm.

With the other rotation group on vault, which lasts less than ten seconds per gymnast, it's a quick turnaround between floor routines. Before I know it, I'm on the podium waiting for a Windy City girl to finish vaulting. I keep jumping in place, and when she lands and salutes, I walk out onto the middle of the floor mat.

I gulp. The green light flashes. I salute. I drop into my starting pose. The bell dings. After only a half second of dead air, the creepy opening chords of the theme from the movie *Saw* turn the arena into a terrifying 1880s insane asylum. It's time.

Every floor routine tells a story. Tumbling is only part of what we do out there, because there's this pesky little thing called artistry that we also need to master. I've never truly been able to grasp it, but neither do most gymnasts. Occasionally someone will show up with the performance quality of Maddie Ziegler in the "Chandelier" music video, but in general, we're athletes. Not *performers*.

Not primarily, anyway. How can we be? Dancers literally exist to tell stories through movement. Gymnasts are a different breed. Everything in this sport is a rule, and if there's one thing we know how to do, it's following those rules. That rigid conformity is great when we need to execute a perfect double back, but it makes us naturally terrible when it comes to freedom of expression.

Or at least that's what it's like for me.

Most girls get routines that match their personalities, which helps with the performance aspect. Emerson's routine is dramatic and elegant and flawless. Ruby's is loud and sassy and exciting. What does it say about me that mine is straight out of a horror movie?

The background story behind my routine is based on the journalist Nellie Bly, who went undercover at an asylum to expose the doctors for abusing patients. In my routine, I'm locked up in an old asylum against my will. I decide I need to escape, and I spend the rest of my routine trying to break free. Near the end, I find the evil doctor, steal his keys, and lock him up before busting out, ready to tell the world about his crimes.

It's super weird, so thankfully no one outside of our circle really knows about our routine stories or that they even exist. Watching my routine, you probably wouldn't guess any of that is going on in my head, but for us, simply having some sort of plot and the emotions that come with it — horror, fear, anxiety, and determination, in my case — helps us convey something through our dance. Honestly, without mine, I'd be totally clueless.

Polina actually even choreographed facial expressions into mine, assuming if I saw the expression as a "skill" and not an "emotion" I'd be better suited to capturing it. As usual, she was right. The facial expressions now come just as naturally to me as a pirouette, and I don't even have to think beyond the movement.

Today, I vow to give it my all. I don't want the crowd to politely applaud my tumbling. I want them fully involved and along for the ride the way they are for Ruby and Emerson. I'm in it to win it.

The music and the choreography carry me at the start of the routine, and I try to remember everything Polina has ever told me about making a routine great instead of good. I don't want to walk into the corner before running into my double arabian simply because I'm supposed to. I want the story to bring me there. I want to feel the desperation of my reimagined Nellie Bly as she flees the cages that oppress her.

One tumbling pass after the next, I inch my way closer to the escape, and when I finish the routine posed on the floor with my arms triumphantly up in the air, for once, my exhilaration is about more than me finishing without screwing up. I feel like I *am* Nellie Bly, so happy to be free.

A single tear rolls down my cheek and the people in this crowd lose their shit.

"What did you do with Amalia?!" Natasha screams as I run to her. "That's what you call a *breakthrough*."

Most of the girls and coaches in my rotation group congratulate me on what is easily my best floor routine ever. Actually, I don't even know if it was technically good, but I don't care if I screwed up every skill. This is the most I've ever been able to let myself find freedom in this sport. It's a sweet release. I'm pretty sure this is what drugs are like.

***

"Up next on vault, from Malkina Gold Medal Academy, Amalia Blanchard!"

Salute. Visualize. Run. Block. Fly. Flip. Twist. Land.

That's vault in a nutshell, over and done with in eight seconds. Like most of today, it's over before I even know it's happening, and my only memory is the step I take forward on the landing. It's annoying, but it's not the make or break factor of me making this team. For once, I'm weirdly okay with it not being perfect.

Ruby, who stuck her own Amanar as the first up in this rotation, comes over to celebrate with me when I come off the podium. Natasha gives me a tight hug and doesn't even bother with notes or corrections. She knows I'm not listening.

In the background, Irina Borovskaya is again mentally falling apart on bars, just like she did at nationals. I'm kind of watching it go down, but I'm not really processing it because every emotion in the world is spreading over my mind, body, and soul.

"Three falls," Ruby whispers when she comes off again, whacking her armpits on the low bar during her pak. Ouch. "Think she'll get back up for more?"

I shrug, too busy watching the somber conversation between Irina and her coach. She wants to get back up. He tells her to kiss her dreams goodbye. She pouts, bursts into tears, and because she's a rule follower, salutes the judges just like she's supposed to, signaling the abrupt finish to what is probably her last routine ever, before she runs off the podium and out of the arena.

When you're so mentally rattled that falls begin to happen on every single skill, most coaches will pull you after your third time down, the way Irina's just did. Who knows what kind of devastating injury the next fall could bring? Your score's already in the toilet. It's better to pull you off than to let you keep going, putting your neck on the line.

Knowing there's no way she's in the Olympic picture after this, I can't help feeling a little rush of excitement. She's the reigning world bars champ and some of my toughest competition for a spot. I'm almost mad at myself for finding this glimmer of happiness out of what is a truly brutal end to her career, but I can't help it. Anyone in my position is in a crappy spot between elation and sympathy, but that's gymnastics. Not everyone can win.

Finally, it's Emerson's turn. I'm done for the day, so I let myself watch, and I know she'll hit this. Finishing on vault is kind of the best thing ever, because if you know what you're doing, there's basically no way you'll screw this up.

"Have you been watching the scores?" I ask Ruby. "Think she can beat you?"

"She won this competition the second she walked into the room," Ruby beams, not taking her eyes off of our teammate. "You got this, Em!"

Emerson isn't the most powerful and her vaults always finish a bit short, but tonight, a near-perfect day gives her the adrenaline she needs to get that extra boost off the table. She's clean in the air, lands perfectly straight and center, and doesn't move her feet a centimeter on the finish.

The crowd erupts as Emerson jumps off the podium into Sergei's open and waiting arms. He gives her a whirl around and then lifts her back onto the podium so she can wave to the crowd. They eat it up.

When her nearly impossible score of 16.1 finally comes up, her name moves to the top of the rankings. Her combined all-around total between Friday and today is 124.3, a little over a point ahead of Ruby for the title, which seals the only automatic spot on the Olympic team. *Emerson is an Olympian.* It's official. And it's surreal.

I see Maddy's name in third, which is a bit disappointing considering I was in third place after the first day, but I'm next, in fourth. It's a spot higher than nationals, and almost guarantees me a spot on the five-member team.

"All athletes must clear the arena," one of the floor managers informs us before I can process anyone else's scores. "Please head to the locker room, and the selection committee will meet you there when they're done determining the team."

"Oh boy," Natasha grimaces, finally succumbing to her nerves. She's usually the queen of staying cool, so this is next-level dramatic for her.

Right behind her, Ruby drops a series of f-bombs and no one stops her.

The selection process is basically over at this point. It's not just the one meet this weekend that decides our fate. Everything we did this season, from national team training camps at the farm to smaller competitions like the open and nationals, those were like our tests in the school year. This weekend was just the final exam.

If Irina had had a better overall season, today's bars meltdown probably wouldn't have been a big deal, but she was also a disaster at nationals in addition to losing her mind at the farm on more than one occasion, meaning she hasn't proved she can handle the pressure of competing at the Olympic Games. There's a difference between fluke falls and gymnasts who mentally can't compete, and today Irina showed that she is the latter. You can't trust someone like that in a three-up three-count team final where every score counts into the total. There's no way Vera can take her.

So everything we've done this year matters, but you never know. Even if Vera and the other members of the selection committee had their minds set on a team, there's always the possibility that someone who was on the "maybe" list jumped into the "definite" pile after an especially strong performance this weekend.

The fourteen of us nervously file into the locker room, which we don't even really use, since we get ready in our hotel rooms.

An assistant from the women's national team program explains that Vera and the rest of her committee — there's a board of four people who choose the major international teams along with her — will spend about ten or fifteen minutes finalizing the team before meeting us in here and telling us who makes it. At that point, the five Olympians and three alternates will be ushered back out onto the floor podium to celebrate in front of the crowd, and then it's time to meet with the media for the first time as members of the 2016 United States Olympic team.

We each pull on our Team USA warmups in dead silence. The excitement on our way back here has turned into full-blown anxiety, which for some people is manifesting itself as rage. When Beatrice trips over Maddy's backpack, Maddy nearly punches her in the face, and Emerson snaps at a caterer for not having Greek yogurt, even though she has literally nothing to worry about with her spot already secure. Things are rough.

I sit on a bench, jiggling my leg up and down nervously until Ruby comes over and presses her hand against my thigh to get me to stop.

"Whatever happens today, I'm so proud of you," she says. "You came in this season as the girl who didn't make nationals last year and now you're walking away one of the best gymnasts in the country. Remember that."

"Thanks, Rube," I whisper back.

The next ten minutes are murder. By the time Vera marches into the room with her entourage, I feel eighty years old. The rest of the girls rush to stand in line and I follow suit, still so new to this that I'm always a step behind, like a tag-along little sister.

"As you know, selecting the Olympic team is not an easy decision," Vera starts. "You are all talented, hard-working, world class athletes who have been training in this sport for more than half of your lives. Many countries struggle to build five-person teams and we have enough top-level gymnasts for two. We are lucky that depth is the biggest problem the US women's gymnastics program has, though it is bittersweet, as we will unfortunately leave several of you behind when you all truly deserve to be there."

Oh. My. GOD. Just *say it already*, I want to scream. Spit it out, lady!

Without further ado, the 2016 United States women's Olympic gymnastics team includes Emerson Bedford of Vanyushkin Gymnastics, Ruby Spencer of Malkina Gold Medal Academy, Maddy Zhang of Windy City Gymnastics, Zara Morgan of Reynolds Gymnastics, and Sophia Harper of Nashville Gymnastics. The reserve gymnasts are Amalia Blanchard of Malkina Gold Medal Academy, and Charlotte Kessler and Olivia Nguyen, both of Windy City Gymnastics."

I hear my name, but I know it came after the girls who made the team. I'm not one of the five. I'm an alternate. Technically I'm an Olympian, but I'm not *really* an Olympian. I'm a kind-of Olympian.

Almost everyone in the room is talking and crying, but I hear no individual words. Only noise.

Before any of us have time to really react, floor managers are shoving bouquets of flowers into our arms while pushing us into a line so we can file out into the arena in the correct order, alternates last.

Everything's a blur. The crowd, the confetti and balloons raining down from the ceiling, the screaming, the crying...I play along because I know I'm supposed to, even though I don't feel like I'm actually living any of it. It's like I'm looking down from above and seeing this other girl experience it all.

I'm not crying. Neither are Charlotte or Olivia, I realize. We're kind of in a limbo of having made it but not really, and so we have these big, confused smiles on our faces, but no happy tears like the girls on the team, and no sad tears like the girls still in the locker room.

The five who did make it, they're bawling like babies. They'll get to compete in Rio. They'll get to live their dreams. I won't.

I won't compete in Rio.

I didn't make the Olympic team.

Monday, July 11, 2016
25 days left

It's impossible to remember everything that happened last night.

Ever since the naming of the team, I've felt like a ghost watching my life from another dimension, and even going back and looking at clips on YouTube doesn't make it feel real.

On the podium during the celebration, there I am, smiling. In interview clips with reporters afterwards I'm "so grateful for the opportunity" and I "hope I can represent the United States as best as possible if they need me to step in."

I played it cool. Even after talking to the reporters, when everyone came up to me to give their congratulations, I thanked them with a big smile on my face, as if I'm truly honored and straight up lucky to get an alternate spot.

In real life, the only thing I understand is that I didn't make the Olympic team. I was never actually on the team, so I know deep down I didn't technically *lose* anything here, but I can't shake the feeling that a piece of me is missing.

Vera threw everyone for a whirl putting Sophia on the team. We all knew Emerson and Ruby were gonna make it, no matter what. They've been the best all-arounders in the country all season and are virtually unbeatable. That was set in stone. Maddy, yeah, she was third at trials and is consistently a top all-arounder, she has irreplaceable scores on her best events, *and* she'll probably win vault gold pretty easily, so she was a given.

But the combination of Zara and Sophia is totally bizarre. I mean, I guess it makes sense. You have the three best all-arounders plus two specialists, Zara for vault and floor and Sophia for bars and beam. It's the perfect way to piece together the puzzle.

Zara can be kind of a disaster on her other two events, though, and Sophia doesn't even train vault or floor! What happens if an all-arounder gets injured after the deadline to swap in an alternate? They'd have to put Zara up on her bad events and Sophia wouldn't even be able to be a replacement on the events she doesn't do.

This is what Natasha and Polina kept ranting about over dinner. Natasha actually thinks Vera blocked me from the team because it would seem too political to have three girls who train at her daughter's gym all make it, but what does that matter if I'm one of the proven best? If I placed last and made the team over girls who were clearly better than me, then yeah, that's a problem. But I was fourth. *Fourth.* If I had made it, I would've deserved it, right?

I convinced my coaches, teammates, and parents that I'm totally fine. The truth? I'm a mess. Here it is, four in the morning, and I'm sitting in a now freezing bathtub running through every possible thing I could've done wrong this season that led to Vera deciding I wasn't worth it.

We have a team breakfast meeting in four hours and a photo shoot after that, and all I can think about his never getting out of this bathtub for the rest of my life.

"You know I'm proud of you," Natasha had said once we got back to the hotel, pulling me into her room. She reiterated everything Vera said earlier about the decision being about who best fit the team, not about talent or ability. In some scenarios, I was the perfect choice for a spot, but a ton of work went into figuring out the *best* scenario, and it doesn't include me.

"Bias aside, I would have chosen you over Sophia in a heartbeat," Natasha griped, shaking her head. "Sophia's good, but they're going to want an extra vaulter out there just in case, and she can't give them that. I don't want to go as far as saying she made it on her name and former Olympic glory because she did have a great trials. But had she not been on the 2012 team, had she not won the all-around gold that summer, she wouldn't have been a top choice. Maybe it was pressure from the Olympic Committee? Maybe she has upgrades coming that we don't know about? Honestly...her inclusion on the team makes very little sense to me. But no matter what, I'm proud of you and you should be *so* proud of yourself. I know it's not what you wanted, but a year ago if you asked if I ever thought you'd make it this far, I would've said hell no. You completely blew me and everyone else out of the water, and you absolutely deserve to be on this team."

She says it to make me feel better, I know, but in the end I only feel worse. If I had been a disaster, if I had low-difficulty routines, if I couldn't mentally compete, if I had zero chance at all, I'd be able to accept my fate.

But getting this close and being as good as the girls who did make it? I had the best performances of my life this weekend and I'm on pace to peak at exactly the right moment, and I was tossed aside. Forgive me for being overdramatic right now, but I'm a teenage girl, so get used to it. This is so unfair, and the pain is literally unbearable.

I shiver, realizing I've now been in the tub for over four hours, doing who knows what. Thinking? Moping? My phone is turned completely off, buried somewhere in the blankets on my bed so I wouldn't have to deal with all of the congratulatory texts and tweets and snaps. Or worse, the *pity* texts and tweets and snaps. It felt so good to disconnect. I don't want to face anyone until I've had a few days to sulk.

Wrapping a towel around my wrinkled, goosebumpy flesh, I tell myself I'll get over it. I know I will. I could stay upset about this forever, quit the sport, and move on, but no. I'll go off to the farm with the rest of my Olympic teammates and train hard knowing full well I'll never get to compete my routines, but I'll still do the job I was given because I'm Amalia Blanchard and I Don't Quit.

For now, though? I'm going to sulk and I'm going to be pissed off and I'm going to bitch and moan and hate the world until I don't feel like doing these things anymore.

When I'm dry, I replace my towel with a ratty old t-shirt of Jack's that I must have subconsciously packed as a comfort item. I wrap the towel around my head and climb into bed, not caring that my hair will look like crap in the morning.

My head drops onto the pillow. I need to force myself to sleep for the next three hours, when I have to get up and be bright and shiny once again. My eyes well up, and I let myself cry, the tears rolling down my cheeks with no fight on my part to hold them back. Like a baby, I cry and cry and cry until I eventually tire myself out and fall asleep.

***

"Congratulations again to the 2016 US women's Olympic gymnastics team," Vera announces to a hotel conference room full of the five team members and three alternates, our coaches, a million parents (minus my dad, who had to fly back early this morning), agents for those who have them, and all of the staff from the USGA who will be part of this process. There's the media crew, a medical team, national judges, administrative directors, and even the CEO, who told us earlier how great it is to have both the reigning world and Olympic all-around champions on "the best team this country has ever seen." I stifle a yawn.

With all of the ass-kissing and celebratory speeches out of the way, Vera launches into the more boring technical aspects of today's meeting while we eat breakfast, the non-gymnasts digging into pancakes and French toast dripping with sugar and maple syrup while we gymnasts stick to egg whites and fruit. It's less than what we'd normally eat at home, but there's something terrifying about going to town on massive quantities of food in a room full of people who exist solely to judge you.

"You'll have three days back at home." Vera flips through some papers on her clipboard, going into the schedule that will keep us together for the next month. "You will report to the national team training center this Friday, and we will train as a team for two weeks. We will fly to Rio on the 28th, arriving the morning of the 29th. The time difference isn't much, thankfully...in Rio, they're only two hours ahead of central time, so we should be fine with a week to train and adjust to life there prior to our official podium training date."

She clears her throat before continuing. "If you are an alternate, the two weeks spent at the farm apply to you as well, and you will fly to Rio with us. Once we arrive in Brazil, those who are credentialed members of the team will depart for the Olympic Village in Barra di Tijuca. Sadly, alternates and their coaches are not allowed to stay in the Olympic Village, nor will you be allowed in the training halls or in the athletes only areas at the arena. Instead, we have rented an apartment in Ipanema where a local gym has graciously invited to host our athletes. You'll remain in Ipanema unless called upon to replace one of the members of the team. We have until the end of our podium training date to name a replacement. Following that time, if you are not needed to help the team, you'll be free to return home. You may also stay in Rio and watch the competition. Based on my previous experiences, there will not be much interaction between those in the Village and those in Ipanema, but we will have a member of the national team staff act as a liaison between the two sides."

I fight to hold back my tears through my pasted-on smile. The one thing keeping me going in all of this was the fact that I'd at least kind of get an Olympic experience. Not being allowed in the Village or the training halls, I won't even have that. A crappy Airbnb or whatever nowhere near the arena? And with Ruby on the team, Natasha will be in the Village with her, meaning I won't even have my coach at my side.

Don't get me wrong, Polina is great and everything, but she doesn't get me the way Natasha does. Natasha knows how to handle me, but Polina often gets frustrated. She hates that I don't pick up on everything right away and that I struggle to figure out how to make corrections work for me instead of just doing them perfectly as she yells them at me.

Polina prefers working with the trained seal robot gymnasts who automatically do everything exactly the way she wants, and she can't deal with me when I get stuck in my head. But Natasha knows exactly how to unlock the door, pulling me out and helping me shine without getting annoyed even when I'm being the biggest pain in the ass.

I need Natasha there with me. I can't do it without her.

I should quit.

Vera is still going on and on about the logistics of the next few weeks, while the coaches — and even a few parents — are taking vigorous notes. I sigh and sip my water, and then search for my gum. Chomping on that will keep my mouth busy so I can stop yawning, which is what I'm probably doing in every single photo snapped by the social media guy. I can't wait to see all of the pics of me looking heinous with captions like "no wonder she didn't make the team!"

Shut up, brain.

"We would like to send out an official team photo along with a press release sharing information about each of the ladies on the team, so we'll take care of that once breakfast is over," an assistant from the USGA media team says. "We have faux-Olympic leos for each of you, and the process will be quick and painless so those of you with early flights don't have to worry about missing them. Thank you, and congratulations once again."

"Is this everything you've ever dreamed of?" Ruby grins, biting into a piece of toast. She's the one daring soul ignoring the unwritten rule of "no carbs in front of Vera."

"Yeah, totally!" I smile back, feigning excitement. "It's the best day of my life."

Okay, yeah, that was taking things a little too far.

"It's cool that you get to come to Rio," she adds, testing the waters by mentioning the whole alternate situation. "In 2012, the alternates had to train at some gym in the middle of nowhere, eight hours away from

London, and this year some countries won't even send their alternates at all because they have no idea where to house them. So even though you can't...you know, be in the Village, or whatever, at least you basically get a free trip to Brazil! Ipanema, too...that's a way better area than where we'll be. Beaches everywhere. I'm jealous."

I don't respond, pretending I'm super interested in fixing one of my gladiator sandals, which I never tie correctly, leaving the straps dangling childishly against my ankles.

"You okay?" she finally asks, and I yawn in response.

"Sorry, just exhausted. I didn't sleep at all last night. Way too excited."

Thankfully, we're summoned over to pick up our fake Olympic leos, the real ones kept a state secret until the team debuts them under the lights of the arena when they compete. I dump my paper plate into the trash, spit out my gum, and skip over with the rest of the girls.

Once, when I was little, my mom and I were driving to Idaho for a competition. We got so insanely hungry on the road home, she finally gave in to my whining and stopped at a McDonald's for the first and last time in my life. She wouldn't let me go to the playground, though, which is basically the entire point of eating there.

At first, I sadly watched from our booth, trying to have a good time with the tiny plastic toy that came with my meal, but then I imagined I was the little boy speeding down the curly slide and the little girl burying herself in the ball pit, and it almost felt like I was in there with them. My imagination isn't what it was when I was seven, but now I'm trying to trick myself into thinking I'm actually one of the girls on the team.

Worth a try, but the magic no longer works. Now I need to suck it up. The Olympics aren't going to happen for me. Face it. It's over. I can't be a jerk about this. As pissed off and upset as I am, I'm still a part of Team USA and I need to at the very least feign happiness for my teammates so I don't ruin this for them.

I slap a smile back on my face, "ooh"-ing and "ahh"-ing over the cheesy stars and stripes leos along with the other girls, who are already discussing going for a bold team-bonding red lipstick to complete the look. I want to roll my eyes *so badly* but I fight it.

The next few weeks are going to kill my soul, and there's nowhere I'd rather be right now than at home in my bed, but I need to stick this out. I can't give up on something just because I didn't get what I wanted. And if I'm along for the ride, I might as well make the most of it.

I'm going to pretend I'm one of the five. I'll train like I'm leading this team to gold, like they could never make it happen without me. I'll support my teammates. I'll become better and stronger. I'm gonna make Vera wish she never overlooked what I have to offer.

I'll be the best damn alternate the world has ever seen.

Tuesday, July 12, 2016
24 days left

"You haven't said one word all morning! Are you feeling okay?"

"Mom, you're suffocating me," I moan over a glass of orange juice. "I'm exhausted. And I'm not a baby. Don't you have to go to work?"

"You're only home for three days and then I won't get to see you again for a month. I took the whole week off. I want to spend time with you."

I groan. "I'll be at the gym for most of the week," I remind her.

"So I'll get work done at home while you're there, and then I'll be here to make you dinner when you get back," she says cheerfully, ruffling my hair. I instinctively jerk away from her touch, *the incident* with her coworker in this very kitchen last weekend always on my mind. Was that really only a week ago? It feels like two hundred years.

"You really don't have to," I mumble.

"Sweetheart, I won't see you again until August. If your father can't be home for you, I should be."

"Dad has to work," I bluntly respond. "You should, too."

"Shush." She busies herself with dishes and sorting the mail and whatever else moms do when literally everything else is done but they have to be doing *something* mom-like at every second of the day to keep the world from imploding. "Oh, before I forget, Jack wants to know why you're not texting him back."

"Oh, balls!" I jump out of my seat, realizing I haven't turned my phone back on since before Sunday's meet. I know, a teenage girl without her phone for this long?! Shocking. But contrary to popular belief, not everyone is a stereotype. My middle-aged dad spends more time on his phone than I ever have.

"Language!" my mom yells as I book it upstairs. "And I still want to talk to you about making the team!"

I roll my eyes, dig for my phone at the bottom of my bag, and plug it into the charger that lives under my windowsill. After a few minutes, the little black apple appears in the center of the bright white screen and I aggressively tap my fingers against my knees until it gets to the passcode screen.

I have 389 texts, and roughly ninety percent of them are from Jack, live-texting the competition as he saw it on TV. There are millions of screen caps from the podium celebration and then a "congratulations" message with a whole screen full of emojis. After that, he asks me to call him a few times, and then his last text from earlier this morning just says "um...hello?"

I'm an ass.

"Sorry sorry sorry sorry sorry!!!" I text. "Got home late last night and zonked! Dinner tonight?"

I sigh, hard, and lean back against the side of my bed, my legs just long enough so that my feet touch the wall. As badly as I want to see Jack, I don't want to talk about what happened. I like keeping things light and breezy between us, and am so not in the mood to get all deep about my feelings right now.

My mom barges into my room while I'm still waiting for Jack to respond.

"Knock much?"

"So?" she says excitedly, ignoring my attitude. "I haven't gotten to talk to you at all yet! Are you still on cloud nine?"

She doesn't get it, at all. She thinks an alternate spot is just as good as getting on the team, because I'm still "part of the process" and all that. I only saw her for a few minutes after the team meeting yesterday, but she was, like...*actually* proud of me, not just pity-proud.

"Yes," I lie, staring at my phone so I don't have to face her. "I can't believe it."

"You sound less than thrilled." She crosses her arms and walks over to me. "Are you hitting your surly teenager phase? I'm honestly excited if you are. I thought I raised you from four to forty overnight and I was almost sad about never getting to enjoy the drama that comes with having a fifteen-year-old daughter."

"Calm down, Jerry Seinfeld. I told you downstairs, I'm *tired*, and out of whack. Once I get to the gym and have a normal schedule again, I'll be back to my old and wise grandma ways."

My phone buzzes and I swipe wildly at the screen. Jack.

"Dinner's good, Olympian! Where to? I can legally drive now, in case you were looking for an accomplishment that tops making the Olympic team."

"Omg awesome!!!!" I respond, using way too many exclamation points and looking psycho. "But you can just come over here maybe? My mom is home this week and wants to spend time with me. She's making all my fave meals."

"I'm there," he texts back immediately. "Lemme know when you're home from gym."

"Actually, can we do tomorrow night?" I write. I definitely still need another day to get over myself. He responds with a thumbs-up emoji and I breathe a sigh of relief.

"Jack's coming for dinner tomorrow," I announce to my mother, who smiles, squeals, and claps her hands.

"I'll make it extra special." She runs out of the room, probably going off to watch a thousand Tasty recipe videos to discover some wild new way to turn a chicken carcass into a gourmet meal.

Practice isn't until two today. I lean back against my bed and scroll through my list of texts, deleting them without opening any. Every "congratulations" is mocking me.

I probably would've reacted better to not making the team at all. Being an alternate is an honor, but it's all work and no reward, and you're constantly reminded of your failure of not making the actual team.

As much as I try to be happy and positive and brave about everything, at this moment I don't know if I can actually handle it.

***

"Finish what you're doing and then line up on the floor!" Sergei calls out during conditioning at the end of our first training session back.

I grunt through my last set of leg lifts and jog over, tugging on my warmups as I go. I spent the entire day doing nothing around the house but dreaming of myself going up to Natasha and telling her I want to retire from elite.

"I want to give up my alternate spot and go back to level ten," I say in my fantasy, calm and without a care in the world. No more forty hour weeks in the gym, no more daily mental freak-outs, no more passive aggressive fighting to be noticed over a dozen other girls...seriously, elite was the dumbest decision I ever made. If I quit, I can relax and focus on staying healthy for NCAA.

My heart flutters as I contemplate actually saying these words to Natasha. Would she murder me? She would. She would literally murder me. Has anyone ever actually turned down an Olympic alternate spot before? Everyone tells me most people would kill for this opportunity, and here I am whining about it not being good enough for me.

But really, I can't spend the next month feeling like crap and pretending everything is perfect while watching other girls live their dreams. I want to be mature and awesome about this, but I'm not mature and awesome. I should fake an injury or something.

"Amalia, can I see you before you leave?" Natasha asks, pulling me aside after Sergei goes through the training and travel plans for the rest of the week. I didn't pay attention for even a second. Does she know I want to quit? She can totally read my mind sometimes. It's actually freaky.

"Sure," I say, super casually, dropping my bags to the ground. Ruby raises an eyebrow but I smile brightly. "See you tomorrow!"

Natasha closes her office door behind us and I sit meekly in a chair across from her desk. I've never been to the principal's office, but based on my extensive knowledge of bad teen movies, this feels just like that.

"I know I told you how proud I am. It takes real talent and strength and passion to make something like this happen, and I've never seen any other gymnast have suck a quick turnaround in this sport. You're a special kid."

"Thanks. I'm honored to get this opportunity. It's a dream come true." Amalia? More like I'm-a-*LIAR*. Thank you, I'm hilarious.

"I also know how much you've been beating yourself up for not making the team."

My smile fades and I gulp.

"Amalia, anyone in your situation would be disappointed. The chance of an alternate replacing someone on the Olympic team is incredibly slim and hasn't happened in the US since before you were born. I've seen girls compete vault with leg fractures and swing bars with dislocated shoulders because they didn't want to lose their Olympic spots, no matter how badly they were hurting. I don't want to dash whatever hope you have left, but the likelihood of you getting to compete is low."

"I know."

"I'm sure you do. I wouldn't have brought it up, but you weren't...*you* today. You hit your routines and did all of your conditioning, but you were only going through the motions. Now isn't the time to go through the motions, though, okay? Because even if your chance of competing in Rio is less than one percent, that's still not nothing. It's still reason enough to be at your best. I can't take you to the training camp looking like you're over it. Vera would kick you out of the gym, give your spot to a girl who didn't make it, and you'd never be invited back to the farm. I need you to decide right now if you want to go through with this."

Now is my chance. This is my way out. My moment of truth.

"I want it, okay?" I blurt. So much for quitting.

"You're the best all-arounder among the alternates, and almost all of your individual events are better than what the others can do. You're the best option to replace any gymnast who goes down. But if you start slipping, Vera will turn to Charlotte or Olivia. If you're going to be an alternate, you need to be the best alternate for the team."

"I understand."

"So you'll come to practice at a hundred percent tomorrow?"

"Two hundred percent."

"Nothing is bothering me," I lie again, though my voice sounds way too over-the-top to be genuine. "I'm just exhausted."

"Sure," Natasha rolls her eyes. "Okay, go home and get some rest. I'll see you bright and early tomorrow, and I expect you'll be back to your old self?"

"Absolutely."

"Good. Remember, Olympic team or dead last, I couldn't be prouder of everything you've done this year, okay?"

I nod and walk out of her office with a pathetic little wave before heading outside to my mom's car.

"How did it go, Olympian?" she asks as I climb into the back, sprawling out across the seat.

"Perfect," I lie again for the millionth time in the past ten minutes, hoping for an otherwise silent ride home, though I'm sure my mom will ask eight hundred questions about my day.

I didn't quit. I wanted to, or thought I wanted to, but no matter how bad it gets, deep down I know I can't. Natasha actually asked me if I was done, giving me a way out, and I said no before I even had a chance to think. I want to be here, no doubt, and as much as this sucks, as much as the next month is going to make me feel like crap, I got this far. If there's even that one percent chance that I could still compete in Rio, I can't give up on that.

I've made my decision.

I'm going to suck it up.

Wednesday, July 13, 2016
23 days left

"Good, Mal! The rebound was awesome, but you still had that slight hesitation breaking up your fluidity. You'd probably get credit, but if you make it a little more smooth, the judges wouldn't have to think about whether to credit it or not."

A little out of breath, I nod at Polina, and walk back to the end of the beam. I take a deep breath and try to mentally prepare yet again for my side aerial to Onodi combination, performing the two difficult acro skills one right after the other without stopping. When you do something like this successfully, hitting two or more skills fluidly with no break between them, the judges reward you with a connection bonus on top of the difficulty points for the skills.

I get an extra one or two tenths for all of my connections, but if I pause for even a second, it doesn't count. Since the majority of my routine is made up of connections like this one, how fluid I look can be the difference between my untouchable 7.2 D score or a more average 6.4.

When I'm ready, I raise my arms and swing them forward, my body following through. The momentum takes me into my side aerial, which I land without any wobbles or missteps. As soon as my feet smack against the smooth, hard surface of the beam, I push off again, launching backwards into my Onodi, a back handspring with a half twist. I land upright, facing the end of the beam closest to Polina, who looks happy with my progress.

"That was perfect. What went through your mind to make it work?"

"Nothing, actually," I admit, shrugging. "No mental cues. I just went for it."

"Sometimes that's all it takes," Polina winks.

I've worked hard at practice this morning, though mentally I'm still not where I should be. The physical effort is there, at least, and it's showing. But mentally, I'm still somewhere else. Home. In bed. Sleeping.

"Okay, one more full routine, five dismounts into the pit, then move to floor, sound good?"

"Yeah." I hop off the beam, walk to the chalk bowl to dust on a bit more, and return for my mount.

The rest of practice goes swimmingly, and Natasha looks pleased with my attitude adjustment, even though it's mostly a show for her benefit. When I finish floor, Emerson and I pair up to work on flexibility while Ruby goes to spend some time with the treadmill.

I sit in a pike position, reaching my hands to my toes while Emerson plants herself on my back. Teamwork.

"How are you doing?" Emerson asks after a moment.

"I'm great."

"What did Natasha talk to you about yesterday?"

"Nothing, really. She just wanted me to know I should keep my expectations low about getting a chance to compete for the team."

"Yeah, it's definitely not going to happen." I twist my neck around and glare at her. "What? It's not. Do you want me to lie to you and tell you it will? It's easier to deal with the inevitable disappointment if you don't have any expectations going in. Unless you're planning on pulling a Tonya Harding, you're done."

"Gee, thanks."

"If it was me in your situation, I'd be pissed, not gonna lie. But I'd also do my job and then move onto the next thing. No reason to dwell."

"Easier said than done. Get up."

Emerson climbs off of my back and we swap places, me sitting a little more forcefully than necessary. Oops.

"Jesus, Mal, don't Tonya Harding *me*. Breaking my spine isn't gonna get you a spot," she snaps. "Listen, you came out of nowhere and beat a ton of girls for this. It's not like you spent years winning world medals and then blew it, like Irina, or got injured weeks before, like Ruby in 2012 and Bailey this year. You came up a nobody as the youngest kid in the mix, and you worked your way almost to the top. That's awesome. If someone like me got alternate, that would suck. But you, you're actually *so lucky* to be in this position. Just be grateful. So many girls would kill to be you."

I get up and storm off to the locker room, pissed and frustrated and annoyed and over it. Over everything. The worst thing is that I'm not even mad at Emerson. The only person I can be angry with is myself.

***

"I know this isn't champagne, but in honor of your brilliant accomplishment, a toast is required." Jack smiles, raising a champagne flute filled to the brim with grape juice.

My mom raises her own glass, filled with wine, and I lift my baby cup of milk, directing it to the center of our dining room table. I wish my dad was here to celebrate, even if this is the lamest party in the history of the universe.

"To Amalia!"

I blush and take a small sip of milk, the perfect complement to the chicken saltimbocca and asparagus my mom whipped together.

"I'm going to eat upstairs in my room," my mom smirks as she stands up and lifts her plate. "There's a Duggar marathon on TV."

Cute. I'm pretty sure most mothers of teenage girls don't actively force them into awkward date-type situations, but since I waited almost sixteen years to discover the opposite sex, my mom is almost too excited to make me and Jack happen.

"How was practice?" Jack asks in between bites.

"Meh," I shrug. "Fine. Now that the team is set and everything, it feels kind of anticlimactic, I guess. Like, a week ago, I still had something to work for, and now it's over and everything seems kind of pointless."

"Pointless? Mal, should I remind you that you're training for an *Olympic team*? An Olympic team which *you made*. I can think of about ten billion adjectives that describe this and pointless isn't one of them."

"I don't know. Maybe it hasn't sunk in yet."

"Maybe."

We eat in silence for a few minutes and I pretend to be super interested in the design on the rim of my plate. My mom sure knows how to pick dinnerware.

"Is everything cool?" Jack asks. "Between us, I mean."

"What? Yeah, everything's great!" My voice once again sounds way too chirpy for anyone to possibly believe. "Why wouldn't it be?"

"I don't know. Things just feel weird. You didn't answer my texts this weekend and you *always* answer my texts. I know you were competing, but I didn't hear from you for a long time after you finished. And now, I don't know. You seem distant or like you don't want me here."

"You're like the one person I actually *do* want to be around," I blurt, my cheeks turning pink. "I mean...everything's crazy right now. It's overwhelming, like I need a break from being around people. I'm mentally exhausted. Trust me, if I didn't want you here, you'd know.

Not because I'd *tell* you, but because I'd passive aggressively make up excuses. That's how I roll."

"I get it," Jack nods. "That's how I feel most of the time, and why I prefer Friday nights on my laptop over going out to parties. I see people all day at school or at camp. That's more than enough."

I laugh. "People suck."

"I don't think people suck. I get along with pretty much everyone. But constant interaction is exhausting. Sometimes it's just good to be by yourself."

"Yeah," I agree. "Especially like...I spend all of my time with people who are so outgoing and have these huge personalities and are always fighting to be in the spotlight. Emerson and Ruby, they're literally too much sometimes. It wears me out."

"Welcome to the introvert club!" He clears his throat and holds his fork up to his mouth like a microphone. "So, Amalia, tell me how it feels to be going to the Olympics?"

I roll my eyes. "Hilarious."

"No, for real! Obviously, you're happy, but, well...are you happy?"

"Yes, of course I'm happy. I don't know how to describe it, but *happy* is a word most people would use, right?"

"I don't think it's possible to sound less happy while trying to convince people you're happy," he teases. "Come on, what is it?"

"I told you, it's shock. I swear, I'm happy." As I say this for the millionth time, I realize how sick I am of pretending everything is sunshine and bubbles and rainbows. "Actually, I'm not. I'm sorry, I don't want to complain because I get that being an alternate is a big deal, and part of me really is happy about getting this far, but an even bigger, brattier, more selfish part of me is pissed about not going all the way."

"Whoa," he whistles. "Okay, yeah, that sucks. I don't know what to say to make it better. There probably isn't anything I *can* say...nothing that would fix anything, anyway. I will say that you deserve to feel this way. You wanted something, you worked hard for it, and you didn't get it. Anyone would be upset. You're not childish or selfish for feeling that way. You're human."

"I'm human."

"How does your job even work? What is the purpose of an Olympic alternate?"

"I'm a replacement option. I train with the team as if I'm going to the Olympics, and then if someone gets horribly injured or starts sucking or something, I go in and take her spot. Well, one of the alternates does. There are three of us so it might not be me. But yeah, it never happens, so I'm basically doing a crap ton of work preparing for nothing."

"But it could happen?"

"Yeah. It won't. But yeah."

"Well, if no one gets injured or anything on their own, I'm happy to rig the vault," he shrugs, and I burst out laughing. "Or poison! I'm sure I could find some sort of recipe online. I did get an A in chemistry last semester."

"A recipe for poison," I laugh. "That sounds like the name of a Lifetime movie I'd *love.*"

"*A Recipe for Poison: The Amalia Blanchard Story.* When a desperate gymnast doesn't make the Olympic team, there's nothing she won't try to make her dream come true...including *murder.*"

The harder I laugh, the funnier I think it is, and before long I can't breathe and have tears running down my face.

"Thanks, Jack," I manage, wiping my eyes. "I needed that. Ever since Sunday people have been telling me how awesome this opportunity is, and how lucky I am, and how a million girls would kill to be me. I know if I sounded ungrateful for even a second, I'd get so much crap for that. Thanks for getting it."

"Always."

We finish our food and Jack coughs nervously.

"Wanna watch a movie or something?"

"Uh, I figured that was a given. Movie nights are our thing. A literal Netflix and chill."

Jack turns red at my mention of "Netflix and chill" and I follow suit. We're truly perfect together.

"I, uh, wasn't sure because that was…before? Now that we're, I don't know, dating or whatever, it seems weird to keep things the same."

"Dating?!" I almost spit out my milk. "Was this…this was a *date*?"

"Well, yeah." He looks at his fingernails, but shockingly, they don't give him a way out of this. "We said that once you made the team, we'd give this a shot. I thought that was why you were ignoring me this week, like you were afraid to give it a try, but then you invited me to dinner…"

"Oh my God."

"…I just thought it was a date, I guess. Our first date."

"Our first date," I repeat, slowly.

Holy. Crap.

Friday, July 15, 2016
21 days left

"Over ten thousand girls compete in the sport of gymnastics every year, and every four years, eight of those girls get to call themselves Olympians. This year, three of these eight train right here in our beautiful city of Seattle."

The crowd that has gathered outside our terminal at the airport applauds Mayor Ed Murray, who stands at a makeshift podium set up right outside the entrance. Our flight to Minneapolis is in a few hours, and from there, a car service will take us to the middle of nowhere in Wisconsin, where we'll spend the next two weeks training before going to Brazil.

"Ruby Spencer and Emerson Bedford moved here, over a thousand miles away from home, to train at one of the best facilities in the country, the Malkina Gold Medal Academy, owned by Olympic gold medalist Natasha Malkina. Amalia Blanchard, born and raised right up the coast in Lynnwood, is making history as the first US Olympic gymnast to hail from the state of Washington."

More applause from the crowd. My teammates and I stand at the mayor's side in our Team USA warmups, which will come off the second we go through security, quickly swapped in the bathroom for leggings, hoodies, and Uggs.

"Thank you for joining us in wishing these young women safe travels and the best of luck on their journey to Rio 2016. Girls, we know you will make Seattle proud."

Red, white, and blue balloons release from behind the mayor, but because this is an airport and it would probably be dangerous to let hundreds of balloons up into the sky in a place where planes are constantly taking off and landing, they stay tethered to the podium by long silver ribbons.

The crowd applauds one more time, we wave and smile and sign a few autographs, and then security escorts us into the airport.

My mom and Jack meet me inside for our final goodbye. I won't see either of them again until after my job ends in about three weeks, which is so weird to think about. I'm used to traveling without my family, but I've never been away this long before.

"Oh, Amalia." My mom grabs my face in both hands, tears welling in her eyes. "Have an amazing time, and don't forget to FaceTime me every single day with updates, okay? I don't want to have to google you to see how you're doing."

"I will, mom." She kisses me on the top of my head and then hugs me for about an hour. When I finally escape her grasp, I turn and face Jack. "Well...this is goodbye."

"For now," he grins. "You're going to be so busy being amazing, you won't even have time to miss me. I promise."

"Who said I was gonna miss you?"

After the awkwardness of our "first date" on Wednesday, Jack and I spent all evening together yesterday trying to hang out the way we used to, blobbed out on my bed with the TV on, but the whole time I was a ball of nerves, plagued by thoughts like "should I reach for his hand or will he grab mine?" and "what on earth did we used to talk about, because I can't think of a single thing to say?!"

Once upon a time, hanging out with Jack was so freaking simple, the easiest thing in my complicated life. We could spend hours together not saying a single word and it felt like the most natural thing on the planet.

Now the same situation gives me massive anxiety and I don't know how to behave like a human person anymore, and all because he has gone from my *friend* to my *boyfriend*. I mean, I guess? Is he my boyfriend? I have literally no idea what we are.

He reaches forward and gives me a quick hug. An eighth grade school dance hug with about a foot of open space separating us.

"Text me," he says as I reach for my bags, which he carried in for me. "Call if you can."

"Yeah, if the farm actually has service. Love you guys," I add, emphasizing "you guys" so it doesn't sound like I'm telling Jack I love him. I'm pretty sure two days into our "relationship" might be a bit too soon.

"Have a good flight!" my mom calls as I walk away. I turn back to wave and Jack is giving my mom bunny ears, which is so immature and looks so ridiculous. I can't help giggling.

"I'm not going to miss you either, by the way!" he yells.

"Who cares?! I'll miss you even less than you miss me!" I shout back.

Actually though, I'm gonna miss him so freaking much.

***

The flight to Minneapolis is a relatively quick one, and even though it's smack in the middle of the day, I fall asleep the second we reach the magic three-minute window that takes my brain from "we're definitely going to crash" at take-off to "I love flying!" once we're at a safe 10,000 feet. I don't wake up until Ruby pokes me in the ribs as we're about to land.

"So, you and Jack?" She raises an eyebrow.

"What? Everyone knew it was gonna happen eventually."

"I figured you'd wait until after the Games. You've always been pretty serious about that whole 'no boyfriends' rule. Like when you thought I was secretly hooking up with Sergei?"

"That's different. He's a *coach*, and an older man. Jack is my age, we've been best friends since we were babies, and we're both total losers when it comes to dating. Everything's exactly as it was when we were just friends, except layered with eight tons of crippling anxiety."

Ruby laughs. "Remember when you were totally losing your mind over Max? It's hard to believe that was only three months ago. You've come so far, little one."

"Ugh, *Max*. I forgot he existed."

"Too bad the boys aren't doing their pre-Olympic training at the farm. You could've really gotten to know him. The two of you could've fallen in love and some of your stans would be 'Team Max' and your other stans would be 'Team Jack' and it would be the greatest love triangle of all time."

"Shut up!" I slap her leg. "Is Max on the team?"

"You really don't follow anything, do you? That's okay, I know you've been a little distracted lately. He's an alternate, just like you. The perfect couple."

The guys had their own Olympic team trials two weeks before ours. Their head coach wanted more time working with them as a cohesive team, since they're all good individual competitors but tend to fall apart in situations that require them to compete together. They began their own training camp last week at a gym in Colorado, though I couldn't name a single person on their team if I tried.

"How did Max get alternate?" I ask. "He's terrible."

"Yeah, welcome to men's gymnastics in the United States. It doesn't take much. Also doesn't hurt that mommy and daddy basically fund the men's national program. USGA gives them nothing. Hey, the guys will be sharing your training space in Brazil, though! So...yeah. Enjoy that."

The last time I saw Max was at his parents' place in New York City, when we were there promoting the sport at an Olympic celebration in Times Square. He was a total dick and single-handedly brought feminism back to the 1950s, so thanks to some liquid courage — a couple of sips, I swear! — I ripped him a new one before eating a super expensive meal on his parents' tab and never speaking to him again. Classy. As if the alternate experience won't be sucky enough, I'll now have to see him every single day in Brazil.

"Don't think about it," Ruby reassures me when she sees the panic in my face. "You have Jack. And your training times will probably be opposite. Maddy will be jealous, though! I fully expect her to sneak out of the Village and Uber over to Ipanema to see him. She's always thrown herself at Max."

We land, pile into the small limo waiting for us, and spend the next two hours on the road in relative silence, everyone looking a bit tense with the reality of the next few weeks settling in.

Normally for national team camps, a bus brings everyone to and from the farm in Shell Lake, but with only eight of us coming this time, most of whom will be driving up from Chicago together, the women's team admin staff set up this car for us as a little treat instead.

The farm is totally empty when we finally arrive just before dinner. Normally the place is overrun by thirty gymnasts, at least sixty coaches, and the fifteen people who make up the staff here, but today it feels like a ghost town. I'm not complaining.

"Welcome back, Seattle!" Miriana Sundstrom, who runs the show on the administrative side, greets us warmly. Usually she's frazzled and can't manage anything more than pointing hurriedly at the bulletin board with our bunk assignments, but today she helps us pile our luggage on a trolley and personally walks us to our rooms.

"Coaches, your rooms are the same as usual," she says, handing out keys. "Girls, because you're here as part of a US team, Vera assigns the bunks rather than you sticking to your club teammates. Looks like Emerson and Ruby will be together anyway, so no disruption there, and Amalia, odd man out, you're going to be with Zara. She's already here."

I look at Ruby and start to panic a bit. I *always* room with Ruby, but she shoots me a look that says "chill" and I bite my cheek. You're not a child, I tell myself. Stop acting like one.

"Go get settled. Dinner is a little late tonight so we can accommodate everyone's arrival times." Miriana smiles. "See you in the dining hall at seven."

I knock on the door to warn Zara, in case she's changing or meditating or cooking meth or something, and then swipe my key and slip in quietly. I've never said more than a few words to Zara, who's my age. Like me, she kind of snuck onto the scene this season after not really being well-known as a junior. She's super strong on vault and floor, but aside from that, I know almost nothing about her because she's pretty quiet and barely even talks to her teammate from her gym, let alone anyone else on the national team.

This will probably end up being incredible, I realize. Ruby's always so loud and crazy in the room when she's not asleep. Now she and Emerson can torment each other and I can live in bliss without a roommate who requires more attention than air or water.

"Hey!" Zara grins when I walk in. She's short with well-defined muscles, even for a gymnast. She has thick and curly chin-length hair, her smile is warm and inviting, and though she's sixteen, she's so tiny and adorable, you wouldn't guess she's a day older than eleven. She's actually almost identical to Rue in the movie version of *The Hunger Games* at closer glance, which is oddly comforting. Her skin's a bit darker and her muscles are nine billion more pronounced, but otherwise she and that actress could be twins.

"How have you been?" I ask. "Congrats, by the way. I never got to really talk to you after trials."

"Thanks, I'm good. I thought you'd be on the team for sure."

"Yeah," I sigh. "But I'm lucky to be here anyway. Did you guys just get here?"

"This morning. My coach was so excited, he had us booked on a flight at five. We were the first ones here."

"You're from where again?"

"Oklahoma born and bred!" Zara smiles. "I would've committed to OU when I was five if they let me."

"Oh, I *love* Oklahoma's gymnastics program. I almost died when they won nationals this year."

"Both of my parents went to OU. Not as gymnasts, but I've been a Sooner since I was in the womb. I went to their camp every single year when I was a kid and verbally committed to the team when I was thirteen. Everyone said that was way too young to make a big decision like that, but I was never even going to consider another school. Have you committed yet?"

"No. I have a couple of offers, but I'm waiting because I want Stanford. Even though the athletic department wants me, you have to get accepted academically before they extend an offer. I won't be able to apply until next fall, but I'm a little worried because what if I don't get in but by that time all of my offers at other schools have disappeared?"

"You could always verbal at another school and then change your mind if you get Stanford."

"Yeah, true. I'd feel like a dick for saying yes to a school and then backing out, though. Of course, I could always go pro. I bet I could make *so* much money as a gymnast who will never step foot into the Olympic arena."

Zara laughs. "An agent talked to me after nationals but I said no way."

"Yeah, someone got in touch with me as well. I considered it but now I'm glad I didn't go that route. I had a meeting set up, but when I got a concussion I realized how lucky I was because what if I met with them a week earlier and I signed and gave up my college eligibility and *then* I got a concussion and didn't make the team? As it worked out, I ended up not making it, so I'd be totally screwed right now if I'd signed. No endorsements *and* no scholarships."

"I can't imagine." Zara shakes her head, and then yawns. "I can't believe I've been awake this long. Wanna head over to dinner with me?"

"Yeah, sure!" I tidy some things by my wardrobe and plug my phone, almost at zero battery, into the jack closest to my bed.

Zara holds the door open and grins as we walk through. I like that she's opening up already, and I get an overwhelming feeling of happiness, glad fate brought us together. We seem to have a lot in common, so I can't wait to get to know her better.

It'll also be nice to have a friend on the team who is my age and isn't from my gym. Ruby and Emerson are awesome, but sometimes I feel like gymnastics is the only thing we have in common. With Zara, I don't feel like an annoying little sister tagging along and not understanding half of their jokes. Maybe this whole thing won't be as bad as I thought.

Saturday, July 16, 2016
20 days left

"Welcome to the 2016 Olympic training camp!"

The eight of us stand up straight, lined up from smallest to tallest, chins up and arms behind our backs. I figured everyone would be all chirpy and giggly and excited to get started today, but breakfast was dead quiet. Even Ruby and Emerson are totally freaking silent, which is actually horror movie levels of terrifying.

Dinner last night ended up being more casual, with Vera giving a little speech about us needing to "be a team" and support each other and blah, blah, blah. I'm still not sold on this whole thing, but I'm trying to at least not be a brat about it.

"Today's morning practice will be modified, used to help us acclimate to what will be a rigorous couple of weeks," Vera starts. "We'll do the national team warmup, light conditioning, and then twenty minute rotations on each event. Vault will be a few timers with the focus on the block and the rise, nothing serious. On bars, we'll break down routines into a few parts with our eyes on alignment, angles, and technique. Beam will have a quick skills warmup before two routines apiece, and then on floor we'll do two or three of each tumbling pass."

No one says a word or even nods. Even the coaches, standing in their own line behind Vera, are statues.

"I met with all of your coaches after dinner last night, and we came up with a plan for the next twelve days," Vera continues. "Tonight's practice will be another modified, with a few select members of the media here before and during so they can get footage for the Olympic broadcasts. Tomorrow, things get tough. We will do two-a-day trainings tomorrow and Monday, and a quick morning practice Tuesday followed by a mock competition on vault and bars that evening. We will repeat with two modified trainings on Wednesday, then two-a-day Thursday, two-a-day Friday, and on Saturday we'll have a morning training with a mock competition on beam and floor in the afternoon. Sunday is a day off, and you can thank your coaches for that gift. Monday and Tuesday are two-a-days, Wednesday is a full mock competition day, and Thursday is our travel day with practice in the morning, packing in the afternoon, and then we leave for our airport."

Aside from a little fist pump from Natasha during the "day off" part, no one breathes. I can tell Ruby wants to laugh but she doesn't dare with Vera staring at her from five feet away.

"You have all earned your spots here and deserve to be here, but the hard work is not over. Most mountain climbers don't die trying to summit Everest. They die on the way down because they spend too much time celebrating at the top, not realizing their work is only halfway done. You have reached the summit, but you still have a long way to go. You must still finish strong and make it safely back to base camp, which for you is the Olympic Games. If you start to falter or give me a reason to remove you from the team, I will have to do it for the benefit of the team. An Olympic team is only as strong as its weakest member."

She pauses for a moment, and then narrows her eyes. "Well?" she barks.

"Thank you, Vera. We are prepared and ready to win!" We're all perhaps a little too enthusiastic with our required and rehearsed shouting, but Vera's face softens and she claps her hands together proudly.

"Warmups begin in five minutes."

That does it. We bolt from our lineup, stripping off our leggings and jackets along the way before rushing back to the floor to do our pre-warmup warmups, little stretches that will help us limber up before the hard stuff starts.

"Who would've thought Vera was such an Everest junkie?" Ruby laughs as we settle in our spot to stretch.

"Dramatic much?" Emerson rolls her eyes. "She probably read *Into Thin Air* last night or something. What an analogy."

I laugh, and then realize our little circle of three has expanded to include everyone. We're no longer an exclusive MGMA party, but now rather a whole big Team USA party, every club coming together instead of going to war. In addition to the three of us and my roommate Zara, there's also Sophia from Nashville and the Windy City girls, Maddy, Charlotte, and Olivia.

Everyone goes quiet until Maddy finally speaks up.

"Awkward much? But we better get used to it. Team bonding and all that."

"Yeah," the usually quiet Zara pipes up. She said she's trying to open up more at this camp so she can have a good relationship with her teammates and be able to show more of a personality once she's interviewed on every TV network under the sun. "I don't have anyone from my club team here with me, so if y'all could adopt me, that would be great."

Everyone giggles and Ruby puts her arm over Zara's shoulder. "You can be my mini-me," she offers. "Vera would be *thrilled* if my obnoxiousness rubs off on you."

"Just what we need," Emerson jokes, kind of. "*Two* of you."

"Enough chitchat!" Vera bellows from the other side of the gym. "Get to work!"

That command carries weight in here, and we all scramble into position before she can continue yelling. If we can't find other ways to bond, at least we can share our common fear of a seventy-year-old woman.

***

For practices, we split into two groups, groups I'm affectionately referring to as "the real team" and "the fake team." Guess which one I'm on?

The real team trains in the order they'll compete in qualifications at the Olympics, beginning on floor and going through to vault, bars, and beam. They have Vera watching over their every move alongside the head coaches of each gymnast and the national team event coach for whichever apparatus they're doing.

My group starts on vault and ends on floor, and we only get the event coach and our secondary club coaches, since Windy City's head coach is with Maddy and Natasha is off with Ruby. It's okay. Polina will do.

Everything goes about as well as we can expect. All of the gymnasts here look fantastic, and honestly, there's so much talent in this one room, the rest of the world is gonna be in for a world of hurt when Team USA takes to the stage in August.

Vera's been pretty distant outside of training, though you can tell her eyes are on us everywhere we go. Even though she isn't rotating with the alternates in practice, she's still somehow watching everything we do. I never believed my mom when she said she had eyes in the back of her head, but I kind of wouldn't be surprised if Vera somehow had a pair surgically implanted.

"Focus, Amalia!" Polina yells at evening practice. "You're not hitting a single handstand!"

We're only doing basics on bars, a couple of skills but concentrating on the so-called "little things" like hitting handstands at a perfect 180 degree angle and pointing our toes at every moment. They may *seem* like little things, but if you have eight handstands in your bars routine and each one is a few degrees off, that's almost a point gone from your execution score. The little things matter, and I'm apparently failing at getting them right.

"It feels like I'm right over the bar!" I whine when I hop off. "I'm casting up the same as always, and even though I'm adjusting a little, I know I'm at a straight angle."

"Nope," Polina shakes her head. "You're at least ten degrees short. Next time you go up, squeeze back a tiny bit more than you currently are. If you feel like you're straight up and down but your body looks short from my view, I want you to reach a point where maybe you feel a little arched. You won't be. You'll be straight from this angle, I promise."

I sigh and chalk, sigh and chalk.

"Is she always such a bitch?" Olivia asks.

I don't know much about Olivia, aside from the fact that she and Charlotte used to be Emerson's little minions. When Emerson left for Seattle, Maddy became their new queen, and they're now bona fide sidekicks, like the Crabbe and Goyle to Maddy's Draco Malfoy. Maybe I can Harry Potter my way into the situation and bring them over to the good side.

"She's not a bitch," I retort. "She's just Russian."

I peer across the room over to beam to see if I can get a glimpse of Ruby or Emerson, but NBC's gigantic cameras and boom mics are blocking my view. During the Olympics, they'll use a bunch of footage from today's practice in their lead-up to the competitions, highlighting a few random conditioning exercises and maybe a hard fall or two in order to dramatize the back-breaking heartache we gymnasts face on a daily basis. If they're lucky, they might even get tears! Then they can cut to the competition with everyone kicking ass and bam, they have a story. Juxtaposition. Narrative. I paid attention in freshman English.

"One last time, Amalia. Do your final two skills and the dismount. When you go up into handstand, think *pull back* and then feel yourself go up and over the bar."

"Okay," I mutter, slapping my hands on my bare thighs to get rid of the excess chalk. I mount and go into my first handstand, expelling a bit more energy casting up, hoping to get it perfectly vertical. I feel like I'm arching too far over, though, and I doubt myself, breaking my swing.

"Don't get down!" Polina yells. "Kip cast back up, swing through a giant to get your bearings, and then start over."

I swing under the bar a few times to build momentum, kip cast into a short handstand, swing down, tap into a couple of giants, and then on a third giant, take it slow when I reach the handstand so I can try to feel this thing out.

But it's no use. I have the same problem. It feels like my legs are going too far past where they should be aligned with the rest of my body. I can't hold onto it, and I have to jump off.

"You were *right there*," Polina huffs, blowing her hair from her eyes.

"I couldn't balance!" I almost yell back. "It felt like I was completely arched over and about to fall."

"I took video so you can see how wrong you are. Go practice on the single rail floor bar before we finish today's practice, please."

I stomp the whole way over, getting more and more frustrated, which makes me less able to do anything productive. A handstand on the high bar is a baby skill. No wonder I didn't make the team. I'm literally trash.

Handstand drills on the floor bar are at least physically easy, and I have a semi-good view of beam from here, where I stalk Emerson and Ruby, who are laughing with Natasha and Sergei between sets. The camera crew catches each and every moment for what I'm sure will be used in the inevitable "Ruby versus Emerson showdown" montage aired during the all-around final.

Watching them have so much fun here while I get bitched at by Polina for being human garbage who can't master a level six skill sucks.

I hate this, I hate this, I hate this.

Tuesday, July 19, 2016
17 days left

"I had a fibula fracture once," Zara grins. "That was my worst. I was twelve. My coach wasn't spotting me on bars, I missed my Tkachev, and I like, drilled my leg into the mat and landed on top of it with my full body weight. It felt like it totally snapped in half."

"That's *nothing*," Olivia rolls her eyes. "I had an *open tibia fracture*. As in the bone *did* snap in half, *and* it punctured the skin. During a competition. There was blood legit everywhere and while I waited for the medics I was just staring at the bone wondering how it was possible I could have bones outside of my body. I was in total shock. The doctor didn't know if I'd ever get full use of my leg back."

Maddy guffaws. "Literally every word out of your mouth just now was a lie."

"Was not!"

"I was there," Maddy snaps before turning to the rest of us. "It was an ankle dislocation and she bled on the floor because she also stubbed her toe really bad."

"It was *way* worse than that."

"No. It wasn't."

"Save your energy for the gym," Sophia yawns, pushing her chair back and standing up, only half-finished with her lunch. "I'm taking a nap."

At twenty-two, Sophia is the oldest on the team, and we've taken to affectionately calling her Grandma because she's always sleeping and talking about her hip pain. I can't help thinking that most girls her age are recent college grads looking for jobs, drinking a ton of beer, and singing that Taylor Swift song repeatedly, and yet here she is, hanging out with a whole mess of immature weirdos.

"Mmm, a nap," I yawn as well. "I'm exhausted. I think Vera drugged the chicken."

"I'll walk over with you," Sophia offers. She won the Olympic all-around gold in 2012. I was only eleven then, and developed the biggest girl crush obsession, so I'm a little terrified of casually hanging out with her even though she seems like the nicest person alive.

She's also the person who technically beat me for a team spot. It's technically not her fault, but I can't help secretly despising her a little.

"How's the farm treating you?" she asks as I toss my paper plate and empty cup of water into the trash.

"Not too bad!" I lie. The two-a-day practices yesterday and Sunday almost killed me. Our workouts here are shorter than our workouts at home, only about four or five hours total compared to the seven or eight hours I spend each day at MGMA. But at home, there's a lot of downtime, and Natasha makes everything pretty relaxed.

Here, we're working our asses off nonstop, like when you set your Oregon Trail pace to "grueling" and everyone dies of exhaustion not even halfway to the Willamette Valley. Every muscle in my body is screaming out for me to give up this sport and spend the rest of my life watching TV on a cloud of pillows. The ice bath is my new best friend, and I want to sleep twenty hours a night.

"I've been coming here for a decade, literally, so feel free to reach out if you have any questions or just want to vent," Sophia says, genuinely kind and supportive. "Trust me, I've been through it all."

"Gee, thanks!" *Gee?* Am I Bobby Brady?

"No problem. World and Olympic team camps are the hardest part of being at the national level, and it never gets any easier, no matter how long you've been doing it."

"What's your secret?"

"Sleep," she grins. "Sleep where you can, when you can."

"Is that even possible with Maddy as a roommate?" I hope she doesn't think I'm being too gossipy or bitchy, but she rolls her eyes.

"Don't even ask. Seriously, I have my earbuds in with a nature sounds app playing thunderstorms every second I'm with her so I can tune her out. I prefer crashing thunder to her voice."

"Sounds accurate," I laugh.

"I was actually hoping to room with Ruby, and I thought Vera might stick us together since we're the oldest, but she has something up her sleeves with keeping Ruby and Emerson together at all times."

"Really? I never thought about that."

"Oh, yeah, there's a total psychological game behind Vera's room assignments. They're as much about the competition as anything. Ruby and Emerson are so stubbornly competitive, they probably make a contest out of who can brush their teeth the longest or something. I can picture both of them at the sink for hours at a time, refusing to relent so they can say they've won, even if they'd be winning the stupidest battle of all time."

"I'm pretty sure I've seen that exact situation play out in the MGMA locker room."

Sophia laughs. "The two of them feeding off of each other like that, they're gonna be out of control competitive when they get to Rio. They'll just keep pushing each other to be even better because they both want to win. No one will be able to touch them."

"What about you and Maddy?"

"Either Vera's mad at me for making so many mistakes this summer and she wants to punish me, or she has a master plan that involves me teaching Maddy to not be the worst person on earth. You and Zara, though, you seem to be getting along great."

"We are!" I grin. "She's awesome. I didn't know her much at all and now we're like best friends."

"I think as the youngest ones here, and as first-timers, Vera wanted you guys to figure this whole thing out on your own and help each other through it. Not that we're not all here to guide you along, but it makes you more resourceful competitors if you're not treated like babies. I was twelve my first time here, and at my club gym, I was the only non-teenager at a level higher than eight. All of the older high school girls in my advanced training group treated me like their baby sister. Then I made it here and everyone treated me like I was twenty. It was a shock, like, *why* isn't everyone telling me how adorable I look in my leo?! I demand attention! But I had to make sense of it all on my own for once, and as talented as I was, that was something I never got to learn back home. I never knew I needed it, and it helped me so much."

"I'm definitely the baby sister at my gym. I get super anxious about everything and you know how there are dogs that warn their owners before they have seizures or whatever? Ruby was basically my anxiety dog. She always knew when I was freaking out before I started, and she knew exactly what I needed to calm me down."

"Which is great," Sophia interjects. "She's an incredible friend. But sometimes you need to go through things on your own if you want to come out stronger on the other side."

"I thought you guys were napping?"

Speaking of Ruby, she comes bounding out of the cafeteria and practically skips over to where we're parked on the benches outside the dorms. I have no idea how she has this much energy on a regular day, let alone after a killer week of training.

"Just chatting first," Sophia says, stretching her shoulders. "Amalia's a much better conversationalist than Maddy."

"My brother's pet frogs are better conversationalists than Maddy. I'm actually gonna go nap as well. Or try to. I might just watch *Grey's Anatomy*. I've been trying to binge it all summer and I just got to the ep with the shooting. I'm kind of dying here. If I miss the mock meet later today, you'll know why. See ya!"

She bursts through the doors into the dorm and Sophia shakes her head. "I can't keep up with her."

We follow Ruby into the hallway at about half her pace and I begin fumbling for my key card.

"See you later, Amalia," Sophia waves. "Thanks for the chat."

"Sure!" I'm grinning from ear to ear as I enter my room. I close the door softly behind me, and lie down on my bed, the thin white sheets feeling cool against my perpetually sweaty skin.

It's been a week of extreme highs and lows, but befriending Sophia tops everything. If someone had told eleven-year-old me that this would be my future, I would have actually died from excitement and I never would've made it to fifteen.

I close my eyes and try to give my body at least a little bit of rest before tonight's mock meet, but as usual, I can't turn off my brain. Candy Crush it is. That's relaxing, right?

***

"You need to be at a hundred percent today," Natasha warns us before we compete. "It's only vault and bars, so without also having beam and floor to focus on, these two events need to be perfect. That's Vera's angle. If she gives you half the workout, she wants to see you go twice as hard."

"Why do we have to work even harder *after* making teams?" Ruby whines. "I'd love to save my slowly crippling body for when it actually matters."

"Vera needs to know that you're always going to be on. You earned the spot, but if you start giving fifty percent, you don't deserve to keep your spot. Vera wants warriors. Robots. She wants you to work harder than you ever thought possible while making it look effortless."

I yawn and roll my neck, which is a bit stiff after staring at my phone for an hour. I may or may not have spent $4.99 of real money on extra Candy Crush lives.

"Am I boring you?" Natasha muses.

"Sorry," I mumble meekly, my face turning red. "Bad nap."

"No excuses. You more than anyone need to prove yourself."

"I'm not even on the team."

"Thanks, Captain Obvious. But if someone gets hurt, you want to be the one Vera calls on. You kick Charlotte and Olivia's asses in this sport. Do you really want one of them going in as a replacement because you decided to give up?"

"No," I whisper.

"Come on, Amalia. Get it together."

I turn my back to my coaches and teammates so they don't see the tears spring up in my eyes. Get it together? I had it together all year and I got nothing. I'm over it.

"Line up!" someone yells, and we obediently run to the mat in front of the vault judges. All eight of us will compete together, in the order Vera's currently considering for the Games. The actual team lineup goes first, and then it's alternate time, Olivia, then Charlotte, then me.

We stand perfectly still at attention for the judges, and then rush through warmups, each of us hitting a timer and then our competition vaults before going up for real. I bounce out of my timer to save my knees and ankles on the landing, and when I hit my warmup Amanar, I decide to bounce out of that as well.

"Nice landing," Maddy scoffs.

"Are you my coach? It's the warmup."

"Whatever."

Maddy's in an extra bitchy mood today because Vera has her second-to-last in the lineup instead of anchoring. Lineups in team competitions are usually set up to build from the weakest to the strongest routine so the scores build throughout the rotation. With Zara last up on vault instead of Maddy, Vera is pretty clearly saying that Zara's the better vaulter without actually having to speak those words out loud.

"She's right, that was a terrible landing," Natasha scolds. "I know you're choosing the most important moments of our collective lives to turn into a teenager, but can you please reschedule your rebellion? Just put it off by a month."

I roll my eyes and slump to the floor, not even bothering with my iPod. When you ain't got nothing, you ain't got nothing to lose, and I'm throwing all of my meet traditions out the window. I don't care.

This is the first time I've actually watched one of my meets in forever, and I'm kind of excited to pay attention and see where everyone stands.

Sophia, who doesn't vault anymore, scratches by touching the apparatus and saluting the judges, but the rest of the Olympic lineup goes up and nails one huge, beautiful, stuck or near-stuck Amanar after another, until Zara caps things off with her Cheng, one of the hardest vaults in the world.

Other big teams may have one Amanar apiece, boosting their overall vault scores a little thanks to the crazy difficulty, but nothing compares to four vaults all bound to reach 15.7 or better in qualifications. That gives us a huge boost right off the bat, leaving a lot of ground other teams have to make up later on.

From Emerson up first down to Ruby, then Maddy, and finally Zara, we are unbeatable on vault and I can't help feeling a surge of pride even through all of my pent-up angst.

Olivia and Charlotte go after the team, which is kind of anticlimactic as they both only have Yurchenko doubles, which are difficult in their own right but not compared to what we just saw.

Finally, it's my turn. I take a deep breath after I salute, but it's mostly so I have air in my lungs for my passive aggressive sigh before I run.

As a gymnast who normally has a million routine rituals, it's kind of shocking even to me that I don't care enough about doing any of them tonight. I'm the most relaxed I've ever been in front of Vera and the judges, so I'm simply just going to do the vault. That's it.

I think it's going to be a mess, but the thing is...it's kind of one of my best vaults ever. Once I hit the table, muscle memory kicks in, forcing me to squeeze my legs tight and jerk my arms in as I rotate through the two and a half twists. My rage strength gives me a stronger push off the table than I usually get, leaving me with more than enough room to get the flips and twists around. I drop to the ground, plant my feet, and throw my arms up. Perfect.

"Amazing," Natasha says, slowly making her way over to me for a high five after I finish. I try to mirror Emerson's levels of blasé, like, who cares? So what if I'm one of the best vaulters here? No big deal, I always nail the crap out of that thing.

But secretly, I'm really excited about how incredible that felt, and I can't help my face muscles literally turning my frown upside down, a smile creeping up from the corners of my mouth.

"It's seriously a shame this team can't have six members," Sophia shakes her head. "That is a team finals-worthy vault."

"Can you get Russian citizenship real quick?" Ruby adds. "They'd kill for a vault like that."

I can't help blushing a bit at all of this praise, but the score — a 16.0 — is bittersweet. It's the best vault score after Zara, and I'm thrilled, but it also stings knowing that it literally doesn't matter.

We move to bars, where I'm again going last. This time the rotation order has Zara going first, meaning she won't go up in qualifications, where only four routines are allowed on each event. Because Sophia doesn't train vault or floor, the other four get lineup spots on both events by default, but on bars and beam, Vera had to decide who got the boot.

If you don't do all four events in qualifications, you can't attempt to reach the all-around final, so even though Zara is better than Maddy on bars, Maddy will get the lead-off spot in Rio because Vera wants her vying for an all-around spot.

Honestly, it's unfair, but Zara doesn't care.

"I could show up, vault, and do nothing else all competition and be totally happy," she had told me after finding out her vault and floor specialist role with the team. "I'm lucky just to be going."

So it's Zara going up first today to get a routine in just in case she ends up being needed, followed by the team lineup order of Maddy, Ruby,

Sophia, and Emerson, which is pretty solid. It doesn't come close to the Chinese lineup, and it probably won't beat the Russians either, but Emerson is basically a guaranteed 15.5 if she hits, and both Sophia and Ruby can get close if they don't have mistakes.

I watch the rotation closely, occasionally yelling out something like "come on, Maddy, you got this!" which is super rare for me, as I'm usually the one quietly hiding from the action.

Even though it's just the farm, it's nice to actually see my teammates "compete" in a sense. Ruby is killing it, her super difficult connections and big skills more than making up for the fact that she's not the most naturally gifted long and lean bars princess like Emerson. As she winds up with a couple of giants before her full-twisting double layout dismount, I scream alongside everyone else, and then explode into applause when she sticks the landing.

"You watched!" Ruby gasps as we high five, and then she grabs her water bottle. "So?"

"Rio 2016 bars medalist," I grin. "Seriously, I know Sophia and Emerson are gonna be tough competition there, and with only two from each country able to get into the final, you're the long shot...but I honestly think you can do it."

Ruby gives me a hug and we lean back against the wall to watch Sophia up next. Like Emerson, she's one of those tall, thin, leggy gymnasts with beautiful lines and an elegance that makes her perfectly suited for bars.

Her routine is one of the most difficult in the world with a 6.9 start value, complete with a million combinations earning a ton of bonus tenths. I think almost all of her skills are connected to one another, which is very Russian of her.

Sophia competed watered-down versions of her routines for most of this year because she had low back pain and could barely bend in half, let alone pike through an inbar stalder, but she whipped out her full difficulty at trials and when I went back and watched the videos, it was hard to be mad at her for getting a spot over me. She was brilliant.

"You got this, Sophia!" I yell during her long wait before she can salute and mount. I can see the nerves on her face, but I don't know why. She had a great warmup.

The head judge finally nods and Sophia gulps, slaps her hands together, and then glide kips onto the low bar to start her routine.

Right away, she looks off, with her inbar full coming super late. Instead of doing the pirouette on top of the bar, she's still completing the turn as she's already swinging down, causing her to miss the connection into her first transition to the high bar, a tenth now gone from her difficulty score.

"Come on!" Ruby screams, practically in my ear. "Control it, Sophia!"

Almost everyone is yelling support, aside from Maddy, who is hiding under what she calls her "time-out towel" after a bad routine of her own.

Sophia gets the next set of connections, a couple of transitions from low to high and then back down again, but from there she's supposed to go right back up to the high bar in a stalder shaposh with a half twist. Instead, she kip casts out of her pak, and does the shaposh half on its own, losing another two tenths in bonus.

At least there are no falls or major form breaks, I'm thinking. If she went for those connections when her mind wasn't fully there, she would've lost so much more than bonus tenths.

Just as this relief pops into my head, I can see her timing is way off on her layout Jaeger, causing her to get nowhere near the height she needs. She catches way too close, doesn't get her dowel over the bar, and she groans as her fingers slip, causing her to fall flat on her stomach.

"It's okay, Sophia!" We keep the support coming as she chalks up again. "Finish strong!"

Sophia cracks her neck, shakes out her limbs, and then mounts the high bar with a boost from her coach. All that's left is her dismount, a super difficult stalder full pirouette straight into a double tuck with one and a half twists, but again she misses the connection, performing the skills separately, probably not wanting to take any risks. Even so, she lands the dismount a tad short, stumbling it around and putting her hands down to finish.

Ouch.

When she stands up, she smiles sheepishly at the judges, and then turns her back to them, making what I call an "I hate myself" face. We all high five her and say "good job" anyway when she comes back, but seriously, that was rough. She lost four of her seven bonus tenths and got two full points off in her execution for the falls alone. Take at least another point off for the little issues adding up, and what could've easily been a score around a 16 on a good day is now going to be somewhere in the neighborhood of a 13 or 13.5 at best.

"I'm glad I didn't do that at trials!" Sophia exhales, resting against the wall. She's playing it cool, but I can tell she's definitely mentally rattled.

My own routine goes well enough. It's nothing special, but it's not a bomb, either, and my coaches look pleased.

In all, even with Sophia's bars meltdown, today is a great first glimpse into how this team will perform in Rio. If Sophia can get over today's fluke disaster routine, Team USA is gonna be tough to beat.

Friday, July 22, 2016
14 days left

"Holy crap! Holy crap. Holy crap?!"

I painstakingly force my eyes to open, and when they focus, I spot Zara standing over her iPad in her underwear.

"What's wrong?" I grumble, pulling the covers over my head. My muscle pain is getting worse day after day with zero breaks in over a week. My day off is usually Sunday, and that's time I desperately need to recover. I'm getting daily ice baths here, and the occasional massage. When I'm not training, I'm trying to rest as much as possible. But I need a full day of doing absolutely nothing or I'm actually going to die.

"The *Olympics*, Mal!" Zara squeals.

"Yeah?" I laugh. It's funny seeing her this excited about something when she usually keeps everything so grounded. "Did you just remember they're a thing?"

"Noooooo. *Look*!"

Zara vaults onto my bed and shows me her countdown app. August 5, the day of the Opening Ceremony, is exactly two weeks from today.

"Holy crap!" I echo.

"Right? Two weeks from today, the Games will begin, and two days after that, we compete!" I notice she kind of cringes immediately after she finishes speaking. "I mean...the team competes. I compete."

"It's okay," I shrug. "Two days after the Games begin, I will cheer you on from the stands, assuming the USGA actually gets a ticket for me."

"What do you mean?"

"Sophia said that in 2012, the alternates didn't get tickets. They trained at a crappy gym far from London, and as soon as the deadline hit after podium training, all three of the alternates flew home right away."

"Wow, that's awful."

"Yeah. I think my parents booked a hotel for most of the Games, though. So, I mean, I'll probably stay even if I don't get to see anything. It's the only real vacation time they'll get all year, basically, so we'll turn it from competition travel to pleasure travel. Shocking, I know."

"Ahhh, yes, the elusive pleasure travel. I think my parents have sacrificed every single second of vacation time to see me compete."

"Same." I yawn and stretch, groaning the whole time. "What time is it?"

"Almost six."

"No *way* did I sleep for almost eight hours and still feel like crap." I yawn again and climb out of the cozy cave my bed has become, but then immediately drop back down and sprawl out.

Like yesterday, today is a double workout, tomorrow is the beam and floor mock competition, and then, finally, praise all that is holy, Sunday is our day of rest.

"Is it bad that I never want to leave this bed again?" I moan.

"Come on, two days! You can do it." Zara tries to pep me up but as much as I try to feed off of her energy like a Dementor sucking out someone's soul, it apparently doesn't work like that.

"I literally can't do anything ever again. It's not even the gymnastics that's killing me. It's sitting down to breakfast with everyone and listening to them saying things and I just can't."

"People are terrible."

"*Yes*. Ugh. I'll give you every penny in my bank account if you knock on Vera's door and tell her we're suffering from explosive diarrhea and need to be quarantined. It's incredibly contagious."

Zara bursts out laughing. "You're disgusting! But seriously, I'd do it for, like...a hundred bucks. *No*, five hundred!"

"Lucky for you, I think I max out at two."

So far the best part of being at the farm has been getting close to Zara, like we were long-lost sisters who found each other here and immediately clicked thanks to some deep genetic connection. We're so much alike, especially with our stupid and dark senses of humor, and I can be moany and angsty without her asking if everything's okay or trying to baby me the way Ruby and Emerson sometimes do.

"Come on, freak," she says, pulling my dead weight out of bed. I slide to the floor and curl into the fetal position. "This should be my conditioning for the day. Get up. Take a shower. And no whining. There's no whining in gymnastics."

I pick myself up, grab my towel, and start toward the bathroom, whining the whole way. Before I push through the door, I turn back to smile at Zara, who winks back, and I'm so ridiculously happy she's here with me, my heart flutters. Without her, I probably *would* be lying to Vera about explosive diarrhea.

* * *

Despite all of my pain and exhaustion, once I get back into workout mode, training goes well and I spend some extra time on floor messing around with passes I've tried in the gym but have never been able to put into routines.

Some of these are dream passes, like a double double and a three and a half, both of which I throw into the pit so I don't smash my legs into pieces. But my double layout is actually pretty damn good on the floor itself, and it would add another two tenths in difficulty to my floor routine. It doesn't sound like a lot, but for me, it's huge.

"Just let me try it," I beg. "There's nothing to lose!"

"You can't just change your routine," Polina scolds. "Natasha will have a fit."

"So? I'll tell her at dinner. If I'm hitting it in practice and want to add it in next year anyway, I might as well try it now in a competition setting with judges and stuff. I'll just take out the double pike."

"If you hit it five more times today, fine. But *you're* telling her, not me."

I dust off my hands and get ready for my next attempt, thinking about where I'll put it into my routine. If I put it directly in place of my double pike, it'd be my third pass, which is a huge risk because I lose endurance as I go through the routine. The best option is probably doing it first and then bumping my more consistent first two passes down a notch, keeping the double tuck as my final.

"Come on, Mal!" Ruby yells from across the room just before I'm about to tumble, and I see Natasha's head whip over in my direction. With a deep breath, I run into a roundoff back handspring and then set into the double layout, two back flips with my body stretched from head to toe. My rotation is quick, my form is solid, and I stick the landing.

"See?" I smirk at Polina. "It's time."

"You still have four more."

"Fine." Instead of running through any of my other passes, I do the double layout four more times, each one as good as the last.

This confidence is bewildering. I'm totally not used to feeling this way. It's almost like the less you care about something, the less your brain tries to ruin it for you.

I look for Natasha across the gym, and instead of making angry faces, she's giving me a thumbs up. Granted, she doesn't know I want to add it in for real and that I'm not just playing around, but I'm taking that as a good sign. I didn't make the team, so I might as well move on and plan for next season, when I'll shoot to make the worlds team. Why not start now?

She doesn't say anything during dinner, but afterwards, when we're all sprawled out in the common room, almost too worn out to lift our fingers to swipe around on our social media apps, she sits on the arm of the couch and rests her hand on my shoulder.

"Polina told me," she starts. "Good plan."

"Really?!" My voice goes high-pitched and Maddy basically growls at me. Whisper time it is.

"I don't see why not. What's the worst that could happen?"

"I could fall and shatter my delicate bird bones and get my second concussion this month and never do gymnastics again."

"All valid reasons," she laughs. "But you did it really well today. I doubt you'll self-destruct, not if it's your first pass. It'll be good to see how you can hit it in a routine, how it would affect your subsequent passes...but I think it's a good decision to try it out. Work it into your full routines at tomorrow's morning practice, and then do it in the mock meet. I trust you."

"Okay, then. Tomorrow."

"You're gonna kill it."

When Natasha leaves, I text the news to Jack, who has no idea what I'm talking about ninety percent of the time when it comes to gym, but he always sends back a supportive little note about how awesome I am. Sometimes that's all you need to spend the rest of your day smiling.

"What's up?" Ruby, who's sprawled out to my right, asks.

"I'm throwing the double layout tomorrow. At the mock meet."

"Holy crap! Mal, that's awesome."

"What's awesome?" Now Emerson wants in, and pretty soon, I have almost everyone gathered around me like I'm Sara telling her wild stories about India in the awesome 90s movie version of *A Little Princess*. Everyone's super excited for me, except Maddy, who's perched on a bean bag chair rolling her eyes.

"Who cares? A double layout? I could do one when I was nine. That's definitely worth screaming about. *Some* of us are trying to mentally decompress."

"Mentally decompress? I don't think your brain works hard enough to have anything to decompress *from*," Ruby snaps back.

"Guys." Sophia gets up and holds out her arms to each side. "Chill. You're both too old for this. We need to at least *try* to be a team."

"Sorry," Ruby blushes a bit, something we don't usually see her do, but she respects Sophia a ton. They grew up on the junior scene together and were always close until Sophia got to go to London four years ago and Ruby didn't. After that, they drifted apart when Sophia made it big; Ruby thought Sophia was phasing her out, but in reality, Sophia didn't want to rub her success in Ruby's face, reminding her of everything she was missing out on.

They became pals again last year when Ruby came out of retirement, and while they're not *besties*, they look up to each other and have a great competitive relationship. So I know Ruby's totally embarrassed about her outburst.

Maddy doesn't apologize, though. Instead, she grabs her magazine from the coffee table and storms off to her room, glaring at Olivia and

Charlotte, neither of whom defended her. Sophia closes her eyes and exhales, reminding me of my mom after a rough day at work.

"I'll take care of Maddy," Sophia says, and she leaves as well.

"I think this party's over." Emerson begins to collect her stuff. "Goodnight, all. And that's great news, Mal."

"Yeah!" Olivia chimes in. "It's awesome. Don't listen to Maddy."

"And she *totally* didn't have a double layout when she was nine," Charlotte adds as the two head to their room.

"Thanks guys." I wave them off and yawn for about an hour. "I guess I should probably go to sleep as well."

"I'll be in later," Zara says. "Ruby was gonna talk to me about my floor."

"What about it?"

"Vera was annoyed with her today because her presentation looked off," Ruby explains.

"Yeah, she thinks I could win a medal there, but not if I don't *do it with meaning*. Artistry and blah, blah, blah," Zara huffs. "It's always something."

"I have the exact same problem," I commiserate. "I've done exactly one routine that hasn't fully sucked. It's not our fault we have zero ability to connect emotionally."

"We're total sociopaths," Zara agrees.

"Well, and it doesn't help that there's no audience in the gym," Ruby reminds us. "But yeah, Zara, you could hit everything perfectly and have the most difficult routine out there, but then lose tenths for something that has nothing to do with my physical abilities. Not worth it."

My phone dings, so I let them talk and I head back to my bedroom, swiping the screen to see Jack's response.

"A double layout?! No way! That's an F skill first performed by Soviet gymnast Stella Zakharova in 1977! Did you know Ukraine holds an annual Stella Zakharova Cup competition in her honor? You should go to the next one and do your double layout. You'd be DOUBLE honoring her!"

I laugh out loud, and curl up under the covers, excited to have more than one bar of service for once, and even more excited to get to chat with Jack before falling asleep.

"Wikipedia much?"

"I'm offended. I'm a natural genius."

"Sounds legit. Face it, you don't know a double layout from a double pirouette."

"True, but I do know that it's important enough to belong at the top of the Flipping Out Forum's all-time favorite skills list, so clearly you are the next Nadia."

"Accurate. Going to bed now. I'm dead."

"Goodnight, Zombie Amalia. You'll kick so much ass tomorrow. Keep showing them what they're missing."

I switch off my phone and smile to myself, unable to stop grinning as I walk to the bathroom to brush my teeth. I'm the luckiest.

Saturday, July 23, 2016
13 days left

"Make her stop crying," Zara whispers to a group of us during beam. "I'm not good at stuff like that. Someone needs to calm her down!"

Zara went up first in the beam rotation at the mock meet, meaning she won't go up on this event during the actual Olympic competition, which she already knew. The actual lineup right now is Sophia, Maddy, Ruby, and Emerson. Vera has been swapping Sophia and Maddy all week, but based on how this morning's training went, Maddy gets the better spot.

It kind of sucks, because Sophia was brought onto the team to be a bars and beam specialist, but if she's in the lead-off spot on beam, she won't do the event in the team final. So...what's the point? She's basically a glorified bars specialist now.

Ruby just finished her nearly perfect routine a minute ago and is still struggling to breathe like a human again, and Emerson's waiting for the judges to figure out Ruby's score so she can have her turn.

Both Zara and Maddy hit their routines, but Sophia is practically suicidal after falling. Twice.

"Her coach is with her now," Maddy shrugs. "She'll be fine."

"Yeah, except her coach is psycho and is probably yelling at her, not comforting her," I retort. "Not exactly what she needs right now."

"I'll talk to her," Ruby says after catching her breath. "After her coach leaves. And after Emerson's routine."

Almost on cue, Emerson mounts the beam and we start cheering for her. There's only so many times in one day I can yell "you got this!" and "come on!" I have no idea how I'm going to survive NCAA, where this sport is ten percent gymnastics, ninety percent yelling.

Like Mary Poppins, Emerson is practically perfect in every way, and beyond gorgeous. For real competitions, we have to wear our hair in tight ballerina buns because coming from the insanely controlling Soviet system, Vera's obsessed with how we present ourselves. But here at the farm, Emerson's long blonde hair is in a ponytail that seems trained to move as gracefully as she does. I want to be her.

Emerson sticks her super difficult double arabian dismount to finish things off, we all scream and high five her, and then Ruby runs off to make sure Sophia is mentally stable enough to make it through the rest of today. At least she doesn't have to do floor.

My fellow alternates Olivia and Charlotte both have falls, and then it's my time to shine, which I do. Not to brag or anything.

Because I'm ridiculous and give no you-know-whats, I give the judges a little wink during my arm wave choreo right before I dismount. Two of them smile at me, which makes me grin as I start my prep, taking away the stress that typically comes before doing one of the most difficult beam dismounts in the world. As usual, I take a deep breath and visualize the skill, but this time I'm totally relaxed going into it.

"Get it, Mal!" Emerson yells when I stick and salute, and I run back to get big hugs from everyone. I'm pretty sure the score will be huge. Probably better than Ruby's and Emerson's.

"How's Sophia?" I whisper, looking in her direction, though I don't see her anymore.

"I think Ruby walked her over to medical. She might be hurt?" Emerson whispers back. "It looks like she whacked her shin really hard against the beam the second time she fell."

My heart flips over. If Sophia's hurt badly enough, they'll start talking about replacements. It's gotta be me, right? The way I've looked this week, there's no way Olivia or Charlotte will get the spot.

I hate myself for thinking about myself before thinking about Sophia's well-being, and I know...it'd be totally bittersweet if I got in because she had some devastating season-ending injury. How could I even be happy in a situation like that?

When the judges finish, we move to floor, where the lineup has gone back and forth all week because everyone's pretty much great. Today, it's Emerson first, then Maddy and Zara with Ruby last.

"I still can't believe I'm first," Emerson groans. "First is the worst. I won't even be in team finals if this is the lineup!"

"It's been changing constantly," I remind her. "If you score higher than any of them today, you'll definitely move up. Just kill it."

"I guess," she sighs.

The judges post my beam score, and it's a 15.8. The highest by half a point and I won't get to compete it. I'm about to celebrate with a high five from Natasha when I spot Ruby running back into the gym. She makes her way over to the floor, and continues jogging in place, hoping to get warm again quickly before it's her turn.

"How's Sophia?" I ask.

"Fine," Ruby responds. "It's her pride more than anything physical. She fell on bars the other day, beam today...with something physically wrong, she has an excuse. But honestly, I think she's just mentally deteriorating. The pressure of a comeback is killer, believe me. Especially coming back as the reigning Olympic all-around champion. It's a ton of pressure, and she's totally feeling it."

"Poor Sophia."

"*Poor Sophia*," Maddy scoffs. "If she can't handle it mentally, she shouldn't be here."

"It's two routines," Emerson retorts. "She hit when it mattered, at trials. Two missed routines at the farm don't mean anything."

"Emerson!" Sergei clears his throat, and Emerson runs to the center of the floor to get into her starting pose. I'm amazed at how quickly she can go from having a normal conversation to turning into a brilliant competitor. I need at least five minutes to get into the right mindset, and she just turns it on and off like an appliance.

I cheer her through a phenomenal routine, and do the same for the girls who follow, though not as enthusiastically for Maddy. She doesn't deserve it.

My turn comes up far too quickly, as it always tends to happen, and I feel a bit more nervous for this compared to my other routines this week, though I'm still nowhere near as bad as usual. In my starting position, I try not to think about what's coming up. I breathe and focus on being in the moment, exactly what Natasha has taught me to do.

The music starts and I turn on the creepy vibes, dancing my way into the corner where I have less than a second to prepare before my first pass, the brand-new double layout.

What I love about floor is that there's so much going on and it all has to be done specifically to the music it's choreographed to, so I don't always have time to visualize everything. Sometimes, I just have to *go. No thinking.*

Considering I busted my head and almost ruined my career on a double tuck in training almost exactly a month ago, a double layout is a huge risk for me, but that was my last pass during an exhausting practice, and this is my first pass while I'm still full of adrenaline after hitting an awesome beam. It's happening.

Roundoff. Back handspring. Set.

I drive my body backwards and think about my cue — up, up, *up!* — to make sure I get the height. I don't believe it's happening until the second flip is fully around and my feet are planted on the ground. Stuck cold.

In the little bit of choreo that comes between this pass and what is now my second pass, the double arabian, I decide to throw a punch front tuck at the end of the arabian if the landing feels good. It's something I've played around with and practiced a million times. I'll feel out the landing on the arabian, and if it's good enough, I'll go for it. Who cares if I sit it? I certainly don't.

The double arabian is like a double front in a tucked position, but with a little twist — literally — that makes it more difficult. I start the tumbling line backwards, but when I set up into the skill, I first twist halfway around before flipping, so the two flips end up going forwards instead of backwards.

I usually land it well enough, but the punch out — which adds a tenth in bonus — is something I've never bothered actually competing because it wasn't worth the risk.

Now that I have nothing to lose, I stick the double arabian with about five feet between me and the white boundary lines that meet in the corner across from me, and without a moment's hesitation, I do an easy front tuck out of it, which gets gasps and cheers from my teammates.

If only I had a surprise with every pass, I think during the middle part of my routine, which involves only choreo and dance elements, none of which I really have to put too much focus into anymore. This middle piece gives me a breather before my final passes, allowing me to both physically and mentally prepare for them, but I know I've got this.

My triple full is a tiny bit under-rotated, but not enough to be devalued by a half twist, thanks to my quick cover-up. I hop back on the double tuck, but keep it from going out-of-bounds, so everything's great here and I'm a badass.

"That was fierce, Mal," Ruby says when I leave the mat, leaning in for a tight hug.

I nod, too out-of-breath to say thanks, and then I turn around. Natasha's there, hands on her hips.

"It's almost like you want me to strangle you," she starts. "But then you hit like that and I can't stay mad."

She leans in for a hug and I spot Zara and Emerson behind her, giving me air high fives.

"Seriously," Natasha whispers into my ear. "You're just getting better and better. Maybe you weren't a lock at trials, but you're sure as hell there now. Everyone knows it. Keep it up, Mal. Anything can happen."

.

Sunday, July 24, 2016
12 days left

"I don't know what happened," Sophia says in our room after breakfast. She played it cool with everyone as we ate, but now she's more vulnerable with only me, Zara, Ruby, and Emerson in the comfort of her room.

"What did the medic say?" Emerson asks.

"I'm physically okay, but it's like my muscles keep spasming and cramping and stuff. It feels like growing pains, you know? Like when you get a Charley horse in your calf muscles. It happened a few times in practice, but nothing like this."

"Is that what happened on bars?" Zara questions.

"No, that was all me screwing up," Sophia smiles. "But on beam, my back spasmed whenever I did anything remotely resembling acro, and my calf muscles and toes cramped up like crazy on everything else. I could barely walk, let alone flip."

"Dehydration," Ruby says knowingly. "Are you drinking nine hundred gallons of water each day? I think that's Vera's recommended amount."

Vera thinks water can solve anything. Hungry? Water. Tired? Water! Broken leg? You *clearly* haven't had enough water.

"Yeah, I should probably drink more." Sophia bites her lip. "I just hope my body can get it together in time for Rio. It would suck to have a routine meltdown there because my muscles are deciding to go on strike."

"Did Vera say anything?" I ask. I want to know for her sake, obviously, but I also want to know what the situation is looking like for me. I'm a selfish jerk, what can I say?

"She won't hold this against me, but it can't happen again. I'm pretty sure if it happens at the full mock meet, she'll definitely cut me. Which sucks, but I get it. Obviously if I can't hit now, she won't be able to trust me to hit in two weeks."

"You'll get there," Ruby says. "Seriously, lots of water. And bananas. That's what my mom always gave me when I got leg and toe cramps like that. Potassium."

"I can't believe it's our day off and we're moping around," Emerson moans, changing the subject. "Does no one have a car? Can anyone drive us anywhere? Literally *anywhere*."

"Like *where*?" Ruby asks. "We're in the middle of nowhere. The nearest mall is a half hour away and it sucks."

"There's that movie theater up route 63," Sophia suggests. "Our coaches took us there once when we were juniors, remember, Ruby?"

"Every movie sucks, though," Zara says, and I laugh.

"We could always go to the lake," I add. "Kayaking or swimming or something?"

"Yes, let's rest our bodies on our one day off by getting in a workout at the lake," Emerson shoots me down. "Sounds like my idea of relaxation."

"I mean, we don't have to do pool conditioning or try to break or personal bests for how fast we swim," I snap. "We can picnic on the beach, read in the hammocks, float around in the water...it's better than nothing. Plus, it's a beautiful day outside, we haven't been outdoors in over a week and desperately need sunlight, *and* we can walk there."

"I vote for Mal's plan!" Zara's hand shoots up. "I'm from a farm in Missouri. I could use some beach time."

"Why not?" Ruby shrugs. "I'm in, too. And hey, Sophia, there's plenty of water at the lake. You'll be all healed up in no time."

"Hilarious," Sophia laughs, hitting Ruby with a pillow. "Yeah, let's do it."

"Okay, Em," Ruby grins. "That leaves you. I mean, you're more than welcome to stay here with your old Windy City buddies, being bossed around by Maddy and worshipped by the other two."

"No thanks," Emerson shudders. "Whatever. I'm in. But I'm not touching lake water, and I first need to drench myself in a gallon of bug spray and the highest SPF sunscreen we can find. The last thing I want is my face on TV looking all splotchy and red."

***

"I already have a thousand bug bites," Emerson whines, swatting at her arm. "I hate nature. Being outside sucks."

"Mosquitos?" Sophia asks, balancing a popsicle and her wallet in one hand and her cell phone and keys in the other. I'm impressed.

"Yeah, they seek me out," Emerson grumbles. "I'm basically the mosquito version of Cracker Barrel."

"You should probably skip out on Brazil, then!" Ruby says gleefully. "You're totally gonna come back with a gold medal and zika."

"I'm not gonna get zika," Emerson rolls her eyes. "First of all, it's winter down there right now. Second, we're going to be near the beach, not in a humid bug-infested jungle. My friend on the Australian team went down for the qualifier in April and said she didn't see a single mosquito."

"But they'll somehow find *you*," Ruby laughs. "Just don't get pregnant and you'll be fine."

"I'll try."

"I can't believe there are athletes turning down Olympic spots because of this ridiculous hyped-up nonsense," Sophia shakes her head. "I'd gladly get zika if it comes with an Olympic medal."

"Like when Ariel trades her voice for human legs," I point out. "Worth it."

"At least you already have a medal," Zara says, slipping out of her t-shirt to show off a ten-pack and machine gun arms in her neon Triangl bikini. I can feel everyone around us gasping in amazement. All gymnasts are muscular as hell, but Zara is like a whole other species.

"True," Sophia smiles. "But I still wouldn't let zika stop me from getting more."

"No more zika talk," Emerson shudders. "You can all joke about it, but you *know* if one of us gets it, it'll be me."

"I can't believe they let us come here by ourselves," Zara grins, happy to switch to a less creepy crawly topic. "I totally thought we'd have a chaperone."

"I'm sure a coach or two will stop by and spy," Ruby rolls her eyes. "But I mean, three of us are literal adults. They can't force babysitters on us."

"Well, they would be right not to trust me right now," I respond, eyes on a fire pit across the beach. "Because they're totally roasting marshmallows for s'mores over there and I'm about to go eat a million of them."

"You *can't* have s'mores!" Sophia gasps, and I think she's joking at first, but her face looks truly horrified.

"Moderation," Ruby smiles, giving a weird glance to Sophia. "I say we do it. We worked out more than enough this week to deserve a treat."

We race to set down our blankets and umbrellas and then run across the sand.

"This is actually a private lunch," a middle-aged man who looks like Santa Claus in a Speedo says, almost protective of his goodies. "You girls aren't from here."

"Dad, we have extra!" His kid, who looks about six or seven, pulls out bags of marshmallows and offers them to us. "Want some?"

"If you don't mind." Ruby, our fearless leader, gives the kid a high five. "We never get treats. And no, we're not from around here. We're actually from all over the country, visiting."

"What made you decide to come to Shell Lake?" He starts prepping five sticks, popping a single marshmallow onto each, and I'm practically drooling after endless meals of bland chicken and fish. "Not exactly a tourist destination."

"We're actually here training for the Olympics!" Zara grabs a stick and sighs happily as she shoves it into the fire.

"Oh, you're at that…what is it? A farm?"

"Yeah, kind of. Half working farm, half Olympic gymnastics training center," Emerson explains, gingerly taking a stick of her own, like someone has just offered her drugs and she wants to go for it but is afraid her parents will find out.

"I'm having marshmallow only," Sophia compromises, noting Emerson's hesitation.

"Wow, the Olympics," Santa Claus muses. "Lemme get a picture of y'all. No one would believe me if I said the Olympic gymnastics team accosted me and stole my s'mores."

With our marshmallows posed over the fire, the five of us grin into his iPhone camera lens, happy for the recognition, however weird. He takes a few shots of us alone and then with his kid before handing out graham crackers and chocolate squares, which Emerson and Sophia decline, though the rest of us are thrilled about the sugar and carbs.

After making small talk for a bit — only so we don't look like freeloaders, which we are — we politely excuse ourselves and head back to our blankets, our reading materials, and our cooler stocked with ice-cold water, fruit, and tuna sandwiches.

"Relaxation mode," Emerson sighs, settling into a comfy position on her blanket, sunglasses perched on her head. "It's not Fiji, but it'll do for now."

Ruby and I share a blanket and a magazine, and Zara paints Sophia's toes while Sophia whips out a book about mathematical theorems, something way beyond my understanding. In addition to being an Olympic champion on her way to her second Games, Sophia is also kind of a genius, and is currently taking a year off from Harvard. Try not to be jealous.

"So?" Ruby is licking the sticky marshmallow goo from her fingers. "What's new with Jack?"

I blush out of habit even though there's not really anything to blush about. "Nothing. It's kinda hard to work on taking steps in our relationship when we've been apart the entire time we've been together. We've been texting, like...almost constantly, though."

"Sexting?" Ruby makes a face and I slap her on the arm.

"*No*. I hate you. Regular texting. He makes me laugh. Whenever I'm having a bad day or when things are annoying, I text Jack and he always has the perfect response."

"You're so adorable, you make me sick. I hate you. You're what, four years younger than me? And I've never been romantically involved with anyone. Neither has Emerson, or Sophia. You've got us all beat."

"I wouldn't say things are *romantic*. I mean, our first *date* was at my house and involved dinner with my mom followed by awkward silence."

"See, but that *is* romantic. When you're fifteen. It's adorably romantic, and when you're all grown up, whether you're still with Jack or not, you'll look back and think *wow*, my high school boyfriend and I were the cutest little couple. You'll *wish* that kind of romance still existed in your life."

"You say this as if you're eighty."

"Physically, I might be."

I laugh, and then lean back onto my elbows, stretching my toes into the sand. It feels so normal, like the Olympics aren't days away and we're just regular people doing regular people things.

"I'm proud of you, by the way," Ruby says, leaning back to get on my level.

"Proud?" I wrinkle my nose. "Why?"

"You're killing it, Mal. I should've known better, but I fully thought you were going to crash and burn here. You seemed so...not you. But you're really just kind of like *screw it* right now and that whole attitude is working for you. You're way less tense and controlling, and opening up like that is a major transformation. It's like watching a different athlete. So many girls in your position would only give the bare minimum, but you're working harder than anyone on the actual team, and really, it's impressive. So yeah. I'm proud."

"Thanks. I...I don't know what to say, really. I'm just trying to make the most of it. I figure what the hell...I'm not fighting for a spot anymore. Nothing I do matters, so it's kind of like I can do whatever."

"I wouldn't say it doesn't matter."

"No, it really doesn't, though. I'm training but not for any meet. Not immediately, anyway. Next season, sure. If I'm lucky, maybe I'll get to go to the Mexican Open or a world cup or something in the fall as a consolation prize. But without something coming up in the near future, I am under zero pressure. It's kind of amazing."

Ruby's eyes sparkle for a second, and then she sits up. "Well, you're doing a fantastic job. And I'm not the only one who's noticing. Trust me."

She grabs her iPhone and turns on some music, my cue to reach for my Kindle so I can read for a bit, something I'm generally too exhausted to do at the farm after a full day of training.

The sun feels good on my skin even through the ninety million layers of sunscreen, but a few pages in, I realize I'm not here to sit back and read.

In a flash of spontaneity, I drop my Kindle, bolt to the dock, and take a running leap to cannonball into the lake.

Before long, Ruby, Zara, and Sophia have all joined me, and then finally, even Emerson climbs up from her spot in the sand, doing a back tuck into the water while laughing uncontrollably, something so un-Emerson, I just want to hug her like crazy.

Despite everything going on around us, in this moment, we are happy.

Wednesday, July 27, 2016
9 days left

Today is the big one.

"It's the final countdown," I sing in my head, complete with awesome guitar riffs, during the lineup before our last mock competition.

Vera's talking about the plan for verification, but I'm more interested in stretching my toes, curling them under my feet and standing on them until it hurts before slowly lowering myself again.

Normally this would be a no-no. No fidgeting. Vera would kill me. But right now, I just don't really care. I yawn without thinking, and then spot Natasha giving me the evil eye.

"Are you trying to get yourself killed?" she asks once we're released from the line.

I yawn again and shrug.

"What's wrong with you?" Natasha swats me on the butt with her newspaper like I'm a puppy who just peed on her shoes. "Hurry up, get out of your sweats."

"I'm last up. I'm staying warm."

"Right. Well, go jump around or something."

I roll my eyes. Clearly, she has more important things to think about — ahem, Ruby — and I'm just the annoying toddler she had to bring along because daycare was closed.

Retreating to the edge of the floor, I jog in place for a few seconds to keep my muscles going. I do a back walkover, a front walkover, and a couple of split jumps, something I'll repeat every few minutes until I go up.

I'm happy with how the past few days have gone, the time at the lake rejuvenating my spirit and making me even more relaxed coming into the final stretch of hell.

During each floor routine, I go through the motions, cheering and high-fiving and making fake sad faces when something doesn't go right, but deep down I know I'm feeling a little crappy because this is it. Aside from training in Rio, the Olympics are basically over for me after this mock meet, and even though I've had time to get used to it and thought I was okay with it, now that things are getting close, it totally hurts.

I pull my leggings off one routine before my own, and then stoically approach the floor like I'm bravely facing my own execution. It's actually fitting given the theme of my creeptastic routine. I get into position, narrow my eyes, and stare right into Vera's soul, me the *Saw* villain and Vera my victim.

"Eat your heart out," I think as the music begins. "You *wish* my routines were going to Rio."

***

"Tell me. *Please.* What is your secret?!" Emerson grovels once we're finished. Because I smashed it on floor. I murdered my vault. I made the bars my bitch. And they might as well start calling the beam "the Blanchard." Basically, I dominated today.

Third place. And if you combined the scores from our first two mock meets, I would've placed third there as well, only a half point back from winning. The third best all-arounder in the country isn't going to the Olympics. Think about that.

"The secret is that she doesn't give a crap," Zara laughs. "Something we all need to learn."

Like she's one to talk. She was fourth today, and if she was a little bit stronger on beam, she would've beaten me. She's naturally one of the most chill competitors in the world.

"You can't teach that," Emerson sighs. "Believe me, I've tried."

"That's the whole secret," I grin. "You just have to completely stop caring, but the catch is that the more you *care* about trying to stop caring, the more elusive it becomes."

Emerson won today, Ruby was second, and Maddy was fifth. Sophia hit a shaky bars set but fell on beam, which was sucky because in qualifications, the team goes up on beam last, always tricky to handle mentally. If she can't hack it here, I don't know how she's gonna handle it in Rio, unless she just needs the pressure of actually being at a competition in front of people with finals spots and medals on the line to make it happen.

After bombing her competition on beam last week and dealing with crazy muscle spasms, Sophia slowly got her life back together and actually had some great practices yesterday and on Monday, but today she showed it's the competition aspect she can't figure out. She cares way too much, she fights way too hard, and she sets herself up to fail.

Ruby spies me tracking Sophia, who's squatting against the wall, head down on her knees, earbuds in, doing deep breathing exercises courtesy of one of her thousands of iPhone relaxation apps.

I know how fried her nerves are and I wish I could swap brains with her or somehow transfer over some confidence so she could just hit her freaking routines.

"Line up!" Vera shouts, and we all run dutifully back to the floor. "Tomorrow we have an early morning practice, and then we have a quick lunch and only a little bit of time after that before we leave for the airport, so you should use this time tonight to start packing your things. We also have the new apparel and gear, including all of the training and competition leotards, which should be waiting in your rooms after dinner. Absolutely *no photos on social media*. I don't want the leotards leaked to the media before we wear them."

I swallow hard. I'll get the same leos and gear as the girls on the team even though I have nowhere to wear it. I'm bummed thinking of my Olympic apparel, some of the leos costing upwards of a thousand bucks, going to waste.

"After dinner, I'm going to speak to each of you individually, you and your head coach. We have a few things to cover before we leave, all related to your gymnastics and what we'll need your personal focus to be as we go into the next and final week of training in Brazil. Thank you for your hard work here these past couple of weeks, and for continuing to build on a strong season."

Vera nods, giving us the okay to grab our things and leave, and it's back to the dorms we go.

"What do you think your *focus* is?" I ask Zara once we're safe in our rooms. I glance around at the tornado of clothing that covers every surface inch of our beds, dressers, and floor, and decide packing just isn't gonna happen. Nap time it is.

"Literally no clue," Zara says. "Not very insightful, am I?"

"Nah, that's Vera's job. You just do you."

"What about you?" she asks.

"Me? My focus will be on putting in the bare minimum, and then getting what will hopefully be the first tan of my life. I don't think I've ever been outside long enough for the sun to actually do anything. I mean, I'm not pushing for skin cancer or anything, but I'd love to not be translucent for a week or two."

Zara laughs. "Keeping it positive. Good."

"Nothing else I can do."

I curl up under the covers, knees to my chest, only slightly sad about how things are going. At this point I've had more than enough time to think about the suckiness that is my situation and it hardly bothers me anymore. I said *hardly*.

"I'll put your stuff near your dresser," Zara the Energizer Bunny says, hands on her hips while surveying the destruction wrought by our hurricane lives over the past couple of weeks. "Enjoy your nap."

"Thanks," I mumble, my body melting into the mattress. Within minutes, it's sleep, glorious sleep.

***

"Amalia, we're going in first," Natasha says at dinner, tapping my shoulder as I finish the chicken, broccoli, and pasta with garlic sauce, one of the tastiest meals we've had since getting here. Mmm, carbs.

"If we go in first, I won't get to see the leos until after!" I whine. "Not fair."

"So you'll get them five minutes after everyone else, pain in the butt. God, you're getting so annoying."

"I love that you can talk to your coach like that," Maddy gushes. "My coach would murder me."

"Mal's not actually being a bitch, though," Ruby explains. "Natasha knows we love being over-the-top ridiculous."

"Whatever. I'm still jealous."

"Okay, Amalia, we're going!" Natasha grabs my elbow, lifting me from my folding chair. "Time to turn on the charm."

I realize as we walk to Vera's office that I've never actually had a conversation with Vera. We've never spoken to her one-on-one. Every interaction has been a post-meet congratulations or a mid-practice criticism, and they've been completely one-sided, with Vera talking and me trying not to die.

Vera is still this mythical creature to me. She was a superstar as a gymnast herself, a legend as a coach, and now she's an icon as the woman who runs the show in one of the best programs in the world. How do you talk to someone like that as if she's an actual person? I don't even know where to start, especially now that I'm not one of her golden five.

Maybe if I'd lived up to her expectations and made the team, we could get to be super close and she'd pinch my cheeks the way she does with Ruby and Emerson and Sophia. Not that they're her BFFs either, but they seem comfortable with her and I want that.

"Welcome, Amalia." Vera smiles almost warmly, gesturing to a comfy chair across from her desk. I feel like I'm at a college interview or something.

I smile back, nervously looking up at Natasha, who refuses to sit. Instead, she stands at my side with her arms folded across her chest, a total power move. She doesn't mean to come off as threatening, but living through four decades of the most epic mother-daughter power struggle ever has put her on permanent edge.

"You've done well at this camp," Vera says, consulting her notes. "Some of your best results."

She peers at me over the top of her bifocals, as if waiting for a response, but I don't know what to say. "How would you say your experience has been?" she pushes.

"Great, I guess," I start. "I haven't really paid too much attention to my scores, so I don't know, like, *quantitatively* how it's going. But my routines have felt great."

"Did you feel the pressure here was similar to the pressure you felt in competition this summer?"

"Not really. Actually, in general, yes, some of the greatest pressure I've ever been under has been here at the farm. But that was before. The competition season happened and that was a lot of pressure, but it was only because I had to make the team. Normally I'm awesome under pressure. I'm a rock. But with the team on the line...I wasn't as confident."

"That's very insightful." Vera seems impressed even though everything that came out of my mouth was super rambly and idiotic. "What did you improve on most while here?"

"Not giving a crap," I blurt, and then I turn seventy shades of red. "I mean..."

Vera breaks out into hearty laughter. Is she having a stroke?

"You remind me of my Natasha. She rubbed off on Ruby, and now it seems she's rubbing off on you. So what does that mean? Not giving a...*crap*?"

"It means...I cared so much about making the team, I psyched myself out sometimes. I still had some great meets. Olympic Trials, I was kind of awesome there. But once the team was out of the picture, I stopped being so intense about everything, didn't force myself to follow all of my crazy rituals, and I just went for it instead. I felt more free and uninhibited."

"Yes, we all saw that. You had a tremendous Olympic camp."

"Thank you, uh, ma'am."

Vera looks down at her notes again. "Amalia, there have been some changes to our team."

My heart explodes into fifty thousand pieces, each of which now beats independently, and I can feel the pulsing all over my body. My temperature rises at least ten degrees, my brain is racing, and my stomach rushes up to my throat.

To my left, I feel Natasha tense up so hard she's going to need a major massage to get her body back to normal. She clutches the back of my chair tightly, her knuckles turning white, while I hold my breath, refusing to let it out again until I know for sure what I think is about to happen actually happens.

"You will be competing at the Olympics, Amalia," Vera says calmly, her icy Soviet eyes piercing into my own. "Right now, the plan is to use your routines on bars and beam in qualifications and in team finals, and we also want to use your vault in the team final so we can let Emerson focus on her stronger events. We think you will be a great asset as we attempt to earn a team gold medal, and we also think you can win a medal in the beam final."

I exhale slowly, my head dizzying a bit and my heart steadily beating faster and faster until it feels like an elephant is sitting on my chest. Am I having a heart attack? Whenever I get little anxiety attacks I naturally assume I'm having a heart attack every single time, but this feels like what I imagine an actual heart attack is. Is my arm tingling or am I just literally *freaking out*?

"Wow. That's. I'm..."

Vera smiles, her lips pressed tight. "I'm sure you're pleased."

Pleased?! I'm so frigging thrilled, I could set fire to the farm and go to prison for life and never stop smiling. I'm floating. I'm fabulous. This is like when Tyra Banks tricks girls into thinking they're going home in a double elimination and then she's like, "Just kidding! You're going to the *fashion capital of the world*!!!!" which is somehow a different city every cycle.

"She's pleased," Natasha says, playing it cool. "We're both pleased, and honored. Thank you, Vera."

"No, thank you. Amalia was originally my first choice for this team, but in Boston and in Atlanta, I saw too much fear and hesitation and nerves. Talent can only get you so far, and I worried Amalia might be a bit too green as a competitor to handle such an intense situation like this one will be. But much has changed. You proved me wrong."

I stare dumbly. I don't think I'll ever be able to speak again.

"At these big international meets, I need to be able to trust my girls," Vera continues. "I didn't know if I could trust you, but it's clear to me now. You are fearless. We just had to see it come out of you. Sophia, meanwhile…"

Uh oh. Me going to the Olympics means Sophia is not going. That's right. Other people exist. I always forget that I'm just a tiny little clump of cells and particles and not the only star shining in my very own galaxy.

"Sometimes experience can work against you. Sophia has done a good job in her comeback, and I have never seen an Olympian return to the sport as dedicated as she did. But right now, she is in a rut, both physically and mentally. I trusted her in 2012, I trusted her at worlds last year, and I trusted this year that her experience would carry her through, especially after her stellar performance at trials. But in training, she has shown that I can't trust her to get back to her top caliber by next weekend. Every mistake takes her deeper into the ravine and she hasn't shown me that she knows how to climb out. Sadly."

I bite my lip and nod. "I understand."

"I'll let you get back to packing. A little bird tells me you haven't even started." Her eyes show a hint of a smile, even though her lips stay still.

"You also have your new gear to go through and try on. Congratulations, Amalia, and thank you for your service to this team. I know you'll make your country proud."

"Thank you. Thank you, so much. I don't think I can express how much this means to me."

"Believe me, I've done this before. I know. Now please, don't say anything on social media, and when you tell your family, make sure they don't say anything to anyone either. We need to put a press release together that will handle this situation...diplomatically."

"Okay, no posting. Got it."

"And don't tell the other girls. I'm talking to Sophia tonight, and we'll have a team meeting about the changes in the morning."

"Copy that. Thank you."

Natasha squeezes my arm the whole way back to the dorms, not saying a word the entire time. Once we're in a safe zone with no eavesdroppers, she squeals so hard I think at least one of my eardrums has exploded. When I pull away from her painfully tight hug, I see she is crying.

"You did it. I knew it. I didn't want to get my hopes up, but I knew it. I love you, kid. Go pack and get some sleep. You're amazing. Congrats."

I whisper goodnight, and then slip into my room, which is thankfully empty at the moment. I need to text my parents and then debate texting Jack, who isn't really family, but he kind of is and it's not like he'd call TMZ to leak the news or anything.

When I take out my phone and start tapping away, I pause, think for a moment, and then turn it off completely. Mom and dad and Jack can wait until tomorrow. My dream, the one thing in the world I've been hoping and praying and working for since I was five, it just came true in the weirdest of ways. For right now, for the next twelve hours, I want this feeling to belong only to me.

My heart still racing, I feel tears start to stream down my face and my whole body is tingling with a million nerve endings all zapping with energy that needs to go somewhere. I pick up my pillow, shove my face into the soft down, and scream.

I'm going to the Olympics.

Thursday, July 28, 2016
8 days left

"Did you see her at all? Or talk to her?" Ruby whispers during our general stretch warmup at the morning practice, our final practice before we leave for Rio, where I, Amalia Blanchard, will compete at the Olympic Games.

Sophia has apparently agreed to take over the alternate spot I'm giving up, but she hasn't been at practice and missed the announcement during the lineup.

It sounded like Vera gave her the morning off or something, but still, I'm worried and can't help thinking it's all my fault even though the decision was completely out of my hands. Judging by Maddy's glares in my direction, I'm pretty sure I'm not the only one who feels this way.

"No," I shake my head. "I didn't want to see her last night, obviously, which is why I didn't leave my room. I can't imagine what it would've been like to bump into her in the hallway or in the common room. She must hate me."

"It has nothing to do with you," Ruby says sternly. "You showed up and did your job. She didn't. No offense to her, it happens, but she was breaking down mentally and physically. She was under more pressure than anyone here. She wasn't eating right, she was dehydrated, she was losing muscle, her body was killing her, she was biting her nails down to her fingertips, she was depressed and anxious as hell no matter how big a smile she managed to paste on…I've been in ruts like that. I get it, and it really sucks for her. But at the end of the day, it was out of her hands and out of yours. Vera made the decision. If people are pissed, it's on her."

The press release won't come out until after we get to Rio. We're all in social media prison at the moment, and we will be until the media team decides how to spin this. Fans of this sport always come up with crazy conspiracy theories whenever something *dramatic* like this happens, so the faster they spin this and get it out in the public, the better it is for everyone involved.

Suddenly, Sophia pushes through the double doors, looking red-eyed and pale. I immediately look away, but it doesn't matter. She's staring at the ground, thumbnail in her mouth.

"Oh boy," Ruby mutters.

"Sophia, please join the warmup," Vera calls out, not lifting her eyes from her clipboard. "You're late."

Still facing away, I track Sophia with one eye, watching her slowly make her way over to the floor, where we are currently knee-deep in lunges. With her long, stringy, unwashed black hair hanging down over her face, she looks like the creepy little girl from the movie *The Ring*. As mentally screwed up as she's been since she got here, this is a new low.

"I hope you're happy," Maddy hisses, again, as if this is all my fault.

"Yeah, *thrilled*," I snap back, trying super hard to not punch her in the throat.

The truth is, I feel *so bad* about how this played out. I get how much this sucks for Sophia and I wish a billion times that Vera had just chosen me after trials instead of playing these stupid "who can withstand the pressure?!" games. We could've avoided this whole heartbreak with Sophia losing a spot she thought she had, and we could've avoided *my* whole heartbreak with not getting it in the first place.

As much as it sucks for Sophia to get kicked off the team, it also sucks for *me* because I have to be all sad and mopey for her because everyone else is sad and mopey for her. If I enjoy myself, I'll look like a dick. I don't get to enjoy the fact that I'm *on the frigging Olympic team*, and that really sucks.

I used to get really annoyed when I'd hear people at school complain about things like grades or boys or not getting cars for their birthdays. Like, there are people in the world with no clean water. There are babies born into unthinkable abuses from which they'll never escape. There are families in my own hometown with nowhere to live, who sleep in their cars. These are real problems. Shut your mouth.

Right now, Sophia is the one whose pain is valid. She is the one experiencing loss. I get that. But my feelings should also be valid, and I hate that I don't get to feel happy just because she's sad. I did something that not even one percent of the people on this planet will ever accomplish and I have to sit here like it doesn't matter.

Taking out my frustration on the floor beneath me, I go extra hard on my straddle jump landings, grunting with each one.

"Careful," Maddy cautions, a bitchy smile on her face. "You don't want to break your ankles."

No, I want to break *yours*.

Sophia is just going through the motions, not saying a word. When it's time to move on to train our events — team girls to floor, alternates to vault — she pauses for a second on the floor before realizing it's no longer where she belongs.

I cringe as her jerk coach barks at her, snapping her back into reality. He's a hardass and makes Vera look like an eight-week-old puppy eating ice cream in a field of daisies. I can't imagine how much crap he gave her.

As she jogs past me to her coach, I try to look away, but she meets my eyes, half-smiling back.

"I'm sorry," she whispers, just as I'm going to say the same to her. Maybe everyone else hates me, but Sophia doesn't. That's all that matters. Maybe this won't be so bad. Maybe I'll even get to be happy?

"Only dance-throughs today!" Vera yells. "When it's not your turn, share the tumble track and go through your passes. Amalia, you're up first."

"You better hit," Maddy says loudly, but not to me. To Zara. "Amalia's only the alternate on floor, but if you're not careful, she'll steal your spot."

Right. Happy my ass.

***

"Your seatmates are the same as your roommates," Vera explains just as our bus pulls up to the Minneapolis-St. Paul International Airport. "Your coaches have your tickets."

"Gimme, gimme, gimme," Ruby says obnoxiously, climbing over the seat in front of her to scare the crap out of Natasha.

"Goddamn!" Natasha screeches. "I'm going to have a heart attack."

She digs through her bag and finds her neatly organized binder, with all of our tickets zipped up safely in a pouch.

"Here, brat," she says, passing our tickets to Ruby.

The ride to Minneapolis was quiet and peaceful, everyone retreating to iPads, Netflix, Kindles, and naps after a long couple of weeks driving each other crazy. Human interaction is overrated.

Sophia emerges from the back of the bus, where she'd curled up in the last row and slept under a giant hoodie without saying a thing to anyone for the duration of the ride. Tomorrow, she'll go off with Olivia and Charlotte to the apartment in Ipanema while I take what she thought was her spot at the Olympic Village. After that, who knows when I'll see her again. Aside from our little moment during practice, we haven't talked at all and I want to make sure we're really okay before all of this happens.

Suddenly, my phone dings and I see a text from my dad. "When's your flight?"

Ruby peers across the aisle, knowing her, most likely hoping to see a sext from Jack or something. "Did your parents totally freak about the news?"

"Oh, shit."

"What?"

"I kinda forgot to tell them."

"*Amalia!*"

"Yeah, I know. I'm the literal worst."

I quickly pull up my dad's number and he answers immediately. "I thought I missed you!"

"No, daddy, we fly tonight. We have a three hour flight to Houston first, and then Rio from there. We're gonna eat at the airport first. Do you know how to...I don't know what it's called, patch mom in?"

"A three-way call? Just look down and hit add call. Come on, you're supposed to be my personal tech support!"

"I can barely use the toaster, dad. I'm calling her, okay?" My dad grunts a response and within seconds, we're all on the line together.

"Is something wrong?" she asks.

"Yeah, actually. We're not gonna be able to do the whole vacation thing in Brazil."

"Oh my God," my mother gasps. "Why not? What's wrong? Are you injured?"

"Well," I start, and then bring my voice down to a whisper so no one on the bus overhears and thinks I'm being a jerk to brag about my news with Sophia nearby. "I'm going to be *way* too busy. Competing at the Olympics."

My mom *screams*. "Amalia, I am *so* happy for you! And proud of you!"

"I had a feeling, kiddo," my dad says. I can almost hear him smiling. "You deserve this."

"How did it happen?" my mom asks. "Did someone else get hurt? That poor girl."

"No, not really. I can't talk about it right now, but I'll tell you later, okay? Oh, and don't tell anyone," I remember to add. "No friends or relatives or anyone. They have to make it official first, with a whole media announcement. Pretend it's a top secret government thing and the KGB will kill you if you squeal."

"We promise," my dad responds. "You can trust us."

"So, I have to run...we have to go through security and everything. I love you guys. I'll email you about ticket info, because I actually get tickets now. Two of them. You guys will get to sit with the rest of the parents. But for now, I love you guys."

"We love you too," they say in unison. "Have a good flight!"

I throw my phone in the bag just as Ruby yells at me from the front of the bus to hurry up. I look back at Sophia and debate waiting for her so we can talk, but I feel too much like a kidnapper plotting my next capture and I back off.

What would I even say?

Friday, July 29, 2016
7 days left

The point of taking this super long flight overnight was so we could get some sleep, but I've been up and fidgeting through almost three full movies at this point. Sleep just isn't happening.

Our head trainer and physical therapist, Michelle, worked something out with the airline so we can be allowed to stretch and stuff in the back of the plane where the bathrooms and beverage carts are. We have a free pass to do whatever we need to feel better whenever we feel like we're getting gnarled up and twisted into permanent pretzels, not exactly what our muscles need a week out from the biggest competition of our lives.

It's four in the morning when I climb over Zara and walk to my own personal gym in the sky, spreading an airplane-issued blanket over what I'm assuming is a filthy floor before lunging and then working my way into a split.

"Point your toes, Blanchard!" I look up and Sophia's there, a blanket of her own in hand.

"Couldn't sleep?" I ask.

"Not with Maddy having a violent seizure next to me. Are sleep fits a thing?"

"She's summoning Satan, actually. She needs an exorcism."

Sophia laughs as she tries some yoga poses, finally settling in downward facing dog. "Ahhh, my hips. Humans weren't meant to sit."

"Yeah, I feel like I need to sit in a split for the next two hundred years to undo the hours I spent in my seat. Hey..." I start, unsure how I want to continue. "I'm really sorry, by the way. I had no idea this was going to happen. I would take it back if I could."

"No, you wouldn't," Sophia shrugs. "Mal, you had nothing to do with the decision and nothing to be sorry about. I'm sure everyone has told you this by now, but you need to hear it from me. Vera kicked me off the team. You did nothing but show that you were the best alternate there, and in my own failure to live up to Vera's standards, you showed that you deserved to compete in Rio more than me."

"I can't help feeling responsible, though."

"If it wasn't you, it would've been Olivia or Charlotte. No offense, but it's not that you were *so good* that Vera booted me to make room for you. It's that I was *so bad* that they had to find a replacement for me."

"You weren't..."

"Yes, I was. I was *so bad*. I fell all the time in practice and in the mock meets. I had zero control over my gymnastics, over my mental game, over my emotions...I kept it professional in the gym, or tried to, but Vera saw I was breaking down. I was way too stressed and never would've been able to pull this off. As much as I hate to admit it, she made the right decision."

"Does it help even a little knowing you've already been to the Games and have medals?"

"Yeah, a little. Not totally, because this was a different dream. You know, coming in as a comeback kid, that almost never happens. When was the last time someone from this country made it to two Olympics in a row? I remember four years ago when all of the 2008 girls tried to come back for London and they were disasters. None of them came close. But I was actually serious about my training and was going to make it happen, which is *huge*. My first Olympic dreams came true, I reached my biggest personal goal in 2012, but this was a different set of dreams and goals and I failed. So it stings. But I'm also rational enough to know how good I've already had it."

I think about Sophia telling me only moments earlier how good she is at "keeping it professional" and hiding her emotions, and I know deep down she's putting on a front now. She's so not okay with this. Not at all. She looks small and beaten down and scared and broken. I wish I could make it better, but nothing I could say could possibly do that. If anything, I'm just going to make it worse.

"What do you think the press release will say?" I ask suddenly, realizing it'll come out any day now and people will know I'm taking over.

"That I'm injured." She pauses, and then shrugs, tensing her shoulders up by her ears for a moment before releasing. "My back. It'll keep me from being productive on bars because I couldn't do stalder work and lost a lot of my difficulty or something. They'll mention that they need to replace me for bars, but that I still have 'value' as an alternate, which explains why I'm still traveling to Rio. It makes no sense, I know. But whatever."

"You're okay with that? Instead of the truth?"

"It's better than the alternative. I'd rather have people think that a physical ailment caused my demise rather than the actual mental breakdown that really ruined me."

We stretch in silence for a few minutes until I finally yawn, get up, and hand my blanket off to a flight attendant, who looks only minorly annoyed at having to supervise us during what is probably his only time to relax on this marathon flight.

"I'm gonna try to sleep for an hour. Totally a good amount of sleep before a full day, right? See you in Rio?"

"Yeah, in Rio," Sophia sighs, massaging her forearm. "I think I have a pinched nerve. Anyway, hopefully I'll get to see you guys for a little while before you go off to the Village and I'm stuck with Tweedledee and Tweedledum."

"Me too."

In the dark, Zara's quiet snores guide me back to my seat. Once settled, I push it back as far as it goes in an attempt to force my body to shut down, but as usual, as tired as my body feels, my mind is on another plane of existence. All I can hope is that we don't have to go straight to training once we land.

***

"This. Place. Is. *Gorgeous*." Ruby presses her face up to the window at the airport while we wait to go through customs. If you squint, you can see the water and the mountains beyond the tarmac.

"It's basically Los Angeles or Florida." Emerson's not impressed.

"There are no mountains in Los Angeles or Florida, jackass," Ruby retorts.

"Actually, there are mountains right outside of Los Angeles," Maddy butts in. "You can see them when you're flying in. I flew in to visit my agent and saw them. They have hills, too. Like…just like the show. *The Hills.*"

"Yeah, not the same thing. Good try though."

We zoom through customs and then a big city bus reading *Especial* on the front is waiting for us outside where it's sunny and gorgeous and in the seventies. We're all in national team leggings and jackets, and as warm as it is, I'm kind of glad for the cover. I'm sweating in places I didn't know existed.

Sophia tugs the back of my jacket and I turn around. "Hey. We're going a different way. I wanted to say good luck."

"You guys aren't even coming to see the arena and everything?"

"Nope. Straight to the apartment. Maybe we'll do a tour or something later, I don't know. But I looked it up on my maps app and we're staying nowhere near you guys."

"I'm sorry, Sophia."

"Stop saying you're sorry. I'll live. Kill it for me, okay?"

"You got it." I give her a big hug, trying to keep from crying as I wrap my arms around her tiny shoulders. "I'll text you, okay?"

She nods and walks over to the small shuttle van waiting for her and the others going to Ipanema. I get hugs and best wishes from Charlotte and Olivia, and then Polina, a crazy sobbing mess, runs to me and squeezes me tight. Even though I'm no longer an alternate, Polina isn't an accredited member of the Olympic team. She'll still be helping out with alternate training, though, as a kind of impartial voice.

"I never in a million years thought you would get this far," she gushes. "You really surprised me. Don't make me regret these feelings of pride."

Wow, a true compliment from Polina. Was it a compliment? Because when I go over it again in my head, it sounds like she was actually fully throwing shade at me. Oh, Polina. I shall miss you most of all.

I drag my giant suitcase — it barely made weight — behind me, balancing my duffel bag on top so I don't have to wear it over my shoulder. My backpack has already claimed that spot.

The driver motions to the open door and we began piling on, each taking our own little row, but lots of swapping goes on as we argue over which side will have the better view.

"Can we take the long way?" I overhear Ruby asking the driver. She whips out her phone and goes over her preferred route, which passes by the beaches rather than going straight through to Barra di Tijuca via the highway. "We're in a beach city and we're never actually going to see the beach. I beg of you. Let us at least see what we'll be missing."

"He doesn't understand a word you're saying," Emerson rolls her eyes. "He speaks Portuguese."

"Duh."

"Are they gonna be roommates the whole time we're here?" Zara asks, turning around to face me. "Because one of them won't be getting out of this situation alive."

The drive to the Olympic Village takes an hour and a half, but the scenic route covered the beaches of Copacabana, Ipanema, and Leblon, the whole touristy coast featuring ginormous Atlantic waves, beachside dives selling drinks served in coconuts, and hot people in the tiniest bathing suits I've ever seen. *So many hot people in almost no clothes.* I mean, I could do without the tanorexic old white dude retirees in tiny bikini bottoms, but otherwise I'm totally here for this.

When we get to Barra, the world turns from Actual Brazil to this Olympic Disneyland version filled with nothing but arenas, training centers, parks, and best of all, the Village, dozens of buildings with thousands of apartments for the ten thousand of us who will begin competing next week. An isosceles right triangle of land dangling just south of the main road, its legs surrounded by water, the Olympic Park is an athlete's dream.

"Welcome to processing!" a chipper Rio 2016 volunteer with an iPad says when we arrive. "Check-in is over there by that Team USA banner; be sure to put on your credentials right away so no one tries to kick you out. Someone will show you to your apartments so you can drop off your bags, and then you'll report to the United States Olympic Committee headquarters to pick up your gear."

The day is a blur. Volunteers are shuffling us around the entire time, not letting us really experience anything on our own, though I'm sure we'll have plenty of time for that in the coming days.

The apartments are awesome, bright and clean with expansive balconies overlooking the Village, each one dangling a flag representing the nationality of the athletes inside. Our apartment has three bedrooms, two beds to a room, with Emerson and Ruby in one, me and Zara in another, and Maddy happily by herself.

At the USOC headquarters, we spend hours trying on clothes and piling up endless amounts of gifts, more stuff than I'll ever be able to carry back home.

We get Ralph Lauren uniforms for the opening and closing ceremonies, an entire duffel bag full of Team USA branded apparel we'll wear on the medal stand and in media appearances, jewelry, sunglasses, sneakers, bags, a blinged-out Olympic ring, and even a special edition Apple iWatch.

It was like one of those TV shows from the 1980s where people ran around stores with shopping carts, taking whatever they wanted from the shelves. Forget medals and glory and bringing honor to your country. I'm totally at the Olympics just for the free stuff.

"Poor Sophia," I sigh while being measured and pinned during a fitting. "Charlotte and Olivia too. It sucks that they don't get to do this."

"They're lucky they're in Brazil at all," Emerson informs me. "USGA is paying a crap ton of money to have them here. The apartments for them and the coaches, the training facility, the private shuttle...most federations have nowhere near enough money to be able to afford something like this, and their alternates have to stay at home."

We're leaving headquarters with more stuff than anyone could ever possibly need when Vera announces that we're heading to the arena. We're not going to practice, thank God, but she wants us to get an early feel for everything so we can get our initial "OMGs" out of our systems now and not when we actually have to train there.

"She has to be kidding," Maddy whines. "We've been traveling and moving nonstop for 24 hours."

For once I agree with her. My eyes are burning, I've yawned thirty times in the past fifteen seconds, and I've only made it through this far thanks to pure adrenaline.

"At least we're not training," Emerson yawns, making me yawn yet again. "It could be worse."

We flash our credentials at the athlete entrance of the Rio Olympic Arena, and guard — yes, an actual guard with a gun and everything, it's kind of terrifying — leads us through security and to the practice gym, which looks like an actual arena on its own. The podiums are carpeted in green and there's a colorful green, yellow, and blue banner around the perimeter, representing the colors of the Brazilian flag.

The actual arena, the one where we'll compete in front of millions of people next week, is like a déjà vu of the training gym, only the space is much bigger.

I know I should be feeling shock and awe right now, but honestly, it feels like all of the other arenas we've been competing in all summer. Actually, it's smaller and way outdated than some of them. I know I'm exhausted to the point of collapse, and I'm sure it'll feel different once there are butts in these seats, but I actually have to pinch my arm to remind myself that we're not in San Diego or Boston or Atlanta. This is Rio de Janeiro. *This is the Olympics.*

"Cool," my brain yawns back. "I'm over it."

Once the tour is complete, we go for an early dinner at the main dining hall in the Olympic Village, where dozens of stations feature every possible food you can imagine...Brazilian, Caribbean, Asian, Italian, American...

"What does the American station have?" Emerson snorts. "McDonald's?"

Actually, shockingly, there *is* a McDonald's on site for the athletes. They're a sponsor. But we stick to sensible chicken and veggies, grab some fruit for the road, and then find our way through the maze of buildings back to our dorms.

Once in my bedroom, I throw my new gear in a heap on the floor, peel off my jacket and leggings, and collapse onto my Olympic-themed comforter, which is this pretty green, teal, and blue ombré blend featuring the Rio 2016 logos for each of the sports represented here.

"Did you see we got free special edition Olympic Samsung Galaxy phones?!" Zara squeals. "And Beats headphones! They're on the nightstand! I have two cell phones! And BEATS! My sister is gonna be so jealous."

I start to respond, but when I lean back and rest my head against the pillow, I fall asleep instantly.

The Olympics, baby.

Saturday, July 30, 2016
6 days left

"Up, up, up, up, up!" Vera yells as I tap through my front giant and release into my double front.

Vera and our coaches are getting super nit-picky as we get closer to qualifications. Right now, they're trying to get more height out of my bars dismount, which involves releasing the bar a nanosecond later than I normally release, and kicking up a bit more to go *up* for height rather than *out* for distance, which is what I apparently favor.

"Good, Mal!" my teammates yell from the chalk bowl when I stick.

There are a bunch of training gyms near the arena, but we're in the one that's basically a mini-replica of where we'll actually compete. The equipment set-up is identical, so we're able to train in pretty much the exact same environment, a huge benefit for us.

Our official podium training inside the real arena won't be until a few days before we compete, so not every team is here yet and things are pretty quiet. Over the next couple of days, some of the other teams will begin slowly arriving to familiarize themselves with the facilities the way we already have, including the girls from the Netherlands, who are in our subdivision for qualifications.

There are five subdivisions total, with four rotation groups in each. We're in the fourth subdivision starting on floor, the Dutch girls start on bars, and then two mixed groups featuring a bunch of individual qualifiers not part of full teams will start on vault and beam. A few of the mixed group girls are here, including the New Zealand gymnast Amy Garry, who knows some of the girls on our team from a few international meets.

We train in the same order we'll compete, so there's some semblance of organization to what can be a chaotic experience. "Olympic order" is traditionally vault, bars, beam, and floor, but since we're starting on floor, our order is floor, vault, bars, and beam, a tricky place to end up since there's a crap ton of pressure to hit, but that's exactly why we practice in competition order. It's like running through a bunch of dress rehearsals before the big opening night.

"You're done with bars," Natasha says after a few notes. "Good work."

"Thanks," I pant, undoing my grips and stuffing them into my bag. "I'm dying."

"Yeah, Vera will do that to you," she grins. "I bet you appreciate me a little more, huh?"

"Always."

I motion through a few back walkovers to get into the feel of tumbling backwards, which after all of my time in this sport still kinda freaks me out. I mean, I get over it super fast every single time, but have you ever thrown yourself backwards onto your hands? On a *balance beam*? It's kind of insane and makes you wonder what kind of drugs the guy who did the first back handspring was on.

The rotation wraps up and we wait for the official nod to walk to beam, where Vera goes over her lineup order. So far today, I've gone up first on vault and bars because I'm not competing either of them, and I was third on bars, with Zara and Maddy going up first and second, Ruby fourth, and Emerson anchoring.

My position on bars tells me I'll most likely lead off the event in the team finals, which is beyond insane, but nothing is as crazy as the moment Vera tells me I'm anchoring beam.

"We will have Maddy leading us off in qualifications, and then Ruby, Emerson, and Amalia," Vera explains. "This will produce the best results."

"Maddy first?" Her coach, Dan Maycomb, has a hint of annoyance in his voice. "So no team final for her on bars *or* beam? Her beam should be in there, Vera. Otherwise she's a vault and floor specialist, and that's what Zara is for."

"She will do the all-around in qualifications," Vera says, slightly annoyed. "That is the job I have given her. That is the job she has earned. Based on her scores and how she looked in training, we only need her on two events in team finals."

"Before Amalia was on the team…" he starts, but Vera cuts him off pretty quickly.

"Before Amalia was on the team, Maddy *maybe* would have done beam in the team final. She has a very strong beam routine, but we only have three team final spots, and all three I've chosen all outscore her. So they will be the girls who compete."

Maddy sniffs, but keeps her face blank, clearly annoyed and upset. But with Vera watching, she only does a quick and sassy hair flip before taking her attitude down a notch. The last thing she wants to do right now is piss Vera off.

I don't know why she's so hurt by not being given a beam spot in the team final. I'd much rather trade my beam team final spot for her all-around qualifications spot, even though Emerson and Ruby are definitely going to be the two who make it into the all-around final. Only two gymnasts per country can qualify into each individual final, so even if Maddy qualifies third overall in the world, if Emerson and Ruby finish ahead of her, no all-around final for her.

The only final I have a shot at is beam, but I'm pretty sure I can beat everyone on my team to get one of the top two spots there. I wouldn't be the anchor if I wasn't able to make that happen. I take a sort of pride in this new and yet super scary responsibility and promise to kick ass extra hard today.

When it's Maddy's turn on beam, she falls within ten seconds of mounting, and on a simple dance element. You sure you wanna keep whining about not getting a team finals spot?

"Get it, Emerson!" I yell absent-mindedly when she goes up. "You got this, Ruby!" I'm never that fabulous at cheering people on, but today I'm so focused on needing to be amazing, I don't really have it in me to help others even a little, so my vocal support is extra dreadful.

The very last American to go up in qualifications. The last person up on the last event. That's me.

When it's finally my turn after an agonizing wait that builds my nerves into tiny explosive devices, I'm afraid that I'm going to be so freaked out I will barely be able to stand still on the beam, a four-inch-wide lump of padded wood that has destroyed more careers than Achilles ruptures and ACL tears.

I gulp, add another coating of chalk dust to my feet in case my nerves make them extra sweaty, and get into position to mount.

The funny thing is, the second I do this, the nerves completely disappear. My body knows what it's doing. My brain is basically like "I've had enough" and gives my muscles total control, like some Dr. Jekyll and Mr. Hyde split personality kind of deal. I can't summon my chill side to take over whenever I want, but when I need it most, like in super high-stress situations like right now, it just happens and I go with the flow.

My teammates are yelling for me the same way I half-heartedly yelled for them, but I hear none of it anyway. Their voices are nothing more than a faint but steady buzz in the background, like the humming noise that makes people focus when they meditate. It helps completely clear my mind, which in turn lets my body do exactly what I've trained it to do for the majority of my life.

With a deep breath before my dismount, I picture myself sticking the arabian double front. When I go for it for real, I listen to the rhythm of my hands and feet against the padding on my roundoff, and use the momentum from my landing to push off the edge. I quickly twist my body around halfway, pull my knees in tight to my chest, wrap my hands around my shins, and then I barrel forwards through the air, flipping twice with just enough time to let go of my legs and straighten my body just as my feet slap against the mat. Stuck.

I know it was a good routine. I'm blind to the little errors, like being a few degrees short on a leap or if the form on my Onodi makes me look like a donkey, but I am fully aware when I really screw up, and I know that didn't happen today.

"You're an *animal*, Mal!" Ruby squeals, running up to me and squeezing the life out of my body. "Beam gold is locked *down*. Everyone go home."

"Shut up," I laugh, wriggling out of her hug. "You'll jinx it."

"That was very good work," Vera says, almost smiling, as she wraps her hands around my neck and pulls my chin up to face her. It sounds like torture, but this is her way of telling us she's happy with us. We actually *yearn* for Vera to crush our windpipes, dig her sassy red claws into our skin, and stare deeply into our souls. It's why we do gymnastics.

"First practice was a success," she declares, releasing me from her iron grip and addressing the whole group. "There are some things that disappoint me, and your coaches know and will spend this next week working on them with you. But for the most part, I am greatly satisfied. Do not be upset if you made mistakes today. We had a very long travel day yesterday and you are all human. But it should not take you long to adjust here, and I will not be as forgiving in the future. We compete in one week, and anything can happen. I have three talented alternates working very hard at a gym in Ipanema right now who would love to step in if any of you can no longer do the job."

Maddy audibly grimaces at this, knowing her work kind of sucked today, but I also wince at the threat, thinking of Sophia sweating it out with no reward over at the alternate gym.

Yes, believe me, I know it's not my fault. She was the one who didn't live up to Vera's standards. I've heard it all before. But it still hurts my heart knowing that *technically* I'm also part of the reason she's off the team. Vera's comments feel like a personal dig.

"Shake it off," I whisper to Maddy as we walk toward the exit to wait for a shuttle back to the Village. "It was only one day."

"Calm down, Judas. You've already stolen one spot. You can't really take another."

I'm taken aback by Maddy's blow, and for a split second, I feel tears burning in my eyes, but then I grab her by the arm and spin her around to face me.

"I was trying to be nice, but I'm over it. Like it or not, I'm on this team, so get used to me. Your little bitch routine won't change anything. It won't bring Sophia back, it won't get you a beam spot in the team final, and it absolutely won't stop you from looking like a garbage monster, which is exactly how you trained today."

Maddy's eyes widen and she opens her mouth to respond, but has no idea what to say. Instead, she turns on her heels, her long black ponytail whipping around over her shoulder as she goes.

Everyone's pretty quiet as we board the shuttle, too exhausted to do much more than scroll through our phones. I put my feet up on the seat in front of me, bending down into a pike stretch, my arms wrapped around my legs and my face resting on my knees. A totally normal way to ride public transportation.

Just then, Ruby pinches my thigh and I'm about to pinch her back when I see her frantically gesturing to the row behind and across from ours. I unwind from my pretzel position and subtly turn my head.

It's Maddy. She's crying.

Whoops.

Sunday, July 31, 2016
5 days left

"Can you believe that in one week from today, we'll be *Olympians*?" Zara rambles excitedly from the ice bath in our suite. "Like, I know we're Olympians right now, because we're at the Olympics, but we compete in one week! One week from right now, we will be athletes who are competing at the Olympic Games. I can't. I can't *even*."

Ruby laughs. "Yeah, it doesn't feel real right now? But I'm betting the whole competing thing will change that."

It honestly doesn't feel real. Ruby's not just saying that. We're only on our third day here, but we've already settled into a comfortable routine that makes it feel like we're at home or at the farm.

Outside of meals and training, we're stuck in our apartment, partly so we can stay relaxed but also so we can avoid the hundreds of people who are all over us whenever we leave this place. Apparently we're a big deal.

Instead of enjoying the Olympic Village, we're in our common room watching Netflix and DVDs, doing recovery treatments like massages and ice baths, scrolling Instagram so we can live vicariously through the athletes who *don't* have Vera locking them up, and that's about it.

None of us have phone service here because the international fees are ginormous. One of the Japanese gymnasts actually got a phone bill for $5000 after playing Pokemon Go on data all weekend, but when his phone company realized he was a national celebrity and the best living gymnast of all time, they waived it and gave him free international data for the rest of his trip.

I have a feeling *my* phone company won't be as accommodating, so I stick to wifi when I can get it, and spend most of my time going back and forth with Jack on Facebook Messenger. With all of the drama over the past couple of weeks, he has been my one grounding force of sanity, and I am hashtag blessed to have him as my rock.

Maddy has been less of a dick since I went savage on her, but instead of being a truly awful human, she is instead more or less ignoring us, so I don't know what's worse. She has her own room in our suite, and she's in there all alone every second she's not forced to be with us.

At least her training last night and earlier today was a vast improvement from our first session yesterday morning. I really would feel gutted if she ended up getting booted from the team this close to the Games, no matter how much I can't stand her. No one deserves that.

"Did you see Amy's new skill?" Emerson asks randomly. She has melted into the bean bag chair, becoming one with it. Even with her superhuman strength, there's no way she's ever gonna be able to climb up out of that thing. "I could *not* stop watching her beam."

Amy Garry, the New Zealander in our subdivision, is awesome on beam, especially given that she comes from such a small program. She totally has a chance at making the final, which would be a huge deal.

"She has a new skill?" Ruby asks. "I *loooove* new skills."

"Yeah. This morning, she was training a side somi into a back tuck, but the back tuck is done *sideways* on the beam. Like instead of doing it down the length of the beam, she does it facing out. Transverse. And *then* she does a straddle jump down to her hands, like a Shushunova on floor, and *then* she does a back hip circle around the beam. I almost *died*."

"Holy crap!" I'm impressed. That's difficult as hell, and super creative too. "She connects all of that?"

"I mean, in training today she had pretty big pauses between the side somi and back tuck, and then between the back tuck and the jump, but even if she does all of those one skill at a time with no connection, it's still awesome."

"I've seen a transverse back tuck before I think," Zara adds. "Actually, I don't know about a back tuck, but I've definitely seen an aerial done across the beam rather than down the beam."

"Yeah, but the transverse back tuck isn't in the code of points, so even if someone has trained it or competed it in a random competition, Amy can get it named for her, so technically it's a new skill."

"That's so awesome," I sigh dreamily. "I've always wanted a skill named for me. Can you imagine? The Blanchard. Everyone would probably expect me to do something crazy on beam, but I'd totally screw with everyone and create a floor skill so people can get all snarky, like, 'can you *believe* Amalia Blanchard has a floor skill named after her even though she sucks on floor?' That would be hilarious."

"I want my named skill to be the most difficult element in the books, something only the baddest bitches would even *attempt*," Ruby laughs. "Preferably something no one could ever legitimately compete again so in a decade commentators can't say something cheesy like 'wow, Susie does the Spencer even better than Spencer herself!' Like a double layout off beam or a triple double on floor or something."

"After winning golds on golds on golds in the next couple of weeks, my ultimate dream in this sport is to compete a tucked double Jaeger on bars," Emerson shrugs as if she's given this a ton of thought. "I'll come back for 2017 worlds, compete it, get it named for me, win bars gold, and then retire."

"No way," Zara laughs. "That's literally impossible."

"Nope," Emerson counters. "I've tried it. It's like doing a double front dismount high enough to be able to reach out and grab the bar again. It rips your shoulders practically out of their sockets, but it's totally not impossible."

"Well, *I'm* gonna be the first person to do a handspring double front half on vault," Zara says. "The first *woman*, I mean. I've trained double fronts and my landing is almost there. My goal is to get the double front at worlds in 2018 and then add the half for 2020."

"I've always wanted to be the first woman to do the Yurchenko triple," Maddy says shyly, peeking out through the door to her room. "I was training it, but didn't want to push it, and then my teammate Bailey got hurt doing it at nationals, so…"

Ruby pats the seat next to her on the couch and Maddy slinks over, resting against the arm and pulling her knees up to her chin. Hell hath frozen over.

Speaking of freezing, Zara leaps out of the ice bath and wraps a towel around her pruny body, shivering as she runs off to our room. "I can't feel a single part of me!" she screams and we all laugh.

"I'm next," I groan, stripping down to my shorts and sports bra before working to refill the tiny inflatable tub. "Can someone pick a movie or something?"

Maddy and Ruby scroll through Netflix while Emerson vetoes every selection and Zara yells more suggestions from where she's changing in our bedroom. When I settle down into the ice, my skin stinging from the cold while my muscles begin singing "Hallelujah" for the relief, my heart is happy with the love I have for all of these weirdo nerds and nothing's gonna mess with my mood.

"Hey, the USGA press release about Sophia is out!"

Or not.

"Lemme see," Ruby says, pulling Emerson's phone out of her hands.

She reads through, scrolling down, taking her sweet time, and the suspense is killing me.

"What does it say?!" I finally blurt.

"Blah, blah, blah, Sophia unfortunately has a back injury, she tried to push through minor pain but she made it worse and after a few training sessions in Rio was forced to withdraw, you're stepping in, Vera said you proved yourself at camp by showing readiness, it's bittersweet, they regret making the decision to replace Sophia but will be overseeing her rehab at the Ipanema training gym and wish her the best in her recovery."

"That's all?"

"Yeah." Ruby switches off Emerson's phone and tosses it back to her. "It's all business."

"Typical press release," Emerson says. "It's the press reactions you have to watch out for. Once the journalists pick up the story, they start speculating and then the fans come up with conspiracy theories…"

"Ugh, I hate this," I moan.

"Actually, though?" Maddy jumps in. "Check Twitter. I searched your name and people are freaking out."

"Good or bad?!"

"They're pretty much all excited about you taking the spot, Mal. Like…everyone loves you."

I turn on my phone and search myself on Twitter, totally flabbergasted at the responses. "I wanted Amalia on the team to begin with," one person says. "I heard Sophia had a horrible camp and they kicked her off because of that," another person writes, and they get a response that says "Sophia made it on her name, but Amalia should've made it on her talent."

"Wow," I exhale after a few solid minutes of reading. "This actually really sucks for Sophia."

"Yeah," Emerson says, still scrolling herself. "People *really* didn't like her being on the team. Who would've thought?"

"I just hope she doesn't read any of this," I sigh.

"She usually stays off of social media," Ruby reassures me. "I doubt she's following any of this."

Shivering uncontrollably, I climb out of the inflatable tub and dump the melting ice into our actual tub. I dig for a pair of sweats, yell out that I'm taking a nap, and curl up under the covers.

"You there?" I message Jack, and he responds within seconds.

"Always. What's up?"

I start typing out everything that happened with the press release and how I feel like crap about Sophia and all of the mean stuff everyone's saying about her, but then I delete it all.

"Nothing," I write. "I just miss you and am having a lame day and needed to hear your voice, or as close as we're going to get to that since we're separated by international waters."

"Lame day?"

"Yeah, no biggie, but my goal was to spend my entire Olympic experience being thrilled about literally everything but little things that shouldn't matter? Turns out they do. There's some shitty stuff happening with team changes and even though it's not really about me, indirectly, I can't help feeling like crap."

"Here's my opinion. Even the most perfect things in life are never going to fully meet your expectations, and that sucks. But remember why you're doing this."

There's a pause in his response, and then a video pops up with clips from a meet when I was eight and fell on literally every event. At the end, my dad zooms in on me standing in the corner sobbing, and then I trip over a bag and take one last fall, splat onto my face.

I crack up laughing and before I can get a response out to Jack, he texts me one more time.

"Do it for her."

Wednesday, August 3, 2016
2 days left

"This is what a well-oiled machine looks like!" Vera beams once we finish up our second training session of the day.

Over the past couple of days, our team has really come together. We are training just like we're hoping to compete, doing a little bit of skill work here and there when problems arise, but for the most part there *are* no problems at this point.

Every single practice, we start on floor, work through our rotations like tiny professional business ladies getting the job done, and finish on beam with the satisfying slap of my feet against the mat signaling the end of another killer day.

Vera is practically in constant shock from these twice-a-day feats of awesomeness. I don't think she knows how to exist in a world where she isn't constantly disappointed by everyone within shouting distance, so our flawlessness is truly messing with her sense of self.

We're gathered at the end of the beam podium for a little group meeting before we have to give up the gym to the next group, but like Monday and yesterday and this morning, I know there's not much to say.

"I am very impressed with how you have all been working as a team this week," Vera continues. "It is not easy to adjust to international competition, especially for those of you who aren't as experienced as others, but you have all passed my test and are exceeding my expectations both individually and in how you are supporting one another. I also appreciate the maturity with which you are handling the questions and news reports about Amalia coming in as a replacement."

I blush at the mention of my name, and Vera clears her throat before continuing. "Tomorrow is our official podium training in the arena, and there will be a press conference after. If you can continue as you have thus far, I have no worries about how well you will do both in the training session and with the media. More importantly, I have no worries about Sunday's competition. That is where our focus must be, no matter what else is going on, but so far you have met every challenge with grace and poise."

She pauses for a moment, and I see a little twinkle in her eye like she's the super athletic female Santa Claus. "After watching things progress all summer, I have an announcement to make. I am happy to say that I have selected Ruby Spencer as the team captain and my daughter Natasha Malkina will serve as head coach."

Ruby squeals, clapping her hands together, and Natasha smirks, as if she knew this wasn't coming. With three Olympic team members training at the gym you own, head coach is in the bag, no matter how many reporters will hound Vera about nepotism and whether she made the decision for the right reasons.

With Ruby, there will be *zero* questions about her new role. The team captain doesn't really have any big responsibilities, but it's usually an honor given to the gymnast who best exemplifies giving her all for the team.

Even though Ruby is one of the best gymnasts we have competing, she would gladly give up all individual accolades if it was for the best of the team, something none of the rest of us would do without extensive whining and posting passive aggressive tweets for a month, minimum.

"I would also like to announce that Friday, the day of the Opening Ceremony, will be a day off from training, and on Saturday we will have only one session in the training gym at the same time we will compete on Sunday. That will be our final dress rehearsal, and just like podium training, we will go straight through from start to finish as if it is the day of the competition."

"Are we going to the Opening Ceremony?" Zara asks hopefully.

"No," Vera says firmly, while athletes and coaches alike emit groans of annoyance.

The Opening Ceremony is the official start to the Olympic Games, where the host country puts on an elaborate show before the Parade of Nations allows every athlete the chance to march into the arena to see the lighting of the flame. It's all about symbolism and tradition and magic and ceremony, but taking place less than 48 hours before we compete, there's no way Vera's gonna let us go. Athletes have to wait around for hours before marching into the arena, and all of the walking and standing around would be killer leg abuse just days before we have to use those legs to win medals. It sucks, but the reasoning for skipping it is solid.

"As much as I would love to let you enjoy the experience of the ceremony and have it inspire you before you compete, you will have to instead find inspiration on television," she continues. "Once the competition is over, you will be allowed to participate in the Closing Ceremony, which is even more fun because you will no longer be under any pressure and you can just enjoy yourselves."

A bell rings, and our training time is up. We grab our bags and make the trek to the athlete's entrance for the shuttle back to the Village, where we have quick ice baths and massages before dinner, the same as every other day this week.

It sounds impossible, but the Olympics so far have simultaneously been the most exciting and the most boring experience of my life, though I'm sure the whole "boring" aspect will change once we stop training and actually get out there and compete.

Natasha plonks down in the seat next to me on the bus, and I congratulate her for getting the head coach gig. Vera's still in charge of everything like lineup decisions, but Natasha will be the one out on the floor with us while we compete, and she'll be in charge of the little things that come up as the meet goes on, as well as the big things, like if someone's looking crappy and has to be replaced last-minute or if there's an injury or something. Pretty much none of these things will happen, but just in case they do, she'll be trusted to make the tough calls.

"Just another job for the resume," she shrugs, though I know she's secretly thrilled about landing this gig. With Ruby's injury and subsequent drama in 2012, having Emerson and Sergei thrown at her just months before the Games, and my whole insane journey, no one deserves it more than her, and she knows it.

"Well, I'm thrilled out of my mind because I could never get through competing at the Olympics without you on the floor with me."

"That is nowhere near true, kid," Natasha smiles. "You are incredible, you know that? I'd bet every cent in my pocket that you'd be the least likely on this team to melt down in a rough situation. That's always been your strength, your super top-notch mental edge. We just had to get those nerves of steel up and running with elite-level routines. It took a lot of work, and there were mistakes along the way, but right now? The way I see things, nothing can stop you."

I bite down on the inside of my cheek, trying to stop a ridiculous grin from bursting through, but in the end I let it out.

"I love you, Natasha." I curl up next to her and rest my head against her shoulder. She wraps her arms around me and squeezes.

"I love you too, robot."

***

"OMG, don't look now, but it's the *Russians*!" Zara gasps at dinner when she spots the five flawless specimens of elegance, beauty, grace, and perfection only a few feet away from our table.

The Russians were a disaster in 2012, falling a million times in the team competition which gave the American team a huge boost, allowing them to win the gold medal. After the Olympics, their government flipped the training system upside-down, replaced all of the coaches, and hired top-level nutritionists, sports psychologists, and personal trainers to make sure the next generation of gymnasts would be in perfect condition.

This year, their team is a squad of five girls, not one older than seventeen, all teeny tiny with white-blonde hair and ice blue eyes. Seriously, I'm about eighty percent positive Putin took the best gymnast they had and made four clones. Everything about them is intense perfection, and even their casual walk through the dining hall looks like a fully choreographed performance, like they're the ladies of Beauxbatons from *Harry Potter*.

Their older teammates went to worlds last year to earn the Olympic qualification spot, but these girls were kept in a bubble. They have almost no international experience, but reports from the training gyms suggest that they're here to destroy anyone and everyone who crosses their path. As a gymnast, I'm terrified of them, but as a gym fan, I'm so insanely excited to watch them compete.

"I thought they weren't cleared to compete or something?" Maddy asks, not taking her eyes away from them. We're all staring, honestly. They're mesmerizing.

"No, that whole performance-enhancing drug scandal thing didn't disqualify them. It ended up being only the track athletes who took the supplements and tested positive, so while they were going to ban everyone at first to punish the entire Russian federation, they eventually decided it wasn't fair to those who were clean, so only those with positive test results got banned in the end," Emerson explains.

"Too bad," Zara whispers. "We're never gonna beat them."

"As team captain, I command thee to shut thy mouth!" Ruby yells, dictator-style, only half-kidding. "We don't know what they can do. No one has seen them compete. Maybe they look like they can murder us by simply staring into our souls like the tiny children of the corn they are, but they've never competed outside of their country. We're the top dogs, the gold medal defenders. *They* should be afraid of *us*."

"I don't know," Maddy shakes her head. "Look at them. We look like schleppy bums eating hot dogs in the bleachers at a Cubs game next to them."

"Speak for yourself," Emerson says, tossing her fork onto her plate. "I look like Daenerys Targaryen, complete with a fire-breathing dragon on my shoulder, and don't you forget it."

I smile meekly at the Russians as they walk past with their trays, and one of them tilts her head towards me, but she either doesn't see me or doesn't care and shifts her gaze back to the front. My heart melts. *I want to be them.*

"Amalia, stop staring!" Zara laughs. "You're going to get arrested."

It takes me a minute to realize that these girls are our competition. I haven't given any thought at all to the other teams here. That's how we train, to think only about what *we* can do and how *we* perform, not about what our rivals are capable of. We have no control over the other teams and what they do on the competition floor, so we stay in our bubble and do our job and hope that it's better than what everyone else is doing.

The majority of the teams here have a zero percent shot at getting a medal. Unless there are absolute meltdowns, it's going to be the United States, China, and Russia on that podium. We're not really fighting for a medal; a medal will happen for us even with a few falls. But we *are* fighting for gold, and if these little Russians are as good as everyone says they are, gold isn't gonna be easy.

"I heard Olya Kuznetsova got a 16.2 on bars at Russian nationals," Maddy gulps.

"Home scoring," Emerson scoffs. "The judges gift the girls on purpose so the rest of the world fears them. I've seen her routine on YouTube. She'd be lucky to get a 15.5."

"What if *our* nationals and trials routines were over-scored?" Zara worries. "What if my floor routine is actually half a point lower out here in the real world than it was at home? I hate subjective scoring. I wish we had robots and lasers instead of human beings."

"Japan's working on it," Ruby laughs. "Stop freaking out! Any score we've gotten so far doesn't matter. All that matters is what we do out there when we compete. If the international judges give us lower execution scores than we get at home, chances are everyone's in the same boat. Their assessment of our routines shouldn't affect how we compete them. Just do your best, fight for every tenth, and you'll be fine."

I've never thought about the outside competition, I've never thought about the outside judging...damn, have I been sheltered during this whole experience or what?!

Maybe it's a good thing. Ignorance is bliss. Going in blind to what my competitors can do might be the thing that saves me from worrying about what I can't control.

But now that it's in my head, it's all I can think about. I push some veggies around my plate with my fork and bite my lip.

"Seriously, Mal?" Ruby rolls her eyes. "Are you really gonna let the potential of some other team undo everything you've done in the gym this week? The competition is about *us*, not them. Guess what? They might win gold. They might be the best team the sport has ever seen. If they're that good, nothing we can do will matter, no matter how good we are. That's how this sport works. But even if they're capable of finishing ten points ahead of us and we have zero chance at winning, we still need to do what we trained to do. We need to reach *our* highest potential and hope that it's enough."

Ruby — ahem, our *team captain* — is right. I have no control over anything but me.

I nod, but sigh nervously, my eyes still glued to those beautiful Russian demons, who even eat like they're performing the *pas de quatre* in *Swan Lake*, everything synchronized and no one missing a beat.

This is going to be a lot tougher than I thought.

Thursday, August 4, 2016
1 day left

"This is going to be just like how we do things in qualifications," Natasha whispers hurriedly to the five of us as we stand in the tunnel that leads into the competition arena. "Everything's the same. It's the perfect way to get your jitters out."

I stand on tiptoe, trying to see over the dozens of heads in front of me into the Rio Olympic Arena, but I get only a glimpse of the green inside. In addition to the 18 gymnasts competing in our subdivision, there are countless coaches, trainers, and medics all waiting to go in as well, and yet the tunnel is oddly quiet, like we've just survived an earthquake and are afraid speaking will make another one come.

We have our whole crew with us, including Vera, our four personal coaches (Natasha, Sergei, and Maddy and Zara's coaches, Dan and Evgeny), Cynthia the judge, and Michelle, our medic slash trainer slash physical therapist slash the woman who never speaks but always knows what we need, whether it's an energy chew or a back rub.

During the Games, only two coaches will be allowed on the floor at the same time, with Natasha the mainstay as the head coach and the others trading off depending on who's up competing, so each gymnast can have her personal coach on the floor when she's up.

While we practice our routines, our coaches will have their own training session, rehearsing the complicated dance that is coach-swapping. Come Sunday, there will be no surprises. Everyone will know his or her purpose and duty to the team, and if anyone screws up, Vera will serve their head on a platter at Thanksgiving.

After what feels like seven weeks of waiting, a bell dings and music starts, welcoming us out into the arena. Going up on floor, we're the last ones in, following two mixed groups and the team from the Netherlands. The stands are empty to the public today, but the media is all set up in their section, quiet but excited to see the reigning Olympic champs in action and probably secretly hoping for us to screw up so they'll have something juicy to report.

Come Sunday, this place will be filled to the rafters with the most enthusiastic fans of the sport, so I try to imagine walking in with thousands of people screaming for us to see if that will get me more into the zone.

It works. A grin spreads across my face, covering up any nerves I felt only seconds earlier in the tunnel. I'm a confident goddess as we march to the folding chairs set up by the floor podium, the thousands of crystals on our brilliant red leos catching the light and blinding anyone within a five-mile radius. We look stunning, and while looks have absolutely nothing to do with how we'll perform today or on Sunday, there's something about these leos that brings me out of my shell. I'm actually *smizing*. Tyra Banks would be so proud.

Natasha calls us over for a quick pep talk, asking us to go all-out on floor with full performances, like we would in front of a crowd. Then another bell dings, signaling us to climb onto the podium and present ourselves to the judges, who aren't there, but we practice like they are.

We go in competition order today, and even though I won't be in the floor lineup during the meet itself, I still get a turn to run through everything just in case, going up first. I get a tiny pang of sadness, realizing this is probably the last time I'll ever perform this routine, and it won't even be for an audience, but the feeling disappears the second I get into position for my opening pose.

The first notes of my music play over the speakers, I take a breath before diving into my choreography, and I get a shiver down the length of my spine.

The only thing I feel right now is ecstatic.

***

"As good as you were today, we do not want to get comfortable," Vera begins, perched in the middle of our couch back at the Village. Yes, it's super creepy having Vera in what is technically my home right now. "Even when there are no mistakes, there is always room for improvement. You are never done working, not until the Olympics are over and you have the medals around your necks."

I sigh, deeply and with satisfaction. Today was phenomenal. Incredible. Brilliant. The best day of my life.

So many other teams had nonstop drama in podium training earlier today, including our biggest competition. The Russians apparently couldn't get through a single beam set without falling, and the Chinese were super messy on vault and floor, but we pushed through with zero disasters or meltdowns. We were golden.

"Remember, teams that did not do well today are the ones that will appear newly charged on Sunday," Vera frowns, bursting my bubble. "They now have a reason to fight and use their disappointment from training to showcase their best work when it counts. We are coming from the opposite place. If we walk away complacent and happy with ourselves today, we have nothing to fight for three days from now. We do not want to come back on Sunday assuming we'll be perfect, so your coaches and I have notes and things to work on for each of you. We have tomorrow free to relax and let our bodies recharge, but on Saturday, we will dedicate practice to fixing all of the small corrections we have from today so we go in sharp and with a mission on Sunday."

We nod, and my stomach rumbles. Our podium training was at 5:30 in the evening, and I haven't eaten anything aside from half a granola bar since lunch at noon. Now it's after eight and if I don't get something soon I'm going to eat my arm.

"Maybe we can talk notes after dinner?" Natasha asks, an angel in human form.

"Yes, fine," Vera huffs. "A quick dinner, and then make plans to talk with your coaches."

I mouth a silent "thank you" to Natasha, who grins and pats me on the back.

"That wasn't for you," she says. "I'm borderline hangry right now and don't want to snap."

Dinner tonight is a rushed affair. Reports of our podium training have reached the masses, and athletes from all over the world are asking us for pictures and wishing us good luck, jumping on our gravy train before it has even reached the station. It's fun to get the recognition, but again. My stomach is empty and eating my insides. Me want chicken.

"This is so insane!" Zara exclaims on the elevator back up to our suite. "I had half of the US women's soccer team all over me."

"My *dream*," Ruby laughs. "I *love* that team."

"Now I know how Michael Phelps feels," I smile.

"It's only going to get crazier when we win," Emerson says with a shrug. "In 2012, the girls who went to the Closing Ceremony said they could barely march because they were absolutely mobbed. The whole thing got delayed because they had people climbing all over them for photos."

"I'm tracking my Instagram followers," Zara says, pulling out her phone. "I have ten thousand followers right now. I want to see how many people add me after each time we compete, like how many I get after qualifications, how many after team finals…"

"You're such a nerd," I giggle, but I've been doing the same thing, going as far as screencapping my follower counts each day to track the rise.

Fame is the one thing you don't prepare for as a gymnast. Your whole life, you're super sheltered, going to school, training, doing homework, and sleeping. Once you get to the national level, fans of the sport start paying attention, but you don't become known outside the sport unless you do something really incredible, like win a million world medals or make an Olympic team.

Before trials, no one outside of the sport knew who I was. I got some buzz there, but it wasn't until the press release announcing my team spot came out that I noticed my follower counts and friend invites increasing.

Once qualifications air in primetime attracting millions of viewers, many of whom have never seen a gymnastics meet before, that's it. Whether I'm fantastic or bomb spectacularly, I'm going to be all over the place and I have no idea how I'm going to handle it.

"Three more days of anonymity," Maddy says, as if reading my thoughts. "After Sunday, we won't be able to blink without some Twidiot calling us disrespectful."

We all laugh, and then I unlock and push open our apartment door, the rest of the gang on my heels. I'm exhausted, especially as I come down from the adrenaline of performing in the arena for the first time, and am totally in the mood to blob out on the bean bag and watch something stupid on TV, but just as I'm about to shut the door, Natasha pushes her arm in and slides it open.

"Remember me?" she grins. "You first."

Yeah. That's right. *Notes.* I cry internally, but then grab bottles of water and lead her into my bedroom, where we sit across from one another on my bed and I prepare to have every good feeling about today totally beaten down.

A gymnast's work is never done.

Friday, August 5, 2016
The Opening Ceremony

"Did you see the video?" Ruby asks excitedly, shoving her phone into my face. "It's *gruesome*."

I haven't seen the video, and I don't want to.

In the final podium training session last night, one of Canada's gymnasts, Anaïs Mignon, had a bad landing on the vault she was hoping would get her into the event final, a tsuk entry with two and a half twists. She had way too much power coming into the landing, and her leg kept twisting into the ground. Instead of a run-of-the-mill knee injury, she completely snapped the bones in her left shin, leaving the lower part of her leg dangling as she screamed from the mat.

"I feel so bad for her, but *damn*, that's an amazing injury," Ruby gushes. "Much better than an ACL tear or something. Actually, it'll even heal faster. All they have to do is re-set the bones and she'll be back in the gym relatively quickly. I know a guy it happened to and he was vaulting again within six months. Like, sucks, but also *yaaaaaaaaas*."

"There's a throne in hell with your name on it." I shake my head, but then laugh at Ruby's misplaced enthusiasm. "You're sick."

"Are they bringing in the alternate?" Maddy asks.

"Yeah, thankfully it happened hours before the deadline," Ruby explained. "The cutoff was by 11:59 pm on podium training day, so they immediately flew their alternate in. She was training at her home gym in Toronto. I guess the federation didn't think they'd need her and so they didn't want to spend the money putting her up in a hotel and finding her a gym here."

"Sucks for the alternate almost as much as it does for Anaïs," Maddy winces. "She's gonna be thrown into the most important meet of her life with less than 48 hours in the village and no podium training? Hopefully she's not a headcase."

"Yeah, I would *completely* freak out if it was me," I shudder. "Sorry not sorry, but I'd almost rather be the one with the injury than the one stepping in with a million tons of pressure taking her place."

"Nah," Ruby says, clicking her phone off. She's definitely been watching the injury video on repeat during this entire conversation. "You're not very self-aware, Mal. You're the only one on this team I'd trust to come into a situation like that and keep your cool. That's literally why you're here."

I blush, and then change the subject. "So, what are your big notes for our final training?"

"Nothing!" Emerson calls from her bedroom, where she's been gleefully flipping through magazines all morning, like this one day off is a free vacation in Hawaii. "I'm perfect!"

Ruby rolls her eyes. "I've been rushing skills, apparently. Not holding things long enough to make them look legit. I need to focus on taking it slow and savoring the moment. Natasha said it's making my bars look messy and that in the heat of the moment, judges are going to go to town on my execution because even if each individual skill is clean, the general rushed quality is making me look like trash."

"Hmm, yeah," I nod, agreeing with Natasha's assessment, and Ruby laughs.

"Thanks, Mal."

I blush again. "I mean, not that you look like trash, but yeah, I noticed your pirouettes were clean but late in one routine, and that's nothing against your form or technique, but only because you were rushing. At least that's easy to fix. Again, it's not like your form is horrible."

"Yeah," she nods. "It could've been worse."

"Evgeny said I'm 'too excited' so I guess that's similar?" Zara adds. "Or like, how did he phrase it…like I congratulate myself too soon for hitting one skill well, and then don't focus enough on the next element. But like, it's the Olympics? So that's probably just nerves. I never compete like that."

"No, you don't," Ruby agrees. "It's okay, we'll calm down by Sunday. And if not, we'll calm down for team finals. At least that's the one thing we don't have to worry about…we can basically have the worst day ever on Sunday but we're still making finals by a landslide."

"Well, I am apparently disgusting to watch on every event," Maddy grimaces. "I mean, I know I'm not, but my coach went on and on about how disappointed he is in me, all because Vera told him I need to watch my line and pay attention to my extension on bars and beam. Apparently in Coach Maycomb's head, that translates to me being ugly and unwatchable. That's the feedback I got, anyway. I'm the grossest gymnast alive."

"Yikes," Ruby says, but she doesn't disagree because that's how Maddy has *always* looked on bars and beam. Looking sharp and clean on either of those events has never been her strong point, but she's not here for bars and beam. After qualifications, she won't even compete them again, so I don't know why they don't just let her focus on what she has to fix on vault and floor, where she actually has a huge chance at making the finals.

"You're up, Blanchard," Emerson yells from her room.

"Me? Umm…the usual, really," I start. "Natasha even said at this point she doubts I'm gonna be able to really make any of these corrections, like they're just ingrained in who I am, so she said to just focus on the overall look of each routine. I have lots of little things to watch out for. I've come to terms with the fact that I'm never going to do a skill perfectly. If I get a handstand exactly vertical over the bar, you can bet my feet will be flexed, and if my feet are perfectly pointed in a handstand, I'm probably going to be a few degrees off."

"Just try to remember every little correction, and if you get them, great, but if you don't, Natasha's right," Zara agrees. "The overall picture. That's what we *all* need to concentrate on."

"Yeah, don't beat yourself up over things that cost a tenth or something, especially if you let worrying about the little things mess with your whole routine," Ruby adds. "You're only going to add even *more* deductions. Just let it go and move on."

I stretch out on the couch, using the arm to help me into an over-split, giving my front leg a few inches off the surface. The day isn't even halfway over, and I'm already *sooooooo boooooored*. A day off sounded great in theory, but right now, I'd kill to be doing something constructive.

At the very least, I just want to leave the apartment and walk around the Village. But Vera has made it *super insanely clear* that we're not allowed to leave our building outside of mealtime.

Suddenly, a spark of genius.

"Vera said no leaving the *building*, but she didn't say we can't leave our room." My eyes sparkle. "Isn't there a game or arcade room somewhere in here?"

Ruby jumps up, elated. She's even more restless than I am. "Anyone up for an arm workout? And by that, I mean pinball and pool."

The four of scramble to throw on socially acceptable clothes and then grab Emerson, who pretends to be against the idea, but I know she's dying to get out. She throws her magazines to the end of her bed, grabs a hoodie, and slips into a pair of flip flops.

"Oh, Maddy?" she says, turning off the light. "Don't listen to Coach

Maycomb. He's a dick and even though I *supposedly* left Windy City because I'm a giant psycho diva who hates everyone and never gave them any credit for my success, I loved it there and totally would've stayed if he didn't exist. His sole reason for living is to make teenage girls feel like crap, and when the Olympics are over, you should kick his ass to the curb. And don't for even a *second* give him credit for anything you've done. You know as well as I do that it's all of his assistants who do all the dirty work while he just shows up at the Olympics and basks in the glory. Why do you think I took Sergei with me when I left?"

"Honestly, because I thought you guys were having an affair," Maddy says, super seriously. Emerson throws her head back and laughs.

"He wishes. Seriously, Maddy. I know things have been crappy between us, but you're doing a great job and you deserve to enjoy this experience. If you let him ruin it, I will be so mad at you."

"Thanks, Em."

It's such a disgustingly precious *Full House* moment, part of me wants to barf, but the other part of me lets loose with an over-the-top "awwwwww" while Ruby and Zara push them to hug it out.

With all of the nonsense and drama over the past four months, I questioned a million times whether we'd make it this far without brutally slaughtering each other in the night. Now here we are, a real team, and there's no one else I'd rather do this with.

***

"The guys are totally at the Opening Ceremony!" Zara whines, whipping her cell phone at us. "So unfair!"

"No, they compete *tomorrow*. They're eight hundred percent not allowed to march a million miles the night before qualifications," Emerson says.

"Just *look*." Zara pushes her phone into our faces and on Sam York's Instagram, there's a snap of all five guys in their Ralph Lauren gear, looking snazzy on the balcony of their apartment. Even though we're technically on the same team, I think I've seen the guys exactly once since we've been here, and to be honest, sometimes I totally forget they exist.

"Read the caption," Emerson rolls her eyes. "It says, 'If we can't be there, we're still gonna watch in style.' See? They're probably watching on TV just like us. They're just as imprisoned as we are."

I unmute the TV just as Gisele Bündchen catwalks her way across the Maracanã Stadium floor, a truly bizarre end to a truly bizarre performance, but hey, what Olympic Opening Ceremony *isn't* totally insane?

"The best part!" Zara squeals. "The Parade of Nations."

"Actually, the most boring part," Maddy moans. "Can't we watch a movie in the nine hundred hours it's going to take for everyone to make an entrance? I haven't even heard of half of these countries."

"You're just jealous," Zara retorts. "Look at how proud everyone is! Dreams are coming true and these people are *living them*. Incredible."

"You're such a weirdo," Ruby laughs. "I love you."

It really does take a lifetime for every country to march through the stadium. Most of us move back to our phones and magazines, though we look back at the screen occasionally when we see people we know, like the few gymnasts whose coaches let them walk and our US teammates from other sports, most of whom we'll never meet.

Even though I've aged a decade and am bored as hell by the end, I feel new life breathed into me when I see the Olympic Torch enter the mix.

Our common room hushes, and I pull a pillow close to my chest, hugging it for dear life as we watch the flame's journey come to an end on the stage here, its fire igniting the giant cauldron, signaling the start of the 2016 Rio Olympic Games.

I get a little choked up here, not gonna lie. I'm sure my teammates would rail on me endlessly if I started to cry, so I hold it in, but when I glance around the room I see tears streaming from everyone's faces and bam. I lose it.

"It's really happening," Emerson whispers, a close-up of the flame bright and magical on our screen.

"Yep," Ruby chokes out. "All this time, none of this experience has felt real, but now? Guys, nbd, but this is the Olympics."

Saturday, August 6, 2016
Men's Qualifications

"Gymnast Sophia Harper, an alternate for the United States women's gymnastics team set to begin their competition at the Olympic Games tomorrow night, has opened up to us about her story of deceit, lies, and betrayal on behalf of the US Gymnastics Association and national team coach Vera Malkina," a newscaster reports in a clip Ruby pulled up on her phone.

"Oh, shit," Emerson gasps. "Sophia is *not* playing around!"

"Shut up and listen!" Ruby hisses.

"Harper, who was the Olympic all-around gold medalist in 2012, was originally named to this year's team but, according to a press release from USGA, she was injured in the team's early training sessions here in Rio, replaced by newcomer Amalia Blanchard, 15. According to Harper, however, the controversial decision to replace her came at the team training camp in Wisconsin and she was forced to play along with the injury story despite training as an alternate in Rio since arriving last week."

The clip cuts to a shot of Sophia, who looks even more pale and thin than usual, sitting on a sofa in a studio.

"No one would tell me what I did wrong," she cries. "I did everything that was asked of me, but I don't know. My coach thinks this was a setup from the very beginning. He said Vera always wanted Amalia on that team, but based on how we performed at trials, it made more sense to bring me and there was no way they could have justified bringing Amalia over me. So they named me to the team, but then immediately thought of ways to swap us, and giving me an 'injury' was their way out."

"Vera's daughter Natasha Malkina coaches your replacement, correct?"

"Yes," Sophia responds, looking down at her manicured nails. "I've proudly represented this country in international competition for ten years, since I was twelve years old, and I won gold medals at the Olympics in London. It's so unfair that every achievement of mine is erased because of something like nepotism."

"And your treatment at the final training camp, could you tell that something was off?"

"Yes. From the moment I arrived at the farm, I was treated poorly. Everyone made mistakes at the training camp, but I was singled out, forced to do extra workouts, and I faced constant emotional abuse from everyone on the national team staff. I went to bed sobbing every night because nothing I could do was good enough, and I woke up every morning afraid to go to the gym."

"When did you find out you would not be competing in Rio?"

"The day before our travel day. Vera called me into her office and told me she was disappointed in me. I could barely speak, I was so upset, but when my coach asked why, she didn't have an answer. She said my performance didn't live up to her standards, which sounded very vague and she couldn't elaborate on that or why my mistakes were so awful when everyone else got a free pass. I said I didn't want to travel to Rio if I wasn't going to compete, but she brought up my team contract and said I was obligated to stay with the team until they released me."

"During all of this, your health started deteriorating, correct?"

Sophia begins to cry again. "Yes. The stress and the pressure was so bad, I was in a constant state of feeling tense and on edge. I couldn't sleep, I stopped eating, I lost a lot of weight, and I could barely make it through practice, I had no energy at all. As much as I wanted to compete at the Olympics, when Vera told me it was over for me, it almost felt like a relief. My body and my mind were completely shot, and I was honestly happy to give myself a break."

"Now that you're back home, are you going to focus on getting well again?"

"Yes, that's my number one priority right now. I don't think I'm done with the sport yet and would love to work on making teams in the future, but when I get back to Nashville my goal will be to get both physically and mentally healthy again, and then I can get back to training once my body and mind are healed."

"Will you watch the Olympics?"

"I don't think I can," Sophia sniffles. "With everything I've been through over the past month still fresh in my mind, I think it will be too painful for me to watch. I wish Team USA the best of luck when they compete tomorrow and later this week, but right now I won't be able to watch them do it because I'll constantly be thinking about how I should be there with them."

Ruby clicks off her phone.

"That's all," she exhales, glancing at me. "I was gonna hide this from you, but you know it'll be the first thing the media brings up. They're probably swarming the Village right now, waiting to pounce on us as we leave for practice."

I chew my thumbnail, thinking about how I feel about all of this. Sophia, someone I thought was my friend and even a *mentor*, going to the press a day before I compete to basically tell the world I don't deserve to be here?

"None of what she says is even true!" I finally blurt. "Like, yeah, USGA was wrong to lie and say she was injured in Rio. They should've straight up said she was replaced the day it happened. But like, I'm not crazy, right? We all saw her in training. Not to be a bitch, but she *sucked*. All camp long, she was a mess. Mentally and physically, she couldn't handle it! Nepotism my ass."

"Why now?" Zara asks from the floor, where she's stretching for practice. "Why didn't she come forward before?"

"After Thursday night, alternates could no longer be subbed in, so Sophia, Charlotte, and Olivia were released from their duties," Emerson explains. "Sophia basically rode out her contract and put on a happy face when she was obligated to, but now that her job is done, she's no longer playing games."

"She must've flown out of here the second they finished their last practice," Maddy shakes her head.

"Yeah, and right to the TV studios in New York," Emerson scoffs. "What a drama queen."

"Drama queen or not, this is a PR nightmare for USGA," Ruby says. "Getting accused of nepotism and emotionally abusing an athlete, even if it's all bullshit...the press isn't gonna leave that alone. And we all know who that falls on."

"Yeah," I laugh. "*Us.*"

"Can I just say it's hilarious that the US men's team is *killing it* for once and is probably gonna qualify in first place which would basically qualify as a historic event and the media's focus is girl drama?" Zara brings up. She's been glued to her phone, checking the live results for the men's competition all day. Our guys are halfway through their subdivision and I've never seen them look so good.

"Let's just be grateful that this is the one sport in our country where the girls actually matter more than the guys," Maddy says.

I pull out my phone and open up Facebook Messenger, scrolling to my conversation with Sophia. We last chatted on the day the press release came out last week.

Amalia Blanchard. How is everything? xoxo

Sophia Harper. Not bad. Keeping a low profile. Happy no one knows where we're training, otherwise our cover's blown and I'd have the media up my butt forever.

Amalia Blanchard. Yeah, what if someone took a picture of you training or something?

Sophia Harper. They'll just say I'm working through the injury, it's not serious, they're still keeping me in mind in case I get better, blah, blah, blah.

Amalia Blanchard. Dumb. I still don't get the lie. So much drama for nothing.

Sophia Harper. They're doing it "for my benefit" or something. Apparently it'll look better for me to be taken down by an injury than it would for them to say I sucked at the farm.

Sophia Harper. Which I agree with, tbh, but yeah. Still so many holes in the story.

Sophia Harper. How's everything going with you? Rockstar yet?

Amalia Blanchard. We've only had a couple of sessions so far but I felt great.

Sophia Harper. Good. I know you're going to be the hero of this team. Just you wait.

Amalia Blanchard. Thanks Soph.

Sophia Harper. I have to run but I'm in your corner, always. I'll be cheering so hard.

Amalia Blanchard. Thanks. That means the world.

In my corner? Yeah right. I'm usually pretty adamant about thinking through what I say or do before following through, but not right now. I type out "why?" and hit send, hoping it makes her realize how much her games hurt me. It's one thing for her to fight back against Vera and USGA, even if she's totally crazy and fully knows why she got booted from the team, but it's another to claw at *my* throat. I've done nothing wrong.

I'm strangely as upset as I thought I'd be, though. Like, I'm hella mad at Sophia, but so far, mentally, I'm still really good. Like, all it takes for Emerson to have a meltdown is her mom showing up at a meet, but my mental game is iron-strong.

So much in my life is crazy right now. My new *relationship* with Jack, my mom being a total hobag, being thrown onto this team as a surprise right before leaving for Brazil, ruining Sophia's life…and none of it has shifted my focus. What's one more wildfire when the whole forest is already burning?

Yes, I'm angry and hurt by Sophia's accusations, but none of that comes into the gym with me. I'm nothing if not amazing at filing and shelving my feelings until I can deal with them at a more appropriate time. Or never! Let's just pretend everything is sunny all the time always, forever and ever.

"Mal, practice time." Ruby nudges me, and I realize I've zoned out, my eyes glued to my Messenger app as I anxiously await Sophia's reply. "Earth to Mal!"

I turn the phone off and grab my bag. "I'm ready!"

"You okay?" she asks, pulling me aside. "This sucks for all of us, but I'm not gonna pretend any of us have it as bad as you."

"Yeah, I'm actually good," I grin, and I'm not faking it. I do feel good. I'm not going to let Sophia take the Olympics away from me. "I'm ready."

"Good girl," she sighs. "But if you need a pep talk at any moment, I am your team captain, and it's my *job* to give you one."

I laugh. "There's no one better at it than you, Rubes."

As we walk through the door, my phone buzzes, and I know without looking it's Sophia. I swipe open the phone, go right to our conversation, and read.

"I'm so so so so sorry, Amalia. I had it all planned out, blaming Vera and USGA for how they treated me, but the way the reporters asked the questions and edited the interview...they're the ones who made it about you. I couldn't back out. If I could go back in time, I never would have agreed to any interview at all. I know that doesn't change things but I never in a million years meant to hurt you. I'm so sorry."

Part of me believes her, and I'm mostly satisfied with her apology, but I'm not ready to let her off the hook just yet because she definitely screwed me over.

I choose not to reply. She'll see that I've read her message, and if she's anything like me, she'll hopefully go into a panic wondering why there's no reply. It's the most passive aggressive revenge possible, but I'm happy with my decisions in life.

The elevator dings at the end of the hall and I slam the apartment door behind me, running to catch up with my teammates.

Maddy's holding the door open for me as I jog. A week ago, I would've pegged her as the one who would try to mentally destroy me at these Games, and now it's like we're in some kind of alternate universe where she's one of my biggest defenders. Life's funny that way.

***

"Once again, you have outdone yourself," Vera says, clapping her hands together. "I feared that with such a strong performance at podium training, you would have relaxed and given up some of your fight, but I see you have all worked at focusing on your areas that needed help, and you looked even better today than you did then. It doesn't need to be said, but I expect you to continue to raise your level even higher for tomorrow, when it counts."

"Yes, Vera," we chorus from our lineup across the podium. Vera looks at Natasha, who clears her throat before addressing us.

"I know the news isn't very positive about our program right now. Frankly, I'm amazed at how composed you were today, dealing with that nonsense, and I hope you are aware that nothing Sophia Harper has said to the press reflects poorly on you. It's all directed at the coaching staff and the big dogs running the show. The world thinks we did something wrong, but we all know the truth, right?"

We nod in response even though I'm pretty sure that was a rhetorical question.

"We have a whole team of people set up to deal with things like this, and they're already putting together a press release that will clear things up. I'm sure the conspiracy theorists out there will continue to badmouth us, and sadly, you guys as well. But don't listen to it. Stay off of social media, don't talk to people who are looking for juicy gossip, keep things light at the apartment tonight with a movie or something...and as cliché as it sounds, keep your eyes on the prize. You guys know what's important and what's true. Let us take care of the rest."

"Yes, Natasha," we say when she's done.

Ruby calls a huddle and the five of us go in together, our hands in the middle of the circle for a simple "Go USA!" cheer before we break it up and collect our things.

"MAG check!" Zara calls, already on her phone. "Team USA is still in first but China is only halfway through their subdivision and they're looking *goooood*. Russia is also in this one, but I think our guys will beat them."

"You're definitely the only person who cares," Emerson snarks, but I'm actually excited for the guys. They had a fantastic day and could potentially bring home a team medal after missing out in London. Good for them.

"I'm still mad Max isn't on the team," Ruby laughs, jabbing me in the waist as we walk to catch the shuttle. "You could've enjoyed Rio together, eyeing each other across the dining hall, sending him secret messages through your interview answers, sneaking down to his room every night...we could've devised a pulley system with the sheets or you could've spidermanned your way down the side of the building with suction cups on your feet."

"I hate you. Oh, and I have a *boyfriend*. Even if Max *was* on the team, there would be no shimmying down buildings."

"Max? Max Oleynik?" Zara asks. "He is *so* hot."

"Little sis, stay away," Ruby cautions. "Trust me. He's gross. I should text him and see what he's up to right now."

"He's probably at some Murray Hill rooftop bar with two money-grubbing cougars buying his drinks," Maddy chimes in, angrily at first, but then she sighs longingly. "I miss him."

"Oh my God, you're pathetic," Ruby laughs, turning to me. "When we get home, remind me to find nice, corn-fed Midwestern boys for Zara and Maddy. Football players. Cute dumb puppy dogs who know how to treat their girls right."

The shuttle finally appears and we have a quick, quiet ride back to the Village. It's late, so we grab food to go from the cafeteria, which also helps us avoid the wandering eyes of every other athlete in there, all of whom know what Sophia is saying about us to the press.

We settle down in the common room with a good old-fashioned episode of *Law and Order SVU* on Netflix. When we're done eating, I do some jumping jacks and push-ups to get out some nerves before brushing my teeth, braiding my hair, and then hugging my teammates goodnight.

I put on my favorite pajamas, navy and cream polka-dotted cotton shorts with a loose knit cream sweater to match. I read a few pages from a terrible book I impulse-downloaded on Amazon. I check my email. I message Jack and my parents to let them know I'm settled in for the night. I jot some notes about the day in my Olympic diary.

With all of my busy nonsense out of the way, I finally feel ready to snuggle under the covers and dream the sweetest of dreams.

"You awake?" Zara whispers. She has her comforter tented over her phone so the light doesn't bother me, but I can see the soft glow through the fabric.

"Yeah," I whisper back.

"Our guys qualified in second," she says, sounding somewhat bummed. "I really thought they could've pulled off first, but China was *so* good."

"That's gymnastics," I yawn. "You can have your best day, but someone else can be even better. Besides, they still have team finals. They can always come back and win there."

"Yeah," she agrees. "And at least they tried their hardest. That's all we can hope for, right? I want to be able to say that every time I compete this week. That we tried our hardest. Even if we finish second, I want to be proud of everything we did to get there."

"We will be proud, Zara. And not only because we tried our hardest or did our best. We're going to be proud because we're finishing *first*."

"Yeah." I can almost hear her smiling from across the room, her voice growing confident as she finishes her sentence. "We're finishing first."

Sunday, August 7, 2016
Women's Qualifications

If you're wondering if it's at all possible to be prepared for that moment when you step out to compete at the Olympic Games, the answer is no.

I've been in Rio for over a week, I've trained in the Olympic gyms, I've eaten dinner one table away from Michael Phelps and snapchatted about three hundred pictures of his face until Emerson threatened to throw my phone into the vat of oatmeal. It's been insane and surreal, I'm not gonna lie, but with our daily routine over the past week, I often find myself going through the motions, not really feeling how big all of this is.

But now we're standing on the floor podium presenting to the judges in our super patriotic American flag leos, silver Swarovski stars shooting along a crimson background while red and white crystals create stripes against the navy. Our hair is in high buns, sprayed so heavily that if we took the pins out, it would stand up on its own. Fresh mani-pedis courtesy of the salon in the village turned our nails into works of Team USA glory, perfect for when we claw our enemies into shreds. We look good, we feel good, and now we're going to bust out the best damn gymnastics the world has ever seen.

Okay, I don't exactly *feel* good. Even though my warmup in the training gym was close to perfection, my stomach has since twisted itself into a small bomb and is currently threatening to burst forth through my belly button, which will totally ruin this ridiculously expensive leo. What have I ever done to you, stomach?

I've paid zero attention to the results from the three subdivisions that came before ours, so I have no idea how China or Russia did. Normally I hate seeing results, but this time, if I knew, I'd have some idea of where they set the bar and would then know exactly what I'd need to do to outscore them.

But *no*, no matter how comfortable I got with watching scores at the farm, it goes against everything I believe in as a competitor. I need to do everything the way I've trained, regardless of scores. The bar I need to reach is my own. Oprah would be so proud of this self-realization.

One of the floor judges is actually *our* judge, Cynthia, the US judge we bring along to every international meet. She's actually trying to lighten the mood, smiling and telling us to have fun and enjoy ourselves, but even though my head is nodding and I'm grinning kind of psychotically, internally, I'm like, fun? *FUN?!* What about this is *fun*, lady?!

When the judges finally give us the nod to go into our touch warmup, I exhale out the air I've been sucking in for two full minutes and climb down the stairs, happy to be alone with my crazy brain while Maddy, Zara, Emerson, and Ruby get their time to bust out some quick tumbling passes before the competition officially begins.

I walk over to the folding chairs along the side of the arena and dig for my water bottle, not because I'm thirsty, but because I need something to do. I don't compete until bars in the third rotation, still nearly an hour away. I should've brought a puzzle or Jenga or something. The camera dudes would be all over that. Think of the memes! I probably won't go down in history as the best Olympic gymnast or anything, but results are nothing. Memes are forever.

I'm so sucked into my world of nonsense that at first, I don't hear the gasp. I don't see the fall. I don't even really comprehend when Michelle, our medic, grabs my wrist and squeezes so hard I later feel it in my bones.

Everything's a delayed reaction, playing in a weird kind of slo-mo. I hear the floor compress and then there's a louder snap, like plywood breaking. I stand up, pulling Michelle with me, and I watch as she lets go of my wrist and runs to my fallen teammate.

I have a brief panic attack not knowing who it is because what if it's Ruby? It can't be Ruby. Not again. I know that in wishing for Ruby to not be injured I'm technically wishing for it to be someone else, but I don't care. Anyone but Ruby.

But Ruby appears at my side seconds later, repeatedly muttering f-bombs under her breath.

"It's her Achilles. I know it. I heard it snap. I'm gonna throw up. It's way worse than mine was. Her foot was *dangling.*"

"Who?!" I practically yell in her face, turning my head back toward the floor. Emerson, easily recognizable thanks to her blonde hair, is standing in the corner facing away from the disaster zone. She competes first and will now have to go up in a matter of minutes with this image in her head.

"Maddy," Ruby exhales, basically suffering from PTSD after watching this go down. "Holy crap."

I don't think at all about what this means for the team. The thought doesn't even enter my head, not when I see Michelle and the paramedics settling a chillingly quiet Maddy onto a stretcher, not when I see Natasha rushing around talking to a small army of officials, not even when Ruby is talking about subbing someone in for Maddy's routines, which you'd think would've gotten my attention since — duh — I would be the sub.

Nope. It's not until Natasha comes running back over to me with a thumbs up, which I think is kind of super bitchy. We're totally screwed and she's like, yay, Maddy's injured? I mean, Maddy could be kind of a dick, but she was really coming around and she's my teammate and she worked her entire life to get to this moment. No one deserves this.

"You're in," Natasha says breathlessly, grabbing my wrists. Between her and Michelle, I'm gonna have bone bruises.

"In what?" I'm dumb. Stanford is absolutely crossing my name off their list as we speak.

"Mal, you're replacing Maddy. You're doing floor. And vault. You're doing the all-around."

***

I've always worked best under extreme pressure. We all know this. It's why I wait until the night before to study or write major research papers. I'm at my best when grades and my entire future are at stake. I'm a champion at performing well with a fire under my ass. But this? This is too much even for me.

"Zara, you'll take Maddy's spots on bars and beam in addition to Amalia stepping in on vault and floor, so all four of you are ending up in the all-around. I was worried, because there's a rule about changing the lineup after it's submitted...it normally comes with a penalty, but I checked with the governing body, and because you guys were technically the alternates for these events and because this is an extreme circumstance, it's okay to swap you in. The only thing is that you have to compete in the same lineup spot Maddy had for your subbed routines, so we'll have Amalia last on floor and second on vault, and then Zara first on bars and beam. Mal, are you warm?"

"What? Yes. Not really."

"Run along the side of the floor and do jumping jacks or something. Thank God we had you tumbling in the warmup gym."

"Natasha!" I practically yell, stopping her rambling.

"Yeah?" She pulls me aside and puts her arm over my shoulder in a mini-huddle.

"I can't do this!" I zip my warmup jacket up to my chin and let my eyes drift to the floor so I don't start crying because I'm three seconds away from a full mental breakdown and if I look at Natasha, I know it'll happen.

She grabs my shoulders and forces me to look up at her.

"You can do this, and you will do this. We have no other choice. Come on, it's not even a big deal. The other three will all go up before you on floor. If they hit — which they will — there's zero pressure on you. They can drop your score. You don't even have to think about it. And if they *don't* hit? You're the first one I'd trust to go in there and give the best performance of your career. No one hits when it counts like you do. I mean, we *could* do it without you and just risk a three-up three-count rotation, but it would suck because you're awesome and deserve this chance. Yes, you, the girl who didn't make nationals a year ago, you're getting an opportunity to compete in the all-around at the Olympic Freaking Games. Besides, you know your vault will score better than Emerson's. Now you have the chance to rub it in her face!"

She's trying to get me to laugh and loosen up, and I'm not quite there yet, but I'm also not in total meltdown mode like I was a minute ago. I bite my lip, sigh, and start jogging in place.

Yes, I'm frazzled, but this is exactly when my training kicks in. Is that a superpower? Getting so worked up and upset that you flip right around and become a total badass? Amalia, you *know* what you have to do. You *know* you will get it done. My brain tricks me into thinking I'm weak and incapable, to the point where I almost actually believe it, but deep down I am a warrior princess and nothing will stop me.

"I'm sorry, Natasha. I can do it. I'll be fine."

"That's my girl. Don't be sorry. It's scary. It's a ton of pressure. But you deserve this. Any other kid in the world, I'd give them a big old 'be a hero, save the team' speech right now but you don't need to think about saving the team. The team will be fine and you don't care about that hero crap. Do this for Maddy. Do this for you."

Emerson's music is starting and I can't watch. I need to not know anything that happens in the next ten minutes leading up to me competing a routine that I both suck at and haven't done in front of a real crowd in a month. Instead, I jog back and forth along the length of the arena, throw a few roundoffs and back handsprings in the corner, stretch, run through my leaps...

...and then suddenly Ruby's music ends and it's my turn. That fast? Three routines have already come and gone? I imagine things went moderately well for everyone, as there were no earth-shattering gasps or moans or screams from the crowd, so all I have to do is hit. That's all.

I speak to no one before I climb the stairs to the floor podium like Marie Antoinette about to get her head chopped off. I probably should've gone with Joan of Arc getting burned at the stake, but I don't really feel like Joan. I'm definitely more of a Marie, like, how did I get here?! I just want to eat cake and play with baby animals all day!

As I stretch into my starting pose, I wonder how Natasha or whoever got the music to the organizers so fast, and then I have a quick heart attack wondering if I'll have music at all. One time at a level ten meet, this girl's music didn't work so she had to compete to nothing but the sound of the crowd clapping. It sounds like aww, cute, everyone came together and made this a special moment, but really, it was the most awkward thing in the history of the world and I will throw myself into a storm drain if that happens to me *at the Olympics.*

But of course, my music kicks into gear without a fuss, and I'm off, immediately forgetting the tragedy I created for myself before actually living my life. Imagine that.

Normally when I compete on floor, I just go with it, focusing on the big picture. My one goal is to simply keep up with the music and not fall, and I forget all of the little things my coaches tell me in training. I don't engage my core on turns, I forget my mental cues as I set into my tumbling, and I've never pointed my feet in a tuck or pike once in my whole entire life.

Tonight, though, I still feel like I'm living in slow motion. I'm actually *calm* and even though the music moves me along like it always does,

I'm taking the time to think about each skill and element as I approach them. See? It's the pressure. It makes me better than I ever believe I can be. If only I had teammates completely blow out their Achilles every time I competed!

I'm doing the choreography bit into the corner before I go into my final pass when my jerk brain steps back and says "Hey, Amalia! Remember when you got a concussion doing this pass in training right before trials?" Gee, thanks.

I take a deep breath, remind myself to keep my body low in my back handspring, exhale slowly, and run.

Nope. No concussion is going to happen tonight. My double tuck is flawless in the air, and as a final eff you to my brain, I stick the crap out of it.

The crowd goes wild, my teammates are jumping up and down on the side of the podium, and Natasha is smiling ear-to-ear, hands on her hips, mouthing "I told you so" when I finish up my choreo and settle into my final pose.

Natasha is waiting for me when I come down from the podium, tears in her eyes and her arms outstretched. She pulls me in for a hug, and whispers softly into my ear.

"Welcome to the Olympics, Amalia."

***

"We're counting your score," Ruby whispers to me as we march over to vault between rotations.

"You're lying?!" I turn around to see her face, but she's dead serious. "Who got dropped?"

Ruby glances behind her, nodding her head in Emerson's direction.

She's stone-faced with her big white Beats over her ears, the cord not even plugged into anything.

"Don't tell me my score, but what did Emerson get?" I hiss.

"She got a 14.3. Nothing majorly wrong or anything, really, just not...what it could have been, I guess? Lots of little things that added up."

"Wow."

"Yeah. Don't think about that, though. She'll come back hotter than ever and destroy us in the all-around," Ruby laughs.

"Sounds about right."

We climb the steps to present for vault, and I already feel a hundred percent more confident than I did when we first came in. A couple of the judges here try to make us feel at ease like our judge did over on floor, and we smile and chat back. It really does make everything better.

The touch warmup goes smoothly, with all of our Amanars and Zara's Cheng easily making us the best vault team in the entire world. I'm going last again here, but I feel way more confident on vault than I ever have on floor, so this is an easy one to brush off and get through without a complete mental catastrophe beforehand. Once it's over, I get to finish up on bars and then beam, my best event last. It's smooth sailing from here on out.

Emerson goes up first again, and I'm chill enough to watch this time. She's clean in the air, but probably ten degrees under-rotated, and she has to take a small step forward to steady herself. Not her best, but it'll still be a big score.

I go up next, and what can I say? I do my job. I focus all of my energy on keeping my hips straight, my legs together, and my arms tight into my chest so I can twist quickly before opening up into the blind landing. I flare my arms out as I sink my feet into the mat, bending my knees slightly to absorb the impact, and then I take a baby step in place to keep it secure.

"You murdered it!" Natasha screams over the roar of the crowd as I rush off the side of the podium into her arms. "Your best ever in the air. Perfect body positioning. I'm even happy you felt out the landing, because yes, that counts as a step, but if you fought for the stick you wouldn't have won."

Ruby crushes her Amanar. She practically hits the rafters when she blocks off the table, getting air Michael Jordan would be proud of. She doesn't stick, but the hop is so small, there's not much the judges can take off.

As good as Ruby is, Zara's own vault is the best of all, combining Emerson's beauty and Ruby's power, and she sticks the landing as a cherry on top.

Because she's hoping to qualify into the vault final, which requires two vaults, she does a complicated Cheng as her second vault. This has the same roundoff entry as the Amanar, but before she hits the table she does a quick half turn and then blocks off into a front layout, completing one and a half twists in the air before landing. Somehow, she makes this one look even better than her first.

I don't look at any individual scores, but when our team event score flashes, I see we get a 47.7 which is going to blow every other team out of the water. Zara no doubt outscored me here because her own Amanar was the definition of perfection, but I wouldn't be surprised if my score was higher than Emerson's or Ruby's, meaning my score would once again count into the team total while one of theirs gets dropped. Unreal.

"You were awesome, Zara," I say, giving her a big hug as she savagely attacks half a granola bar for recovery.

"Well, I would have given you a perfect ten!" she squeals, returning my hug with a high five.

"Please judge me on bars because that's where I'm really gonna need the Zara Bonus," I joke.

Ruby gives me a hug and we go back and forth complimenting each other for being awesome, and then Emerson, who has retreated into her emo brain and is for some reason having the worst time ever at the Olympics, hugs me like a great aunt would hug you at a funeral.

"You okay?" I ask.

"I'm fine," she says through gritted teeth.

"Come on, Em." I pat the seat next to my own and she sits down while we grip up for bars. "You're doing amazing so far?"

"I'm literally last in the all-around out of the four of us right now."

"Yeah, hello, you're literally only tenths behind and we did your two weakest events, obvs. We'll get to bars and beam and you'll explode past the rest of us. None of us can do what you can on bars."

"Sure," she rolls her eyes.

"Just have fun with it. I know it sounds stupid or basic or whatever but everything is so life or death for you."

"In case you haven't noticed, we're competing at the Olympics, which is pretty much as life or death as it gets. Seriously, why is everything so easy for you? Everything just works out for you all the time and you never have to worry about a damn thing. You look at me now with your big 'who, me?' eyes like you're perfectly shocked that you're doing as well as you are, and it's totally genuine so I can't even hate you for it."

"Nothing has been easy for me, Em. The opposite. I have a lot of bullshit in my life right now and I'm in a fight with my own head every second of every day."

"Yeah, but you *win*. My head beats me every single time."

"Listen, okay? Like, yeah, the Olympics are important as hell, it's the biggest competition of our lives, blah, blah, blah, but that doesn't mean we have to plow through it like we're storming the beaches of Normandy. I know it's counterproductive to tell a stressed-out psycho to relax, but really, just try. This is a once-in-a-lifetime experience, and if you spend the whole meet letting yourself get upset about everything, you're going to kick yourself when you're eighty, which is hard to do and that's how you break a hip."

"*Friends*?" she asks, and a little tiny baby infant Jesus smile crawls onto her face when I nod. We've definitely watched way too much TV this week.

Emerson exhales as she slaps the velcro down on her grips. "I'm gonna kick your ass, Mal."

"You better. It's no fun competing against someone who doesn't at least try."

***

Emerson gets her groove back on bars, where she goes up last for our team.

For the last two events, Zara is now in my shoes, having to go up and hit two routines she hasn't competed publicly in a month. I could tell she was a little flustered on bars, but she's more like me when it comes to dealing with nerves, though, turning them into firecracker energy and using them to her advantage rather than letting them suffocate her to death (hi, Emerson).

She may not be the most natural bars gymnast, but she made it through with only minimal scarring, and we won't have to count her score anyway, not with the rest of us hitting.

Ruby and I both slayed bars, with Ruby's set probably the best she's ever done and I'm pretty sure the judges had a heart attack watching her insanely difficult skills. A bars final spot was a long shot for her, but now it looks like it's actually going to happen.

But Emerson is the bars hero for our team, and shows Ruby up with her own performance that is about as excellent as anyone could've asked for. Even the Russians and the Chinese will struggle to match her perfection, so she's looking at a potential bars gold if she can keep that up. I'm so proud of her for fighting back after her lower-than-usual floor score to position herself alongside Ruby as the top two gymnasts going into the final rotation, which will also easily secure all-around finals spots for both of them.

Despite all the drama, Team USA heads to beam looking like a gold medal squad. Right before we have to go up for the touch warmup, Natasha nods to Ruby, our captain, who pulls us in for a quick group huddle.

"I've been thinking all meet long about what to say here, guys. We started out today with just about the shittiest possible thing that can happen in a gymnastics competition. Not only did we lose a teammate and her huge scores on vault and floor, but we watched it go down and then had to immediately get back in the zone and forget it happened. But we've done an incredible job bouncing back, and Zara and Amalia have stepped into their additional responsibilities flawlessly."

Zara and I look at each other and grin, and Natasha rubs my back like the proud mama bear she is.

"Beam is the mental event. No gymnast wants to start her meet on beam, and no gymnast wants to end here. Yet this is where we stand, all because some guys in suits drew our competition order out of a bingo numbers ball. We can't fall here. We can't wobble, we can't stumble, we can't miss connections, we can't screw up. This is it, everything we've worked for, coming down to ninety seconds for each of us. We're making the team final no matter what, but how we look on beam right now could mean we get to walk back into this arena on Tuesday as the team to beat. Let's finish strong for Maddy. On the count of three..."

"One, two, three, GO USA!!" We raise our hands high and then clap as we run to the podium to present to the judges before the touch.

On beam, Zara is first up, and I'm fully back to being unable to watch anything. Instead, I listen for the rhythm of her feet against the apparatus, and for the crowd's reaction when she lands each element. I can practically hear her deep exhale as she preps for her dismount, but when her feet smack safe and sound against the hard blue mat, I know we're good.

"Perfect leadoff, Zara," Ruby says with a high five as she runs up the stairs for her own set.

"You killed it." Emerson smiles and hugs her, and I join in next with my own congratulatory high five.

One down, two to go. I walk to the side of the podium where I'll be less distracted, and get to work going through the motions of my routine, the same routine I've done hundreds of times over the past year, the routine that got me on this team.

I listen to Ruby's set the same way I did with Zara's, and I try not to get too excited when I hear the crowd react. I know it's great. It never was not going to be great. Come on. It's Ruby.

Ruby triumphantly runs off the podium straight into Natasha's arms. I watch the celebrations and when the moment is right, I run back and give her a big hug.

"You got this, Emerson!" I yell.

This is it. The last routine before I go up. I really can't deal with it anymore, so I go completely into my head, not watching *or* listening, but when she preps for her double arabian, Ruby reaches for my hand and squeezes. She has the same effortless landing as she always does, and the crowd bursts into screams. I know she stuck it.

"See?" I tell her when she comes down the stairs. "The Olympics. No big deal."

"Yeah, just another meet," Emerson laughs, finally able to enjoy herself now that the pressure is off. Not only did she just contribute a huge score to the team, but the all-around final and maybe even a beam finals spot are now in the bag for her as well.

I quickly stretch my hips, about to climb the stairs to go up for my own routine, which will wrap things up for our competition today, when Emerson grabs my wrist.

"Give 'em hell, Mal."

***

This is it.

I'm on the beam podium waiting for the judges to calculate and turn in Ruby's score, hyper-aware of the fact that all eyes will be on me super freaking soon.

This is my event, the reason I'm here, the routine the TV announcers will call a "must-watch" routine. I'm nervous, but I know I'm not going to make a single mistake. Have you ever felt something so strongly in the depths of your soul, like nothing in your life has ever been more crystal clear? I've been a human person on this planet for almost sixteen years, and all five hundred million of those seconds have formed the path that brought me to this one moment where I will do the thing the universe has written in my stars, and everything, everything will be worth it.

Down to my left, Ruby is celebrating the end of her competition with a cookie, which I can see her stuffing into her mouth while she attempts to escape the embrace a weeping Natasha has locked her into.

A few feet away, Emerson is pacing, fully freaking out. Once her score is in, we'll know who qualifies first and second into the all-around, and I don't know how Emerson will react if she's second.

I mean, she's in the final either way, so it's not like she lost the all-around gold based on today. When qualifications are over, everything starts from zero, and she and Ruby will once again go head-to-head. They've gone back and forth all summer, Ruby getting first place one day and Emerson getting it the next, so today's ranking is actually pointless, deciding only that they'll make the final, not who will win.

When Emerson's score comes up, I blind all of my senses, ignoring the crowd and Ruby and Emerson and Natasha and everything except my own breath, counting as I inhale and exhale, and thinking about how weird breathing is and how it's a thing that we do all day and night and yet we never think about doing it.

Except I'm thinking about it right now. Meta. Yeah, I'm about to compete on beam at the Olympics in front of everyone in the whole wide world and my brain has decided to think about how I never think about breathing.

And then I start to laugh. I glance at Natasha, who looks at me quizzically, like she's afraid the pressure has finally gotten to me and that I'm having a full-blown breakdown, but then she smiles and does a not-so-subtle performance of one of the chicken impressions from *Arrested Development* and I laugh even harder.

The green light flashes.

An announcer says my name.

I salute, my mouth in a big dumb grin. Usually, I force this smile for the judges while thinking "would *you* be smiling if you were me, jerks?" but today, it's all genuine, nothing but love.

There's nothing to fear.

***

"Mal, you were *amazing!*" Ruby gushes as I hop down from the podium.

"For real," Emerson grins, giving me a hug of her own. "You're easily gonna qualify first into the beam final."

"Thanks," I blush, and then spot Natasha, who is sobbing. Or *still* sobbing, I should say. I'm assuming she hasn't stopped between Ruby's routine and my own.

"I'm so proud of you, kid. Seriously, what a day. You worked for it. You did it. I love you, Mal."

"I love you too, Natasha." She hands me a cookie and a bottle of Gatorade so I can refuel and recover. Now that my day is done, I want to be fully present to experience everything that comes next.

The media frenzy around us right now is insane. There are dozens of cameras from television stations all over the world shoved into my face, trying to capture my expression when my score comes in, but I try to ignore them.

After a few sips of Gatorade, I walk back over to where Emerson, Ruby, and Zara are standing, near the side of the floor podium, where they're cheering for our New Zealand pal Amy Garry. Natasha follows, her hand on my shoulder as if I'm a four-year-old she's trying not to lose in a busy supermarket.

A roar comes up from the crowd, and I smile to myself, knowing it's for my score, but I don't look up yet. I want to savor this moment and think about scores later.

From the corner of my eye, I see Emerson move away from us and over to her bag, crouching down in front of it like she's searching for something. She gets up, grabs her bag, and heads out through the tunnel, probably to the bathroom. Really? *Now*? She couldn't wait another five minutes for this rotation to officially end? Some cameras follow her, but most stay glued to my face, so annoyingly close I have to stand on tiptoe to see over them so I can watch the rest of Amy's routine.

"You got this, Amy!" I yell. She's doing awesome, and her routine is super fun to watch. It's not the most difficult tumbling, but she's such a natural performer, and everyone here is enjoying her routine.

I feel Natasha's hands land gently on my shoulders. I turn around to smile, but she moves her hands to my head and aims it back toward the center of the arena.

"Look," she whispers.

"What?!" I have no idea what she's doing right now or why she's being super creepy. She moves one hand to my chin and raises it to the ceiling where the scoreboard hangs, listing the all-around rankings from the four subdivisions thus far today.

My eyes dart in a frenzy. I don't know what I'm looking for. The board only has our all-around totals, not our event scores. My beam score only flashed for a minute after the judges turned it in, and I didn't look, so I'm gonna have to wait until we get the full score sheets to see it.

I sigh and let my eyes scroll the all-around rankings. I probably got a personal best or something, which would be super cool, to say I got my best all-around score ever at the Olympic Games.

First on the board is Ruby. I mean, duh. Emerson was great today, but with her floor score lower than usual and with Ruby actually on fire, she was never gonna bounce back to get first. It's okay. Thursday's final is another day. She'll get her revenge.

"You did it," Natasha whispers, a million camera flashes going off inches from my eyes and blinding me. Next to me, Ruby throws one hand over her mouth and grabs my hand with the other.

And then I realize what Natasha has been trying to tell me.

Second place isn't Emerson.

It's *me*.

"Amalia, you're in the all-around final."

Results

Olympic Trials Day 1 — July 8, 2016

1. Emerson Bedford, 61.6
2. Ruby Spencer, 60.9
3. Amalia Blanchard, 60.7
4. Maddy Zhang, 60.4
5. Zara Morgan, 60.3
6. Irina Borovskaya, 60.0
7. Charlotte Kessler, 59.8
8. Olivia Nguyen, 59.6
9. Amaya Logan, 58.7
10. Beatrice Turner, 58.1
11. Madison Kerr, 57.7
12. Kaitlin Abrams 57.1
13. Brooklyn Farrow 56.4
14. Sophia Harper, 31.4

Olympic Trials Day 2 — July 10, 2016

1. Emerson Bedford, 62.7
2. Ruby Spencer, 61.9
3. Maddy Zhang, 60.8
4. Amalia Blanchard, 60.1
5. Charlotte Kessler, 59.5
6. Olivia Nguyen, 59.4
7. Zara Morgan, 58.9
8. Madison Kerr, 57.8
9. Brooklyn Farrow, 57.2
10. Kaitlin Abrams, 56.4
11. Amaya Logan, 56.3
12. Beatrice Turner, 55.9
13. Irina Borovskaya, 51.4
14. Sophia Harper, 31.0

Combined Olympic Trials Totals

1. Emerson Bedford, 124.3
2. Ruby Spencer, 122.8
3. Maddy Zhang, 121.2
4. Amalia Blanchard, 120.8
5. Charlotte Kessler, 119.3
6. Zara Morgan, 119.2
7. Olivia Nguyen, 119.0
8. Madison Kerr, 115.5
9. Amaya Logan, 115.0
10. Beatrice Turner, 114.0
11. Brooklyn Farrow, 113.6
12. Kaitlin Abrams, 113.5
13. Irina Borovskaya, 111.4
14. Sophia Harper, 62.4

Olympic Team Camp Verification 1 & 2 — July 19 and July 23, 2016

1. Emerson Bedford, 61.8
2. Ruby Spencer, 61.7
3. Amalia Blanchard, 61.2
4. Zara Morgan, 59.9
5. Maddy Zhang, 59.1
6. Charlotte Kessler, 57.3
7. Olivia Nguyen, 56.6
8. Sophia Harper, 24.9

Olympic Team Camp Verification 3 — July 27, 2016

1. Emerson Bedford, 62.1
2. Ruby Spencer, 61.9
3. Amalia Blanchard, 60.8
4. Zara Morgan, 60.5
5. Maddy Zhang, 59.7
6. Charlotte Kessler, 59.4
7. Olivia Nguyen, 58.7

8. Sophia Harper, 29.1

Olympic Qualifications (U.S. Only) — August 7, 2016

1. Ruby Spencer, 61.9
2. Amalia Blanchard, 61.5
3. Emerson Bedford, 61.4
4. Zara Morgan, United States, 59.8

Acknowledgments

After finishing my first book last year, I never thought I'd be able to write a second, but then I got such a positive reaction, I was truly shocked and honored and instantly inspired to write again, which truly proves how much I thrive on compliments and attention.

Thank you to everyone who read *Finding Our Balance* and told me it was good and motivated me to turn back to this project. Thank you to the members of the gymternet who has supported me and all of my projects from day one. Thank you to my friends who make life fun and keep me from working too hard.

And as always, thank you to my family for always encouraging me to follow my dreams, no matter how insane or outlandish they sometimes are. Mom, Dad, Ricky, and Sarah, I love you and am so grateful.

About the Author

Lauren Hopkins began writing about gymnastics for *The Couch Gymnast* in July 2010, and spent four years there as the US expert while also contributing to *International Gymnast* magazine, GymCastic, and as a guest on several blogs. In 2014, she created her own website, *The Gymternet*, now one of the most popular gymnastics sites providing exclusive coverage for the most enthusiastic gym nerds. In 2016, she also began working as a freelance gymnastics reporter for *SB Nation*, and she was a researcher for NBC's digital gymnastics coverage, including for the post-competition live recap show, *Daily Dismount*. Lauren's first book, *Finding Our Balance*, was published in 2015.

A New England native, Lauren is a 2014 graduate of Columbia University. She currently lives in New York City and she loves the Red Sox unconditionally.

www.laurenhopkinsbooks.com

Please visit my website for more about this and any upcoming books as well as special fan surprises, including full competition results from all featured meets!

WHEN IT COUNTS

Copyright © 2016 by Lauren Hopkins

This is a work of fiction. Names, characters, places, and incidents are either the product of the author's imagination or are used fictitiously, and any resemblance to actual persons, living or dead, business establishments, events, or locales is entirely coincidental. This edition published by arrangement with Gymternet Productions.

Made in the USA
Middletown, DE
17 December 2016